Lethal Evidence

Lethal Evidence

Jonathan G Rigley

authorHOUSE®

AuthorHouse™
1663 Liberty Drive
Bloomington, IN 47403
www.authorhouse.com
Phone: 1-800-839-8640

Published by AuthorHouse   02/23/2013

ISBN: 978-1-4817-8516-7 (sc)
ISBN: 978-1-4817-8519-8 (e)

Unfortunate Events
~ Chapter One ~

Rumbling through the air at thirty two thousand feet above the ocean, it was becoming obvious to the passengers that flight LA 1872 was in trouble. The Airbus A340 just an hour into an eight hour flight heading from Germany to Denver was vibrating badly and leaning to the port side. Ellie who was in seat 36a could see smoke erupting from one of the engines. "Stewardess, Stewardess!" whispered Ellie.

"Just a moment," said Diana.

Diana Burton was a 43 year old senior flight attendant with more than 20 years experience and had been flying with Lufthansa for the last six years. Diana was a lean 5' 10" with jet black hair expertly fasten back into a French braid. With a slightly pale complexion, high cheek bones and plush lips made her look caring but a little sad.

"Hi my name is Diana how can I help you?"

"The engine, look the engine, there is smoke coming out of it!"

Leaning forward across Ellie, Diana could indeed see the number one engine on the wing tip pummelling with smoke down the left hand side of the plane. Her heart sank immediately as she thought the vibrations and listing was due to heavy turbulence.

"I'm sure there's nothing to worry about. Can I get you a drink or maybe a pillow?" At that moment the 'Fasten Seat Belts' sign lit up as the plane shook violently.

It was a cool mid September day with only 136 passengers on board. Some of the passengers were holiday makers while others were on business trips. The atmosphere was tense but calm with most passengers just looking at each other looking for comfort or signs that everything was okay but it wasn't and they knew it. Flight LA 1872 was in trouble and needed to land straight away but on a transatlantic flight the nearest, largest airfield was over forty five minutes away.

This was the first time Ellie Fox had flown transatlantic and she was feeling very scared. Ellie was a very slim 5' 7" fashion designer with long blonde hair and a cheeky cute face. She had deep blue eyes wearing a white shirt with a black mid riff belt with large buckle and black pin stripe trousers, she really looked smart. At 27 years old and single Ellie had put relationships on hold while working hard to promote her designer label and was about to explore the American market for potential customers.

After Diana had assured Ellie that everything was okay, she made her way back up the aisle towards the cabin. The plane shook and lurched with some of the passengers screaming in terror. Brian who had seen Diana talking to Ellie shouted out "Miss, Miss!"

"Yes Sir?" asked Diana.

"What's the smoke coming out the engine and why are we bouncing around so much?" Brian who was flying back home had been on a business trip to the UK in the security sector, he'd had a smooth flight out of Heathrow to Düsseldorf in Germany. Now lurching around and shaking Brian was becoming really nervous.

"It's just really bad turbulence Sir, nothing to worry about." Diana said trying to hide her own nerves.

Upon reaching the cabin door she knocked a few times and waited. A minute later First Officer Nathan Taylor opened the door, "Come in Diana," said Nathan. In the left seat was Captain David Benson. David was a strapping burly man with muscular arms, tanned skin, black side swept hair and a moustache. Both the First Officer and Captain wore black polished shoes, black trousers with crisp white shirts black ties and black epilates on their shoulders.

Nathan who's a bit shorter than David with blonde streaked hair, short but fashionable, closed the cabin door and returned to his right hand seat. Nathan then picked up the headset and microphone, flicked the communications switch to PA and pressed the transmit button. "Ladies and Gentlemen this is the First Officer Nathan Taylor; we are currently experiencing some technical difficulties. While I can assure you that everything is under control we do need to work through these difficulties. I shall endeavour to keep you up to speed." He then released the PA button and picked up the flight ops manual from the tray in front of him.

"Take a seat Diana," said David with a concerned sound in his voice. Diana sensed something was seriously wrong.

"David what's happening? One of the engines is smoking like hell and the passengers are shitting themselves."

David a 56 year old flying veteran with nearly thirty years under his belt had known Diana since the flight academy. Over the years they had become very close friends with a special bond. Sometimes after a long haul flight Diana and David would meet up for a meal and drink, and explore the local towns and do a little window shopping. Although David wasn't married, he had never thought of Diana as more than a close friend but he did sometimes think that she would have liked it to be more.

They had probably become such close friends as they had both lost both their parents some time ago and sought some form of comfort from each other. David never spoke much of his parents which gave Diana the impression that he didn't get on too well when they were alive or maybe there was something else.

"Diana we are up shit creek big time, the number one engine caught fire and ruptured the hydraulics. We are losing fuel pressure to the other three engines and the rudder control is nearly down. We are trying to contact the emergency frequencies but there's no reply. We think that when the cowling was blown off the engine, it damaged the lower side of the airframe and severed the communications link."

"Christ David, are we going to be okay," said Diana.

David sensing the tremble in her voice and her nerves thought for a moment. Not wanting to sound more distressed. "I think so Diana but we are in a bad way and need to make an emergency landing but the nearest strip is over 40 minutes away due south of Iceland. Any joy on the radio Nathan," said David in a formal manner.

"No nothing, I'm switching to the international distress frequency on 121.5 MHz," said Nathan

"I'll take over from here Nathan"

"Yes Captain".

"Diana I want you to prepare the rest of the flight crew and prepare the passengers for an emergency landing," just then the plane shook violently with a loud bang. 'Whoop Whoop, Warning Warning, Whoop Whoop'.

"Captain we have a Master Alarm and engine No4 is overheating."

David leaned forward and acknowledged the ECAM computer. All modern aircraft are fitted with many safety devices and computers. The main computer system is an Electronic Centralised Aircraft Monitor (ECAM). The ECAM monitors and lists all faults and to some degree recommends a course of action. In the event of an engine overheat the thrust is pulled back to idle for thirty seconds. David reached across to his right and gently pulled back on thrust lever No4. Nathan looked down at the ECAM on his side it was showing a warning. Engine No4 fire! The ECAM then reported back to overheating.

Seeing that matters were getting worse, Diana wished the Captain and First Officer good luck and went back to the galley to prepare the rest of the flight attendants.

"George" whispered Diana. "I've just spoken to David and Nathan, the situation seems to be getting worse. I believe they are going to make an emergency landing." George didn't know what to say. Having flown as an attendant for many years George enjoyed his job with passion. This was to be his last shift due to early retirement and to spend more time with his family. He could feel his stomach knot and tighten at the fear of what might happen. His thoughts were with his wife Jill and the thought of not seeing her again.

"What we going to do?" asked George.

"Look we need to stay calm first of all. I'm just as scared and as nervous as you but we need to be professional for the sake of the passengers. Come on, we need to update all the attendants and brief them on what is happening." Diana and George hugged briefly and then left the galley to inform and brief the other attendants.

"David, for a few seconds the ECAM had just shown a fire warning on engine No4 but has now gone back to overheating." After a brief discussion it was decided that the No4 engine would be shut down. David reached up and pressed the Engine No4 Master Switch. He could still see smoke out the back of the engine as he was looking out the cabin window. "Nathan, activate the extinguisher on Engine No4." Nathan reached up and flipped the plastic cover marked Fire Suppressants and hit the Engine No4 button. The ECAM was now warning that Engine No4 had failed and that the extinguisher bottle 4a was discharging. "David, I'm trying the radio again," said Nathan with a slight tremble in his voice. With the thought of all what was wrong and the possibility that the communications were down Nathan was becoming more nervous.

"May Day, May Day, May Day this is Flight Lima Alpha 1872 declaring an emergency does anybody read me?" The radio just crackled and hissed for a few seconds. "May Day, May Day, May Day this is Flight Lima Alpha 1872 declaring an emergency does anybody read me?" Again the radio just hissed and crackled. The plane continued to jump around and vibrate badly, David could feel it pulling to the port side.

"Nathan I need some help here." Nathan closed the operations manual and placed it on the tray in front of him. He then wrestled with the joystick to help David level out the plane.' Whoop Whoop, Warning Warning, Whoop Whoop'.

The ECAM was now showing several faults and warnings, 'Primary hydraulic system—low system pressure and low fluid level, wing slats inoperative and flight controls—ailerons partial control only.

Turning to look at Nathan, David could hear a metallic grating noise coming from outside. He leant forward and acknowledged the ECAM "Nathan I want you to go back to Economy Class and visually inspect all engines and check all visible damage. Something's not right back there."

"Yes Captain," said Nathan. He unclipped his safety harness stood up and reached for his jacket. He then grabbed his cap from the back of the door placed it on his head and straightened his tie.

Leaving the cockpit, Diana and George, the Senior Flight Attendants, were preparing the rest of the flight crew in the galley behind the closed curtains.

"So is everybody clear? Smart, Professional and Confident. Put the passengers first and keep them all at ease and assure them that everything is just a precaution and procedure," said Diana.

"Can I just squeeze past you all? Thanks," said Nathan in a very official but polite tone. He walked through First Class towards Business Class and gave Diana a wink as if to say well done.

The plane shook again violently jumping from side to side nearly knocking him off his feet. He straightened himself up and continued on. Close behind him, four of the attendants were following him to take up their positions in each Class ready for the public address announcement. Nathan continued down through Business Class, on the port side, down towards Economy Class near the centre of the plane.

"Ladies and Gentleman please can I have your attention? Due to the continuing technical difficulties we are experiencing the Captain has decided to attempt an emergency landing. Some of you may have seen one of the engines smoking; this in no way affects the performance of the plane and is quite safe. I want you all to ensure your seats and tray tables are in their full upright position, remove any loose jewellery, glasses and remove your shoes and place them under your seat. I stress that this only a precaution and for your safety. One of the attendants will be around shortly to take any hand luggage, laptops etc., and to hand you a pillow. When told too I want you to place the pillow on your lap, bend forward with your hands behind your head like so."

Diana then pointed to George who had taken a seat and was holding his hands behind his head with the pillow on his lap. Some of the passengers who couldn't see properly either stood on their seats or came forward slightly. Josh a little 5 year old boy came running over and tugged on Diana's skirt and said "Miss, missus are we going to crash? I've left me teddies at home, will I see them again? I want me teddies."

Diana knew there was a good chance they were going to crash after what she had seen in the cockpit. She could feel a lump rise to her throat and knots tighten in her stomach. She could feel tears forming in her eyes and gathered all of her strength together to hold them back. She knelt down onto one knee and held his hand. "What's your teddy bears names sweetheart?"

"Scribbles and Fluffy miss cause I don't have Cuddles no more cause mummy drowned him in the washing machine and he fell all apart and now he's gone but I love Scribbles and Fluffy and want to see them again." Josh's mum Sarah came and knelt down beside him and gave him a big hug. Diana squeezed his hand a little and said in a cheeky tone "Now I just happen to know the Captain also likes teddy bears and I don't think he will mind if I let you have one of his."

George sensing Diana's move had disappeared behind the curtain to the duty free and had returned with a brown teddy bear wearing a flying hat goggles with a red scarf. He passed the teddy to Diana behind her back, without Josh seeing him. Diana then pulled the teddy from behind her back and handed it to Josh. His little face lit up and he was smiling so much you could see all his baby teeth. Sarah gave Diana a hug and thanked her before leading Josh back to his seat a happy little boy.

Nathan approached the Economy Class section; he could see the complete cover missing from the No1 Engine and skin damage to the upper part of the wing. With most of the seats empty he walked up closer to the window knelt on the seat and peered down towards the bottom of the fuselage. He could just make out a four foot square gaping hole with wires and cables trailing out of it, he guessed by the size of the hole and the damage to the wing, that the engine had suffered a small explosion ripping off the engine cover which in turn damaged the wing and bounced off into the fuselage. "I've got to get back and tell the Captain" he thought.

Nathan had been a First Officer for just two years, he had spent most of his time being mentored by Captain David Benson and had become very good close friends. He would often join David and Diana during the long stay over's with much enthusiasm. He saw David as a fatherly figure and with his wealth of flying experience hung to his every word. Having learnt to fly at the age of eighteen Nathan had studied for four years at the London University and gained an MPhil/Ph. D. in Aeronautical Engineering and MPhil/

Ph. D. in Avionics. By the age of 22 he had become a flying instructor at the local flying school teaching students to fly either the Piper Warrior PA28's or the Cessna's.

He enjoyed teaching his students both at ground school and in the air, but his dream was to be an airline pilot. He needed to accumulate just over two thousand joint flying hours before he could approach any airlines, and in two years he had done just that. Having applied to Lufthansa, within weeks he was on a flight program and in the simulator. This is where he met David who then took him under his wing. They just seemed to hit it off straight away as if they had known each other and been friends for ever.

Staggering over to the starboard engines, with the plane still vibrating, he could see wisps of black smoke being emitted from the back of engine No4, the furthest engine away. Although he knew this engine had been shut down, he still felt nervous at the thought of flying on only two engines and an overheated smoking engine. Again he knelt on the window seat and peered down.

This time all he could see was damage to the flaps and ailerons his heart sank with butterflies in his tummy. The flaps are slowly lowered in stages during a descent to cause lift and drag enabling the Pilots to land at a safer speed of 166kph instead of a dangerous 230kph. He knew this wasn't going to be an ordinary landing even with all the Captains experience and his own, he knew the odds on surviving a crash landing with this magnitude of danger was not good. Feeling like his whole world was collapsing around him Nathan tried his best to compose himself and started to make his way back to the cabin to inform the Captain of his findings.

Making his way back through Business Class he was stopped by Ellie. "Are you the Captain?" asked Ellie.

"No miss I'm the First Officer or Co Pilot if you like," said Nathan with a smile. Age thirty and single Nathan didn't have much time for a partner or romance as he had always put all is effort into his career. However, when he saw Ellie he started to get butterflies in his tummy. He had not felt like this for a long time and felt a little embarrassed.

"How bad is the situation?" asked Ellie.

Nathan sat down on the adjacent seat and looked straight at her. Ellie leant slightly forward and took his hand. "Please tell me how bad is it? Do we stand a chance?"

"What's you name miss?" Nathan said in a low voice.

"Ellie, Ellie Fox," she gave his hand a squeeze.

"Nathan Taylor at your service" Ellie gave a little laugh and flicked her hair back to one side.

"Ellie, I shouldn't really tell you this but it is not good news I'm afraid. We have two engines failed with wing damage and hydraulic failures. We can land but it's going to be very difficult."

Nathan could see the sad look in her face but could tell she was a really strong person. "Where are we going to land though? We're half way across the North Atlantic Ocean!" said Ellie in a strong but low voice.

"We are about half way between Iceland and Greenland. The airport at Greenland is much larger but slightly trickier."

"How is it trickier?" asked Ellie looking coy but very interested.

"Well the runway is shorter but much wider however there are rocks on either side of the runway. If we should run out of runway we will be met by the North sea."

"It just gets better doesn't it?" asked Ellie

"Well it's not really that bad, but the chances are that we will be diverting to Keflavik in Iceland, it's not as wide but it is longer and safer," said Nathan.

Giving his hand another squeeze and leaning a little closer, Ellie asked Nathan "Will I be able to see you again? Maybe before we land or afterwards?"

Nathan could tell Ellie was taking a bit of a shine to him. Although not really ethical, Nathan had started to get more butterflies in his tummy and felt a little something towards her as in, 'love at first sight'. Ellie handed him one of her business cards with her phone number on it. Nathan took it and reached into the back right hand side of his trouser pocket and pulled out his wallet. He carefully placed the business card into his wallet and secured it back into the back pocket of his trousers. He then reached into his inside pocket, pulled out a pen and paper before writing down both his home phone number, mobile number and signed it 'Nathan Taylor'. The plane started to shake and jump around; Nathan sensed the situation was getting worse. "I need to get back to the cabin," said Nathan.

"I know, it is okay, go."

They both stood up, Ellie pulled him closer and gave him a kiss on the cheek and whispered "Thank you for telling me the truth," she too could sense that he didn't want to leave but let go of his hand to let him get back to his job. Nathan gave her a short wave and made his way towards the galley and the cabin. Ellie returned to her seat with her mind still racing around thinking of Nathan. She had indeed taken a shine to Nathan which was unusual as she too had not found much time for a relationship recently. Her previous relationship had been hard and had ended in tears. Maybe now she was trying to fill a gap in her life and was looking for someone who would truly love her. Upon fastening her seatbelt the plane began sinking and rolling to one side slightly. She just held on tight closed her eyes but couldn't stop thinking of Nathan. She wasn't sure why she was feeling this way. Maybe it was the thought that she might die and was feeling scared or decided life was too short to be alone. She could not believe that she had given a complete stranger her phone number while on a stricken plane about to make an emergency landing but one thing she did know was that she now had feelings for him. There was just something about him that she couldn't put her finger on but it was attracting her to him.

Nathan passed though Business Class towards First Class stopping several times to reassure some of the passengers that they were doing their best. Approaching the galley he pulled Diana and George to one side. "Have the rest of the flight crew been briefed?" asked Nathan.

"Yes all the flight crew are now preparing the passengers for a crash landing by assuring them that it is purely a routine so as not to cause too much panic," said George.

"Are the emergency exits covered on the wings?"

"Yes," said Diana "A gentleman down in seat 30a and another in seat 30f both volunteered to open the emergency doors after we have landed and stopped."

"Excellent," said Nathan, he left Diana and George and proceeded to the cabin. He could tell that they were both nervous and scared but he knew that they were professionals and would do their job to the best of their abilities.

He quickly unlocked the door, stepped inside and shut the door behind him. He removed his cap and hung it on the back of the door along with his jacket.

"What's the status David?"

"Engine No2 is running on reduced power and we are slowly losing altitude."

"David that's bad. I can confirm that engine No1 and No4 have shut down but are still burning out, half way back on the port side I can just make out a gash in the fuselage about four foot wide, I could see cables and hydraulics hanging out. The port side wing has skin damage and it looks like the ailerons are jammed."

"I suspected as much," said David. "She is also leaning over due to the power reduction on Engine No2."

Nathan rubbed his hands over his face and up over his hair. After he had made his way back to his seat he pulled his harness over and clicked it into place. He then grabbed his headset from the tray in front of him and placed it on his head. "David, I've been thinking we are close to Iceland and Greenland, I think we would stand a better chance at Keflavik airport in Iceland due to the fact it has a longer runway."

After checking their position on the ECAM, David pulled an air map from his flight case and opened it. After measuring from their current position to Keflavik airport the Captain agreed. "I agree Nathan; turn to a heading of 340 degrees." Nathan adjusted their position as requested. David leaned forward and retuned the UHF radio to 119.30 MHz Keflavik Radar Approach. Checking the secondary UHF, David continued with the distress call. "May Day, May Day, May Day this is Flight Lima Alpha 1872 declaring an emergency does anybody read me?" Again the radio just hissed and crackled. "May Day, May Day, May Day this is Flight Lima Alpha 1872 declaring an emergency we are 300 nautical miles due south and bound to Keflavik airport does anybody read me?"

Nathan turned to look at David and said "It's no use David I think the communications were knocked out when the engine cover blew off." David didn't say anything but just stared ahead.

"May Day, May Day, May Day this is Flight Lima Alpha 1872 declaring an emergency does anybody read me?" asked David. He was about to transmit again but the plane lurched nose down forcing the auto pilot to disengage. David instantly grabbed the controls and tried to pull the nose back up.

Nathan also grabbed the controls to assist. It felt like a sky scraper was hanging from the nose of the plane it was so heavy. The sudden descent had put them at 28000 feet before they managed to pull the nose back up. David clicked the autopilot back on and wiped his brow. It was now obvious that the hydraulics to the rudder and elevators were failing. Nathan reached forward and took hold of his operations manual and started to thumb through it looking for anything on rudder or elevator failure while David continued the distress call.

"May Day, May Day, May Day this is Flight Lima Alpha 1872 declaring an emergency does anybody read me?" asked David again.

"Lima Alpha 1872 this is International Air Distress, please state your location and souls on board repeat Lima Alpha 1872 this is International Air Distress, please state your location and souls on board." Nathan swung round sharply to look at David in utter amazement.

"Thank god!" said David looking at Nathan. David checked the readout on the ECAM way-points then clicked the radio transmit button "International Air Distress this is Lima Alpha 1872, where are two nine zero nautical miles south of Keflavik airport with one four six souls on board including flight crew."

"Lima Alpha we copy your location and one four six total souls on board. Please state your emergency."

"Nathan could you bring up the diagnostics for me?" asked David. A few seconds later his computer was listing all the current diagnostic faults and was flashing red. David again clicked the transmit button

"This is Lima Alpha 1872. Engines No1 and No4 are dead and smoking, the cover on engine No4 blew across the port side damaging the wing, ailerons elevates and flaps before making contact with the lower fuselage tearing a four foot hole, splicing cables and hydraulic pipes. We have a part electrical failure on bus No1 and are losing rudder control. Engine No2 is on reduced performance," said David feeling very nervous.

"Stand By 1872."

David looked at Nathan and said with a slight tremble in his voice "When you look at it all like this, it sure hits home how screwed we are."

Nathan just shook his head not really knowing what to say.

"Lima Alpha 1872, are you reading."

"This is Lima Alpha 1872 go ahead," said David

"1872 you have intermittent communications' failure. Turn to a heading of 355 degrees and descend to twenty thousand feet."

"Received, Lima Alpha 1872," said David. Both David and Nathan took hold of the thrusters and slowly pulled them one eighth of the way back. Looking at the altitude they could both see that she was slowly descending through 25000 feet. Continuing to descend Nathan reprogrammed the new heading into the flight computer and the plane started to tip slightly to the right and began to turn for a few seconds. The ECAM was showing that they were two hundred and forty nautical miles away from Keflavik. Approaching 21000 feet, both David and Nathan again took hold of the thrust levers and pushed forward to regain control and airspeed until they levelled out at twenty thousand feet.

"Lima Alpha 1872 this is International Air Distress."

"Lima Alpha 1872 receiving," said Nathan.

"1872 Keflavik airport is on standby with all runways clear and the emergency services ready to roll. You are close to military bases and have so much damage that you will be escorted by two F18 Hornets to help assess further damage and guide you in, they are on route and should be with you shortly."

Nathan clicked the transmit button and in his official tone said "This is Lima Alpha, message received and understood." Before he had released the transmit button two F18's blew past either side of the plane and crossed in front spinning around to settle in front of the plane, one of the F18's started to pull away again but this time rocked his wings up and down. This was the interception communication for 'follow me'

"Lima Alpha 1872 this is Flight Lieutenant Johnston to your port side. We are one three five nautical miles from Keflavik airport and need you to do an emergency descent to 8000 feet and decompress"

"Understood, Lima Alpha 1872," said Nathan. Both David and Nathan took hold of the thrusters, "fifty percent," said David as they both gently pulled back.

Descending through 19000 feet to 18500 feet David realised they were not descending fast enough. He leant forward and disengaged the auto pilot. Nathan clicked over the UHF onto intercom PA and clicked the transmit button. "Ladies and Gentleman this is the First Officer Nathan. Due to continuing technical difficulties we are now under escort by two military jets. We need to make an emergency descent which will take a few minutes. Please make sure you stay seated and that your seat belt remains tight and fastened thank you." David turned to Nathan and acknowledged the announcement he had just made with a wink and tipped his head slightly as if to say well done.

"Are you ready?" asked David.

"Yes ready." David pulled hard on the controls to the left, as he did the plane eventually banked over sharply. With the assistance of Nathan he then pushed hard forward to push the nose of the plane down but the controls were so stiff it was taking some doing. After a few seconds the nose dipped down and they began to lose their altitude rapidly. Continuing their descent Nathan reached up over his head to the right and started to adjust the in cabin pressure down slowly to decompress. Usually, if the cabin pressure is reduced too quickly it can result in your ears popping or worse a burst ear drum so he was careful not to reduce it too quickly.

Approaching 11000 feet David started to pull back on the controls and levelled out the wings. They both then increased the thrusters slowly back to full power. It took a few minutes to pull the nose back up and level out at 8000 feet. Having pulled level there was a large crack from the passenger compartments. Nathan undid his harness and jumped up making his way to the cabin door. His heart was racing and he felt very nervous. Opening the door he could see past the galley and into First Class where it became apparent that all the emergency oxygen masks had deployed.

He could see Diana and George racing round with the rest of the crew reassuring the passengers and rolling the oxygen masks back up into the head space above them. With a sigh of relief he turned round closed the cabin door and made his way back to his seat. "Bloody oxygen masks, looks like the dam lot has just deployed" Returning to his seat he pulled over his harness and clipped it together. He then reached over and took hold of his headset and placed it over his head.

"We should have taken them off automatic," said David.

"Lima Alpha 1872 this is Flight Lieutenant Johnston."

"Go ahead," said David.

"You are now, nine zero nautical miles from Keflavik airport, maintain current heading and power back to reduce your altitude to 100 feet per minute."

David clicked the transmit button and said, "Confirm, maintain current heading and descend at 100 feet per minute."

"Read back correct."

With the thrusters pulled back one eighth of the way, the altimeter read a descent rate of 100 feet per minute. David continued to hold the plane steady as it started to shudder and pull to the left. The ECAM flashed up a red warning of engine No2 diminished performance. "Dam!" said David has he leant over and acknowledged the ECAM message.

"International Distress this is Lima Alpha 1872, our situation is becoming worse. We are throttling back engine No2 and operating on engine No3 only. The rudder control and ailerons are sluggish and near inoperable please advise," said David

"This is International Air Distress, we copy your change in situation, please standby." The F18 in front banked over to the left and down towards the back of the plane. After a few minutes the F18 returned. "Lima Alpha 1872 this is Flight Lieutenant Johnston. You have massive rudder and aileron damage and the port side flaps are jammed. There is a gaping hole on the port side fuselage exposing the hydraulics, cabling and internal fuel lines. I'm afraid there's not much I can do except to tell you to prepare for a crash landing and wish you good luck."

"Lima Alpha 1872, message received and understood," said David has he released the transmit button. David and Nathan just stared at each other for a while before David clicked on the galley intercom. After a few seconds Diana answered, "Hello"

"Diana its David, we are about fifteen minutes from the airport and are preparing for a major crash landing. Stay calm and sharp Diana I need you. Make your final preparations and prepare the passengers."

Diana was now shaking slightly and with a nervous tone said, "I understand David, do your best David and may god be with us."

She then hung up the phone and quickly rounded up all the flight crew and finished a final briefing. "So is everybody clear on what they are doing? Ensure all passengers have removed all loose items and have their pillows in their laps ready, use the PA system if you have to," said Diana with as much courage as she could.

Each of the flight attendants' then made their way to their designated areas to finally prepare the passengers.

Diana slipped forward into First Class and picked up the PA intercom. "Ladies and Gentleman we have begun our descent into Keflavik airport and will be making an emergency landing in approximately ten minutes. Please make sure you have removed all loose objects and stowed your shoes under your seats along with any other valuables. Keep your pillow on your lap at all times during the descent. When the Captain shouts *brace, brace, brace* place your hands behind your head and push your head down into your pillow." Hanging up the PA phone the plane dropped as though in turbulence and started to jump around. Diana carefully made her way back to the galley, took her seat and strapped herself in.

"Holding at 1500 feet, speed 300 knots," said David as he was fighting with the controls. "Activating Air Brakes," said David and reached down to his right and pulled backwards a black lever. Just in front a green light came on. *At least something works*. He thought.

"Lima Alpha 1872 this is Keflavik Radar Approach confirming all emergency services have been deployed, you are clear to descend on runway two zero."

David clicked the transmit button, "Lima Alpha 1872 confirm clear to descend on runway two zero."

"Read back correct I'm now handing you over to Keflavik Tower, change frequency to 118.30 MHz"

"Confirm changing over to Keflavik Tower on 118.30Mhz."

David released the transmit button and retuned the UHF radio. "Keflavik Tower this is Lima Alpha 1872 on final approach runway two zero," said David. "Nathan put the landing gear down and try flaps thirty degrees."

Nathan pulled the lever down on the dash panel marked *landing gear.* Nathan could hear the usual whirling noise as the landing gear slowly came down. He then reached down and set the flaps to thirty degrees, as he did the right wing shot upwards sharply indicating a failure on the left flap. Nathan recognised the flap failure and reset it back to zero degrees. David and Nathan heard the first clunk as the nose gear locked into position, a second clunk as the right port side gear locked into position but no third clunk. The landing gear warning lights were showing two green lights and one red light. Nathan tapped the red light a few times then reset the landing gear again with the usual whirling noise. The thrusters were pulled back to one quarter but the airspeed was still showing nearly 250 knots. Clunk, clunk again the nose wheel and port side gears locked into place but no starboard gear.

"Lima Alpha 1872 this is Flight Lieutenant Johnston, please be advised your starboard side gear has not engaged, I repeat your starboard side gear as not engaged."

Nathan who was now sweating really badly placed his shaking hand on the controls and pressed the transmit button, "Lima Alpha 1872, message received." He released the transmit button and turned to look at David.

David still remaining calm composed and looking as fresh as he always did, said, "I have a visual on the runway."

Nathan acknowledged David and then clicked his transmit button again, "Keflavik Tower this is 1872 confirming a visual on runway two zero. Please be advised we are leaking hydraulic fluid and possibly fuel, the starboard gear is down but has not locked into place." "1872 Message received please stand by."

A moment or two had passed as the radio crackled, "1872 this is Keflavik Tower, the emergency services have foamed down the runway one quarter in and down to the end of the runway."

When the tower finished speaking the ECAM started flashing up an error, Whoop Whoop, Warning Warning, Whoop Whoop. Both David and Nathan could hear the metallic grating noise again, Whoop Whoop, Warning Warning, Whoop Whoop. The plane shuddered and pitched over to the left. David already on the controls was fighting to level the plane out while Nathan checked the ECAM.

"We have engine failure on engine No2!" said Nathan. His hands still trembling Nathan reached over and engaged the engine No2 Master Switch. The ECAM beeped indicating engine No2 failure.

Just a mile away from the runway banking over to the left and shaking violently David and Nathan battled with the controls to try and level it out but it was no use. Approaching three quarters of a mile to the runway the two F18's broke away, one flew up and away to the left and the other up and away to the right, both did so respectively. Edging closer to the runway they could both see the vast amount of flashing blue lights situated up the runway which was glowing off nearby objects. A lump came to Nathan's throat and tears started to come to his eyes. He knew this was it. Coming closer to the beginning of the runway David clicked the PA and said, "brace, brace, brace."

Hearing the brace command all the passengers and flight crew put their hands behind their heads and pulled their heads down into their pillows.

Some of the passengers were crying and a young couple in the front of Economy Class had wrapped their arms around each other with their heads close together in their pillows. Sarah was cuddling Josh with her hand on his back to keep his head down while Josh was holding his teddy tight. Another couple had their young daughter in the middle with both their arms wrapped around her. Ellie had her head partly in her pillow but was looking over the top of it while pulling her tights out of her toes. She too had tears in her eyes and was still thinking of Nathan and what he and the Captain must be going through. She pulled her head into her pillow and closed her eyes tightly.

Flying at 230 knots at four hundred feet David and Nathan knew they were coming in too fast and too high, they tried hard to pull the nose up to lose height but the controls were stiff and not responding. Flying over the blue flashing lights from the emergency services, they pulled back on the thrusters to kill the power to the remaining engine but it wasn't shutting down. Trying desperately to bring the port side wing back up, the plane shuddered again as engine No3 finally shut down.

Passing the beginning of the runway they could see the foam that had been sprayed onto the runway to assist in reducing the chance of an explosion or fire on landing. The plane started to descend slowly at first to 350 feet then 300 feet. Continuing at 210 knots and descending further to 200 feet they knew they were still way too fast but were trying desperately to level out the wings. Descending to 100 feet, the flight computer started up with a digital voice speaking out the altitude; "90, 80, 70." Flying at 200 knots and a quarter of the way down the runway with all the emergency services following, sirens wailing and blues lights flashing, a last attempt was made to level out the wings but it was too late.

Crash Landing
~ Chapter Two ~

The port side wing scraped down onto the runway leaving a five meter wide spray of bright orange sparks shooting up and behind into the night air. Seconds later the rear of the plane touched down causing the port side landing gear to collapse and buckle upwards piercing the bottom of the fuselage before ripping off and spinning out of control behind the plane.

Before they knew what was happening the landing gear had struck the pursuing fire engine smashing through the windscreen and tearing the roof away. The driver was severed in two and killed instantly while the front passenger was decapitated. With his head sliced off, it blew upwards and behind leaving a huge trail of crimson red blood before coming into contact with the ambulance behind. The fire engine jerked round sharply to the right before tipping over and sliding uncontrollably before stopping at the side of the runway. The ambulance following, unable to see anything through the blood smeared smashed windscreen, slammed hard into the back of the fire engine catapulting it over onto its roof leaving the driver partially hanging out the window dead and the occupants crushed to death inside.

The port side wing continued to scrape deeply into the runway shooting white hot sparks up in every direction while bits of the fuselage near the failed landing gear burnt up and broke away. The nose wheels had touched down very heavily sending the plane further off balance until the wing tip gouged forcefully into the edge of the runway shifting and pulling the plane around to the left.

The force of the plane now sliding sideways ruptured the starboard wing fracturing the fuel lines spraying aviation fuel over the back of the plane. The foam on the runway did little to help as flying sparks ignited the spray of the fuel. Instantly the two engines exploded tearing the wing away leaving the plane to buckle and roll over to the right, sliding off the edge of the runway towards a group of private hangers. The rear section of the plane was now burning ferociously with flames leaping out with black toxic smoke billowing out and over the runway.

The eight fire engines still pursuing had nearly caught up when they all activated their external foam cannons. The massive spray of combined foam caught the back of the plane and smothered some of the flames just as the remaining two engines exploded violently sending debris flying in every direction.

Damaged and battered the plane continued to roll over smashing out all the cabin windows before a further explosion tore off the tail section sending passengers flying into the air. Some were crushed to death instantly under the plane while a few others were ripped from their seats and thrown out the windows before it came smashing to an abrupt stop up against the private hangars.

Continuing to burn uncontrollably, thick black toxic smoke had started to fill the cabin. The emergency services carefully made their way through the debris and bodies scattered all over everywhere. Some of the bodies had, had their arms or legs ripped off leaving a trail of body parts and blood soaked corpses. The Fire Brigade started to carefully clear a path through the wreckage when an almighty massive explosion and fireball ripped up into the night sky and shook the ground. The flames from the burning wreckage had inadvertently set fire to the hanger roof sending burning debris swirling around inside the hanger. The maintenance staff didn't stand a chance as the two private jets had exploded ripping open the side of the hanger. The force of the explosion had torn the fuselage and cabin in two. Still trapped in their seats, a few of the passengers were engulfed in flames, screaming and burning to death.

In a matter of seconds the Fire Brigade had the flames under control and nearly extinguished them when it became apparent that there were a few survivors still trapped inside. With the smoke clearing slightly, some of the passengers started to emerge from the middle of the cabin. Looking dazed and dishevelled with torn clothes they were led off to the awaiting ambulances to be treated. The minutes quickly passed by with numerous more ambulances and fire engines turning up to assist, making their way to the smouldering cabin searching for survivors to help lead them to safety.

Amongst all the mass devastation and utter mayhem, nothing could quite prepare the rescue team for what they were about to face. Ian Hughes was responsible for directing the fire and rescue officers to extinguish the rest of the flames and make the fuselage and cabin safe. With the smoke clearing from the inside of the cabin, the fire officers and paramedics began to sift through the bodies to check for survivors. Inside the cabin there was wreckage strewn everywhere covered in thick black soot. Most of the remaining passengers were still fastened into their seats but it was obvious that they were dead. The fire officers carefully cut away the seatbelts and lowered the bodies to the floor, where they were then taken outside. The paramedics were checking everybody for signs of life but so far the body count was at sixty two with only a hand full of survivors.

Having made their way through the first section of the plane it was starting to become darker and darker.

"Trevor!" shouted Ian,

"Yes Sir," said Trevor as he came running over.

"I want you and Gavin to set up the rest of the flood lights as soon as possible. The paramedics are working by torch light and can't see what the hell they are doing. I've called in for more backup which will be arriving shortly. I'll be over at the temporary morgue when you're done."

"Yes Sir?" asked Trevor as he set off to find Gavin and set up the rest of the flood lights.

Ian was a medium built athletic looking guy, which was not bad for a forty-two year old. He had a dark rugged complexion with brown swept hair. He had worked with the airport Fire Brigade all his life and had successfully worked his way up from Fire Officer to Operational Station Manager and finally airport Fire Manager. Ian was no stranger to plane wrecks or mutilated bodies but it didn't make it much easier. Making his way over to the temporary morgue he could see the paramedics had started to recover and tag most of the bodies and limbs that were scattered over most of the field and part of the runway. Approaching the morgue, the remaining flood lights burst into life lighting the entire plane, field and morgue. Continuing to walk, he could see bodies of all ages from a few pensioners near the back to numerous children about halfway back. Most of the bodies were blackened, burnt and virtually unrecognisable.

Having caught up with Ian, Trevor and Gavin were now co-ordinating their efforts inside the mid section of the plane. Although most of the bodies had now been removed they were surprised to see many survivors being tended to by paramedics and the rescue team with some of the passengers making their way to safety unaided. With all the flames fully extinguished, the foam was now starting to dissolve leaving pools of water everywhere.

Trevor and Gavin continued through the mid section towards the front, the shafts of light beaming through the windows was reflecting off the water creating an airy swirling pattern on the ceiling.

Trevor jumped slightly has his radio crackled. "Trevor, are you receiving?" asked Ian.

"Yes go ahead," said Trevor.

"What's the situation inside?"

"We have just passed around ten survivors and can see a few more ahead. What's the current body count Sir?"

"There are one hundred and twelve bodies counted. The National Transportation Safety Board has just arrived Trevor. Continue up front until the whole plane has been searched and report back to me," said Ian.

"Yes Sir. Come on Gavin let's check up front," said Trevor as he clipped the radio back onto his belt.

Setting off, Gavin caught something with his right foot. Crouching down he picked the object up to discover it was a teddy bear. It was wearing a flying hat, goggles and a red scarf. He looked at it for a few seconds wondering whose teddy it was before carefully placing it down on the seats at the side.

"Help, help me!" shouted a weary voice from just in front of them.

Hurrying over Trevor could see a young woman trapped down on the floor between two seats. Her clothes were ripped, torn and soaked with blood while her hair was all mattered covering part of her face.

"Hayley, we need some assistance up here," shouted Trevor who then looked down towards the back of the plane.

"Hang on a sec," she replied. Hayley Spencer was one of the airports on site paramedics. She had worked with Trevor for many years forming a really good working relationship. Wearing the paramedics green uniform she had dark brown hair fastened back into a pony tail and a tanned complexion. At thirty six years old and a mum of two, Hayley prided herself in eating healthy and keeping in shape.

A moment later she came sprinting up the aisle with a trauma kit over her left shoulder and a torch in her right hand. "What we got Gavin?"

"Her names Ellie," said Gavin, "She has a deep cut on her forehead and a dislocated shoulder. We put the neck brace on as a precaution but I don't think there is any spinal damage".

"Hi Ellie, my names Hayley, can you tell me where it hurts the most?"

"My right shoulder is so painful and my bum is killing me where I landed on it," said Ellie.

"Okay my love let me get you off the floor and onto this seat to make you a bit more comfortable."

Once Ellie was seated properly Hayley said, "Your right shoulder is dislocated, I'm going to relocate it but you may feel a sharp pain for a moment okay?" asked Hayley.

"Will it stop hurting once you've done it?"

"Yes it should stop hurting but I won't lie, it will throb a little afterwards. I'm going to give you something for the pain first though," said Hayley. She then took a vial marked *Tramadol* and a syringe from the trauma pack and start to fill the syringe. She then rolled Ellie's shirt sleeve up and swabbed clean the upper part of her arm. "Sharp scratch," said Hayley as she then injected the Tramadol.

Hayley spent the next few minutes cleaning up the gash on Ellie's forehead and applied several butterfly stitches. "There you're as good as new. Right, the painkiller should be working now so I'm going to relocate your shoulder."

"Okay, but do it quick," said Ellie feeling a bit nervous.

Having diagnosed the dislocation as anterior, Hayley stood just in front of her and bent her elbow to ninety degrees and pulled her arm across her chest. She then held her shoulder while she carefully took her wrist and rotated her arm outwards until she felt the joint pop back in.

"That's so much better," said Ellie, "the pain went almost straight away, Thank you." Hayley continued to examine Ellie, taking her blood pressure while Gavin and Trevor continued their way up to the front of the plane.

Slowly opening his eyes, his vision was blurred with a sharp pain above his left eye. He could smell burning and sensed there was smoke in the air. Nathan was still alive and feeling very confused. His shirt was slightly ripped and covered in blood across the top half and his tie was missing. Still fastened tightly in his seat he blindly reached down to unclip his harness and fell forward slightly until he put his arm out to steady himself. He tried to wipe his eyes but his face was stinging from the flying shards of glass.

Once he managed to come to his senses he started to look around. Every window was completely smashed with the glass spread all over. There were traces of smoke coming out of the dash panels which were shattered open exposing the wires behind. It then hit him like a bolt of lightning, the Captain was gone. Peering round he could see the cockpit door was still locked. He carefully made his way over to the Captains seat while trying to keep his balance. He could see his harness had been ripped out at the anchors; his heart sank realising he could only have gone through the windshield. Nathan stood on the seat as quickly as he could and leaned forward and stared out over the smashed window expecting to see the Captain, Captain David Benson his best friend, his mentor.

He couldn't believe what he was seeing. He knew it was early in the evening but outside was brightly lit with blue lights flashing everywhere. He pulled his right hand up over his eyes as the lights were blinding him and continued to look around. There were rescue workers and paramedics all over the place but no sign of David. Nathan was now bewildered, where was David? What had happened to him, was he alive or was he dead.

The sharp cracking sound startled Nathan as he spun round to see the cockpit door burst open. He carefully stepped down from the seat to be greeted by two rescue workers. Gavin and Trevor had been making their way to the front of the plane searching for survivors when they had reached the locked cockpit door. Trevor had tried to kick the door open with no luck but Gavin, being stocky and well built gave it one kick sending the door bursting open. They recognised Nathan as the First Officer by the three gold stripes on his epaulettes. "Sir, are you okay?" asked Gavin as Nathan came hobbling over to them.

"I think so," said Nathan, but he didn't look too good with a large gash on his left leg just below his knee. Making his way to the door he paused as he looked down into First Class.

The intense smell of burning was overwhelming; most of the seats were dislodged and ripped apart. The roof panels were blackened with a few hanging down revealing the masses of cabling in the roof space. Pools of water that had gathered along the floor were sparkling, reflecting the dusty beams of light from the flood lights outside. Most of the overhead compartments had come undone with bags and cases hanging out with the odd coat and jacket draping down.

"What have I done" thought Nathan. Although he knew he wasn't to blame, he felt so guilty at the carnage before him. *Ellie, I need to find Ellie and David*, he said to himself. Trevor helped Nathan out into the galley where he sat him down. He reached behind and removed a first aid kit from his belt. After he had cleaned up the cut on his leg he started to apply a large gauze padded bandage while Gavin cleaned up the cut above his eye. "I think you're going to need a few stitches," said Gavin.

"I don't have time; I need to find my friend and the Captain. Have you seen the Captain?" asked Nathan.

"We haven't but there are many survivors that have been taken outside. I'll glue the cut together as a temporary measure but we need to get you looked at properly," said Gavin. After they had cleaned him up Gavin and Trevor helped Nathan to his feet as he then started to limp making his way down the plane to look for Ellie. With all the burnt panels, ripped out seats and debris all over the place he knew there wasn't much chance that Ellie had survived but he desperately wanted to find her. He started to draw closer to where she had been sat before the crash; he could see a paramedic knelt down tending to a passenger. He started to get butterflies in his tummy and his pulse quickened. Even though his leg was throbbing like mad he hurried as quickly as he could to see who it was.

"Nathan!" screamed Ellie as she jumped up and ran towards him. She had tears in her eyes as she wrapped her arms around him and squeezed him tightly. She closed her eyes as he put his hands on her face. Her tummy was doing somersaults as they both embraced and kissed.

"Do you need a hand Hayley?" asked Trevor as she started to repack her trauma bag. "Yes please," said Hayley as Trevor made his way over to help her pack.

"Ellie, David is missing and I need to find him," said Nathan with a tremble in his voice.

Ellie seeing the desperation in his eyes took hold of his hand and said "Come on, we'll both go and find him. I'm sure he is just fine though so stop whittling like an old woman and come on." Nathan feeling a little more at ease started to chuckle at what she said and wiped the tears from his eyes. Following Hayley and Trevor they all made their way to the planes exit followed by Gavin who had radioed through to update Ian.

"The plane as been searched Sir and more survivors have been discovered. Is there any word on the Captain Sir? The First Officer has been found alive and is looking for him but he is missing and nowhere to be seen," said Gavin.

"I've not heard anyone mention him so if he's not on the plane you could check down the morgue," said Ian.

"Understood Sir," said Gavin as he then replaced the radio on his belt.

Nathan stood in awe at the scene that greeted him before he stepped out onto the field. He started to look around for David but it was just too much for him. There were ambulances and fire engines everywhere with paramedics tending to the wounded and people being taken away on stretchers.

"We need to get you two off to hospital to be looked at properly," said Hayley.

"No, I need to know what's happened to the Captain!" said Nathan.

"Maybe you should go and check down at the makeshift morgue first if you're up to it?" asked Gavin.

"Where is it?" asked Ellie as she took hold of Nathan's hand with both of hers. Gavin spun round to the left and pointed "It's the black canopy tent down behind the fire engine. Lindsey Alden is the officer in charge and co-ordinator. She will be able to help you more." Nathan shook Gavin's and Trevor's hand and thanked Hayley before he and Ellie made their way over.

"Are you sure you don't want to go to the hospital Ellie?"

"No I want to be with you, I'm scared Nathan, please don't leave me."

"It's okay, I'm not leaving you," said Nathan as he leant over and gave her a kiss on the cheek to reassure her.

Approaching the morgue they could see rows upon rows of bodies. Most of the bodies were covered while the others were still being processed and tagged. Near the front row they could see the bodies of some young children one of whom they could see was a little boy. Nathan's heart sank as he walked past and recognised George the Senior Flight Attendant. He just stopped and stared. Ellie too had recognised George and started to sob. Nathan put his arm around her and pulled her head into his chest and just held her. "Are you okay?" asked a voice from behind them. Turning round they were both greeted by a short, slightly overweight woman with dark brown cropped hair and wearing a fluorescent yellow jacket with NTSB (National Transportation Safety Board) on the back.

"I'm Lindsey Alden, the area co-ordinator"

"First Officer Nathan Taylor; I'm looking for Captain David Benson and Diana Burton the Senior Flight Attendant."

After a short pause she said "Well the good news is you won't find either of them here but I think you better come and sit down."

Lindsey then led them both over to a portacabin nearby. Entering the portacabin it felt warm with the smell of coffee in the air. "Take a seat," said Lindsey in a calming voice. Both Nathan and Ellie sat down looking puzzled. After Lindsey sat down she started turning the pages on her clipboard and reading the notes.

"Where's David?" asked Nathan getting anxious.

Lindsey looked up and turned her chair to face them both. "Look, I'm going to be blunt and straight to the point with you," Nathan could feel Ellie shaking as he held her hand. "Captain Benson is alive but in a very bad way, after the plane left the runway he was thrown through the wind shield where he was impaled on a length of metal that had broken off from the fuselage. The metal spike punctured his lung and severed his heart. Although he was pronounced dead at the scene Bruce Bennett the Trauma Surgeon cut open his heart to massage it and then restarted it before stabilising him. He has been airlifted to Keflavik General Hospital. The chances are though he won't make it to the weekend as his heart is so badly damaged."

Nathan was in shock at what he had just heard and couldn't speak.

"What about Diana, is she okay?" asked Ellie

"Diana wasn't so lucky either I'm afraid," said Lindsey.

"Diana has suffered massive internal injuries when she was crushed under the seats with multiple organ failure; she too is currently on a life support machine at the hospital." With his leg still throbbing and feeling shocked, Nathan leaned forward to hold his leg but noticed that blood was leaking from the bandage.

"I think we should get you two off to the hospital to be treated. You should be able to see David and Diana when you get there and learn more on what's happening," said Lindsey.

She then stood up and walked over to the door and opened it. She gestured and shouted over to a paramedic whom came running over. "Take these two over to the General Hospital to be checked out," said Lindsey in a very official tone.

"Yes marm?" asked Danny. Seeing the blood oozing from Nathan's leg and seeing him hobble over Danny took hold of his upper arm and helped him down the steps. Ellie thanked Lindsey then turned to follow Nathan.

"Now then what are your pair's names," said Danny.

"I'm Nathan and this is Ellie," said Nathan in a weary voice.

"I'm Danny Evans; the ambulance is just over here."

With the vast amount of ambulances and blue flashing lights, Nathan wondered how he knew which one was which but just hobbled along with him.

Upon reaching the ambulance they were greeted by Doug Colby Danny's colleague. "Hi I'm Doug, let's get you both inside." he said with a reassuring smile. He then took hold of Nathan's other arm while they both helped him into the back of the ambulance and onto a stretcher. Ellie managed to climb in herself but it was becoming evident the painkillers were wearing off.

"Jump up here," said Danny patting on the opposite stretcher.

"I don't think I can, my shoulder is still killing me," said Ellie.

Danny bent down and pulled a step from underneath the stretcher and helped her up. Once on the stretcher Ellie lay down and turned to look at Nathan. Danny then closed the doors, walked round and climbed into the driver's seat and started the short journey to the hospital.

After Doug had made Ellie comfortable and given her some more painkillers he turned round to see to Nathan. Taking hold of the BP monitor he slipped the cuff up to the upper part of his arm and fastened it closed. The machine started to hum and the digits began to increase on the monitor. "BP 160 over 98 pulse 105. Your blood pressure is slightly high but not unexpected considering what you've been through." Doug then removed the cuff and monitor and packed them away. He then focused his attention on Nathan's leg, he asked "Tell me which part hurts the most" as he started to press his fingers into Nathan's leg.

"Ouch that hurts really badly!" said Nathan as he nearly sat bolt upright.

"It appears you have fractured you fibular bone young man," said Doug.

"What's a fibular?" chirped up Ellie.

"Well, just below your knee cap you have two bones, the tibia which is the thick main bone and the fibular which is a much smaller bone that runs parallel to the tibia," said Doug. "Will he be okay?" asked Ellie looking worried.

"Yes he'll be fine. Don't worry." Doug then walked over to the compartments at the left rear of the ambulance and took out what looked like a roll of plastic.

"What's that for?" asked Nathan nervously.

"It's an air splint. It's a bit like a temporary cast to immobilise you leg and prevent any further damage." Doug then unrolled the plastic and carefully lifted Nathan's leg slightly by the ankle; he then slipped the plastic up his leg to his knee. Nathan groaned as the plastic pulled over the area where the cut was.

"Don't be such a big girl," said Ellie playfully which made Nathan laugh.

Once the plastic cover was pulled all the way up to his knee Doug inserted a rubber tube and started to pump air into it. "It might hurt a little at first and feel a bit tight," said Doug as he kept pumping in the air.

Once fully inflated Doug removed the rubber tube and stowed it in a side draw.

"How you feeling now," said Doug as he pulled a blanket up over his legs and up to his chest.

"The pain, it's really bad," said Nathan wincing.

Doug unlocked the cabinet behind the driver's seat and took out a vial marked Pethidine and then grabbed a syringe from the draw below. "Steady as we go Danny," said Doug as he drew the clear liquid into the syringe. He then administered the injection intravenously in his upper arm. "That will help take the edge off," said Doug with a reassuring smile.

After a few minutes Nathan started to feel all warm and relaxed as the pain started ease away. "That's so much better," said Nathan with a sigh of relief.

Past, Present, Future
~ Chapter Three ~

Upon arriving at the hospital Danny backed up to the entrance at A&E, and then he jumped out and walked round to the back to open the doors. Doug first helped Ellie to her feet before Danny helped her down the steps. Danny then released the hydraulic ramp as Doug pushed Nathan's stretcher onto it. After Nathan was carefully lowered down, Doug pushed him across the short concourse as Danny packed the ramp away and secured the ambulance.

The Accident and Emergency unit was brightly lit with Nurses and Doctors rushing around everywhere. Although the scene looked chaotic, with around sixty patients, it was really well organised. Depending on the severity, the first step is to see a triage Nurse who assesses and categorises the injuries followed by treatment or further investigation. The patient is then either taken into Surgery, to a ward or released.

After Ellie and Nathan were handed over to the triage Nurse, Danny and Doug wished them good luck and left to continue their shift. Having both been placed in private cubicles Ellie and Nathan could still see each other which was reassuring. After being briefly checked over Ellie was transferred down to radiology to x-ray her shoulder and neck while Nathan was still being checked over. "I'm Dr Abigail Winters. Do you have any other pain apart from your leg?"

"My heads still throbbing a bit," said Nathan as he pointed to the cut on his forehead. "Yes I can see that it's been temporarily glued. I'll have Nurse Morgan clean you up and pop a few stitches to your head and your leg, then we need to get you down for an x-ray. I'm going to remove your splint so we can get to the gash below your knee."

"Okay," said Nathan. He still felt very calm and relaxed from the painkillers as Abigail deflated the splint and carefully slid it off his leg. While Nurse Morgan cleaned up the cut on his forehead and started to apply the stitches Abigail began to clean up his leg and also apply stitches. It only took a few minutes before they were both finished.

"How does that feel?" asked Abigail.

"It feels okay. My heads not hurting as much now," said Nathan.

Nathan left to have his leg x-rayed just as Ellie was returning.

"Are you okay?" asked Ellie

"Yes I'm okay." Nathan said as he was then wheeled out.

"I think we can take your neck collar off now Ellie," said Abigail as she studied Ellie's x-ray. "Your shoulder is fine now and there's no lasting damage to your neck either."

Abigail placed the x-rays down on the side and unclipped the neck collar and slowly removed it.

"Thank you," said Ellie with a sigh of relief.

"I'll just get your discharge papers signed and you'll be able to leave," said Abigail as she then left and walked over to the Nurses' station.

After a few minutes, both Nathan and Abigail returned at the same time. Abigail handed Ellie a patient release form and an after-care leaflet. Ellie thanked her and walked across to Nathan's bed and took hold of his hand. "How you feeling?" asked Nathan.

"I'm feeling much better for seeing you," said Ellie with a sweet smile.

Abigail came walking over holding an x-ray and said with a smile, "I have good news Nathan."

Nathan put his hands by his sides and pulled his self upright. Abigail perched herself on the edge of his bed. "The good news is you are well enough to go, however you have a small fracture on your fibular bone. Because it is so small it will heal on its own without the need for a cast, but I am recommending you use a walking stick for a few weeks to help keep the weight off your leg."

"That's excellent news!" said Nathan feeling relieved.

"Nurse Morgan has gone to get you a walking stick and your release papers. Meanwhile there is a Ron Shaw from the airline that's here to see you," said Abigail. Abigail gave Nathan a smile then left with the x-rays.

"Ellie, Nathan, Good Evening, I'm Ron Shaw," said a tall, well dressed gentleman.

Ron was about 5' 8" tall, very lean wearing a black suit, white shirt and black tie with gold rim spectacles on the end of his nose. At fifty six years old he had virtually pure grey side swept wavy hair with a near perfect parting. Ellie looked at Nathan startled as if to say, *how does he know my name?*

"I am acting on behalf of your employers Nathan to make sure you are being looked after and get home safely. I have taken the liberty of booking you both into the Radisson hotel just down the road where a couturier will be waiting to provide you both with fresh clothes. Tomorrow at 11am you will have a private jet fly you both back to London where you will be interviewed."

Nathan just sat with his mouth open in amazement. "Captain David Benson and Flight Attendant Diana Burton, I want to see them."

"They have both been transferred to The London Royal Trauma Hospital about half an hour ago," said Ron.

"Are they okay?" asked Nathan.

"They have both been stabilised but are in a very bad way however they stand a better chance of finding donors over in London. Meantime, if you require anything else use your credit card and you will be fully reimbursed." Ron then removed his glasses, folded them and placed them in his top left jacket pocket before wishing them both well and then leaving.

Both Ellie and Nathan just looked in amazement as he disappeared down the corridor and out the double doors.

"These guys seem to know everything," said Nathan.

"Pity they didn't know the plane was going to crash, I wouldn't have got on it" said Ellie.

Nathan turned to look at her as if to say *behave yourself!* Ellie just smiled with a big cheesy grin on her face.

"Right, let's get you up and cracking," said Nurse Morgan as she returned with some paperwork and a light grey walking stick. She handed the discharge papers and a patient after-care leaflet to Ellie while she helped Nathan to his feet.

"The walking stick will mimic what your left leg does. So instead of putting the weight on your leg you will put your weight on the stick," said Nurse Morgan.

"Yes I think I get it" said Nathan as he started to hobble around the bed.

Ellie put her hand over her mouth as she started to chuckle at him as she came round the bed and took hold of his hand.

Nathan asked Nurse Morgan "What's your first name?"

"Natalie, Natalie Morgan."

"Thank you for your help Natalie," said Nathan gratefully.

Ellie thanked her as well as they both left. Upon walking through the exit doors, the cool evening breeze felt refreshing and soothing. It had been a long day and both of them were tired.

Making their way over to where the taxi cabs were parked, Nathan bent down to the window of one and asked "Do you accept British pounds?"

"Yes Sir, Krona, Dollars or pounds. Where you going?" asked the cab driver.

"The Radisson Hotel?" asked Nathan.

"The Radisson is only about ten minute's away, jump in and I'll take you both over." After the short trip Nathan paid the driver as they got out and made their way to the front counter. "Hi can I help you?" asked the receptionist.

"Ellie Fox and Nathan Taylor," said Nathan.

Looking down the computer screen she said "Yes, you're both in room 136C, I also have a note that you will be seeing the couturier, I will send her up to you," she then printed out two key cards and handed them to Nathan. "Enjoy your stay" she said in a pleasant voice.

Ellie inserted the key card and opened the door to the smell of fresh lavender and a warmly lit room. After looking around she lay sprawled flat out on the bed, "This is perfect," she said as Nathan slumped down heavily on the sofa. A few moments later there was a knock on the door. Ellie jumped up and opened it.

"I'm Charlie Fern; I understand you're in need of a few new outfits?" she said in a posh accent with a comforting smile. She was wearing black trousers, a white polo neck t-shirt and black braces with straight long blonde hair.

"Yes, yes come in," said Ellie a bit stunned.

Charlie stepped inside followed by an assistant that wheeled in a huge rack of clothes. Over the next half hour Ellie was in and out of the bathroom trying on different clothes, underwear and shoes with the help of Charlie while Nathan had already picked out several sets of clothes and was sat on the sofa watching. After they had finished, Charlie gave Ellie a hug and bid her good bye as her assistant left two suit cases and wheeled the rack of remaining clothes outside. After taking a shower Nathan lay on the bed wearing his hotel pyjamas while Ellie was taking a shower. After she had done she emerged from the bathroom drying her hair with a huge white towel and also wearing her hotel pyjamas that were turned up several times at the bottom before jumping on the bed and snuggling up to Nathan under his chin. Nathan reached over and kissed her on the forehead and wrapped his arms around her.

"Tell me a bit about yourself," said Nathan as he looked into her eyes.

"Well my names Ellie Fox" she said with a smile and a chuckle. "I'm 27 and I was born 17th November 1982 in Manchester. I'm 5' 7" tall; I love reading, eating out and girl shopping. I used to live with me mum Linda and my dad Kevin in Manchester until I saved up and bought my own flat in Wollaton, Nottingham. I've been driving for six years and I have one of those new yellow Volkswagen beetles. I spent most of the time studying for my BA in fashion, maths, English and history at the Nottingham University before designing my own brand of clothes to which I now sell in Nottingham and trying to promote and sell over in Europe and America."

"Wow, you're a bit of a smarty pants aren't you, but a yellow beetle? Come on," said Nathan laughing.

"You cheeky bugger!" said Ellie as she playfully jabbed him in the ribs. "It's gorgeous, wait till you see it," she said enthusiastically, "Now what about you? Tell me about you," said Ellie as she turned over putting her head on his chest and looking up at him.

"I'm Nathan Taylor," he laughed, "I'm 29 and was born 28th June 1981 in Nottingham. I too lived with my mother Pat and my father Eric but now I have a house in Nottingham. I studied and gained a Ph. D. in Aeronautical Engineering and Avionics at London University when I then became a flying instructor for a few years until I applied to be First Officer which I've done for the last four years. I've known David and Diana for the last four years and spend most of my time with David when we're not flying together. He's been my mentor, teacher and best friend ever since I started. I to enjoy reading, mainly horrors and thrillers and I can drive but don't own a car; however I do have a motorbike. I like walking and eating out. Maybe I could take you to my favourite restaurant one day?" he said as he looked down at her, but her eyes were closed as she'd fallen asleep. Trying not to disturb her, he reached down and pulled the covers over the both of them and turned out the table lamp before falling asleep in her arms.

The following morning as they both started to wake, Ellie leant over and kissed Nathan and said "Morning gorgeous."

"Good Morning sweetheart, how you feeling?" asked Nathan as he pulled himself up. "My shoulder feels stiff but I slept like a baby, how about you," said Ellie as she sat up. "I'm good; my leg feels sore but not too bad. I'm going to order some breakfast, is there anything you fancy," said Nathan with a smile.

"Anything," said Ellie as she yawned and stretched, "I'm starving."

While Nathan was ordering breakfast Ellie went to the bathroom to get washed up and dressed. After about twenty minutes she emerged brushing her hair "It's all yours gorgeous," said Ellie as Nathan then got up and disappeared into the bathroom.

While brushing his teeth he heard a knock on the door and knew that room service had arrived. He quickly finished up and left the bathroom. Ellie was already tucking into some toast while pouring two cups of coffee. "Sugar?" asked Ellie

"No not for me," said Nathan smiling as he grabbed a sausage and flicked the telly on. "Look the accident is on the telly," said Nathan as he switched to the news channel. "We were so lucky, the report says there were only 34 survivors," said Nathan as he switched the telly back off and went back to the breakfast trolley.

Ellie was already tucking into some bacon while Nathan grabbed a plate. He had taken the liberty of ordering a little bit of everything, Bacon, Poached eggs, sausages, hash browns, beans, tomatoes, mushrooms, fresh sliced fruit and coffee with frothy milk and a jug of orange juice.

"You do know how to spoil a girl," said Ellie smiling.

"Nathan?" asked Ellie looking down at the floor, "There's something I need to tell you." Ellie went over to the sofa and sat down as Nathan joined her. "About three years ago I was in a really bad relationship. I was beaten and hurt, being too afraid to say anything I just went from day to day hoping he would change. He would come in at night drunk, rip my clothes off and force me to have sex. I was so scared I just couldn't see any way out."

"So what happened in the end?" asked Nathan.

"It had been going on for several years before I finally plucked up the courage to do something about it. One night he came home drunk and tried to pull my skirt off, I grabbed the ashtray and smacked him over the head with it. I then called the Police whom came out and arrested him. He's still in Prison serving five years for raping me and domestic violence. I went to several counselling sessions but they didn't really work for me. I sometimes get flash backs but try to hide the hurt and pain he caused me."

Nathan put his arms around her and pulled her close. "I will never hurt you Ellie. I will protect you and look after you."

"Does this mean we are a couple then?" asked Ellie.

"Yes it does, we'll just take things slowly and steady sweetheart," said Nathan.

Ellie had tears in her eyes as she flung her arms around him and hugged him tight. She knew in her heart that Nathan was the one and that he would look after her and take good care of her and how right she would be.

After they had finished breakfast they straightened the room, packed their suit cases and headed down to the lobby. Nathan handed the key cards into reception, signed the invoice and thanked the receptionist. It was a warm sunny morning with a cool light breeze. After summoning a taxi cab it only took twenty minutes to get to the airport. They both got out the cab; Nathan paid the driver and thanked him.

"Where to now?" asked Ellie.

"The Pilots entrance, follow me," said Nathan has he took her hand. Making their way over the main airport concourse they arrived at a door marked private. Nathan took his ID Card out his wallet and ran it through the scanner until the door clicked open.

They made their way through a few winding corridors and past the briefing room before coming out at the private hangars. A brand new twelve seater Challenger 605 Private Jet was sat on the tarmac with the steps down.

"Hi I'm Nathan Taylor and this is Ellie Fox"

"Good Morning, I'm Captain Colin Geoffrey's," said a neatly dress gentleman as he approached them.

After they had shaken hands, Colin said "We are ready when you are," as he gestured towards the steps on the plane. "Come on I'll show you on board."

After they had climbed inside and stowed their suitcases, Colin gave them a brief tour of where the toilet was, the drinks, phone and how to use the entertainment system.

"How longs the flight?" asked Ellie as she looked at Colin.

"The flight time to Heathrow is approximately three hours," said Colin. "If you want to get comfy and strap yourselves in we'll get started?"

Ben Abbot the Co Pilot had already started the flight check list as Colin joined him in the cockpit.

After a few minutes the twin engines roared to life as they then began to taxi to the runway.

"I feel so nervous," said Ellie as she looked at Nathan.

"I've been flying for many years and can tell you statistically it is safer to fly than go by road. The Challenger is one of the safest jets in its Class with a long service history," said Nathan as he took hold of her hand and smiled at her.

Soaring down the runway Nathan looked at his watch. "11.20am, we should be in London by half two." Ellie just smiled at him squeezing his hand. After about half an hour Nathan unclipped his seat belt and got up to make a coffee. He handed Ellie her drink and sat down opposite her as he took a sip from his mug.

"How are you feeling now sweetheart?" asked Nathan as he took another sip of his coffee.

"When we took off, the thought of the crash just hit me and the sight of all those bodies. I felt a bit nervous but I'm okay now."

He leant over and gave her a kiss and said "It will be okay."

Nathan stood up and turned on the LCD television at the front and selected an in flight movie. He then returned and sat down next to Ellie and popped his feet up on the seat opposite.

Touching down on the runway at Heathrow they slowly taxied round to the private hangars where a black limousine was waiting.

"Quarter past two, not bad," said Nathan as they unclipped their seat belts.

After collecting their suit cases and thanking the Captain they climbed into the limousine after being greeted by the driver. They both settled back for the short trip over to the head office. Upon arriving they were met by Ron Shaw again. They both stepped out of the limousine as Ron smiled and shook their hands "I trust you had a comfortable trip?"

"Yes, very comfortable. Is there any word on David or Diana yet?" asked Nathan looking concerned.

"Nothing at the moment but we'll discuss that inside. Shall we?" asked Ron as he motioned to the glass rotating doors.

Having left their suitcases with the receptionist the driver then said goodbye and left. Ellie held Nathan's hand tight as they all entered the lift and made their way up to the third floor. When the lift stopped the doors glided silently open as Ron lead them to a conference room just down the corridor. Ron opened the door and they all walked in.

"Nathan, how are you?" asked a familiar voice.

"Ellie this is my Manager Ben Brooks, Ben this is Ellie"

Ben Brook was a 40 year old operations' manager. He had a rugged and well worn complexion with dark skin and black hair. He had worked for Lufthansa since he was 16 but bitterly hated his job. He was now just working there to keep his pension and health insurance.

"Pleased to meet you," said Ellie as Ben shook her hand. They were greeted by two other officials

Neil Curtis and Harold Gillespie from the airline before being seated.

"Before we begin I must warn you both that what is said in this room is highly confidential, do you both understand?" both Ellie and Nathan nodded. "I'll get right to the point. It is our belief that the crash of flight LA 1872 was not an accident. We believe the engines and fuel were tampered with before you took off." Nathan just stared in amazement.

"Who would do such a thing?" asked Ellie

"We can't be sure at the moment but we suspect it's a current employee of the airline. A letter was sent to us four days ago demanding a large sum of money with a threat to sabotage several of our aircraft's if we didn't pay up. The letter was handed over to the Police who were looking into it. However, now we need to determine the cause of the crash and what led up to it before we think of grounding all our aircraft's. Both your statements will be invaluable to our investigation," said Ron.

"Have the flight recorders been recovered?" asked Nathan.

"Yes they are being examined as we speak," said Neil who was sat to Ron's left.

Over the next few hours Nathan and Ellie both gave statements on their account of what happened from the time they took off from Germany to crash landing in Iceland. Having stopped for a short break, Ellie disappeared off to the ladies while Ron came over to talk to Nathan, "The Company as booked you both into the St Giles Hotel for as long as you need Nathan and a company car is at your disposal. With your help we might be able to catch this person before any more lives are lost."

"Thank you," said Nathan shocked. "I'll do whatever I can to help, but why as the company involved Ellie?"

"During my investigations I noticed that although you were single, you had seen to become close to Ellie. It was decided to take both your statements and treat you as a couple in the interests of security," said Ron

"Why am I getting a feeling that there's more to this than meets the eye? Do you know who is doing this?" asked Nathan in a low voice just as Ellie came back in the room.

"Shall we continue?" asked Harold in a rough authoritative tone.

Everyone then returned to their seats and continued with the statements. Nathan knew something was amiss but just couldn't put his finger on it. His mind started to wander as he wished David was there. He would know what was really happening.

"I think that about wraps it up," said Ron looking at Harold. "Does anybody wish to add anything else or have any questions?"

Ellie shook her head as Nathan paused for a second. "I'm eager to see David and find out how he is," said Nathan.

Ron reached in his briefcase and handed Nathan a mobile phone, charger and a set of car keys. "So we can stay in touch?" asked Ron smiling. "And you'll find a black Audi in the rear car park."

Nathan took the keys and mobile phone and thanked him before himself and Ellie said their goodbyes and headed back down the corridor to the lift. After the lift doors closed Nathan turned to Ellie. "Something doesn't feel right. I have a gut feeling they know who wrote that letter and who is making the threats, but they aren't letting on"

"You don't think they believe it's you do you?" asked Ellie laughing.

"Very funny," said Nathan giving her a nudge. "But something still doesn't feel right."

Having stepped out of the lift, they made their way over to the reception to collect their suitcases.

"Could you tell me where the rear car park is?" Nathan asked the receptionist politely.

"Go through the end door and turn left, then go all the way to the end of the corridor and it's the last door on the right. You will need a key card to get in and out the car park," she said as she handed him a white plastic card.

"Thank you," said Nathan.

They both picked up their suitcases and left for the car park. There were about forty cars in the car park so Nathan pressed the button on the key fob until he could hear the chirp on the cars alarm.

After they had located the car he popped the boot and they both placed their suitcases inside. "Nice car," said Ellie after they had both climbed inside. Nathan carefully backed the car out and made his way to the barrier. He pulled the key card from his pocket and swiped it through the barrier system. The barrier quickly opened as Nathan then drove through.

"How long will it take to get to the hospital?" asked Ellie eagerly.

"About fifteen to twenty minutes, not long really," said Nathan as he looked at Ellie.

Arriving at the hospital they parked up, made their way to the main entrance and to the information desk.

"Hi, how can I help you?" politely asked one of the Nurses.

"Yes I'm looking for David Benson and Diana Burton both from Nottingham, they were air lifted here from the crash in Keflavik, Iceland," said Nathan.

"Are you family or relatives?" asked the nurse.

"I am David's next of kin and work colleague, we were both on the plane with them," said Nathan.

"Okay love, take the elevator to the first floor; they are both in the ICU."

"Thank you," said Nathan with a smile. He then turned and made his way to the elevator followed by Ellie. Stepping off the elevator they followed the signs for the Intensive Care Unit. Nathan could feel butterflies in his tummy as they approached the Nurses Station. Ellie sensing he was nervous took hold of his hand and gave him a reassuring smile.

"We're here to see David Benson and Diana Burton?" asked Nathan nervously. "How are they?"

"Come and take a seat," said the Doctor. "I'm Dr Mark Sheridan and you are?"

"I'm Nathan Taylor and this is Ellie Fox, I'm the First Officer that was flying with David and Diana," said Nathan nervously.

"Okay, Diana is down in theatre at the moment undergoing Surgery, she as a ruptured spleen, broken pelvis and a damaged Liver and Kidney. A recent MRI scan had shown she also has a fractured skull. She is on life support and dialysis but unless we can find a Liver and Kidney donor it doesn't look hopeful."

"What about David?" asked Nathan.

"David is in a critical condition. We removed an eight inch piece of metal from his chest that had severed the main valves to his heart and punctured his lung. The valve is too damaged to repair with the only option of a replacement heart, but to complicate matters more, David's blood group is AB Negative."

"What does that mean?" asked Ellie.

"Only about 1% of the population is AB Negative which will make locating a donor nearly impossible, but we are trying. Both Diana and David are on the donor list, but unless we get access to a supply of organs then it doesn't look too good."

Ellie put her arms around Nathan to comfort him.

"Is there anything at all we can do?" asked Nathan

"I'm afraid that there's not much we can do at this time," said Mark with a sad look on his face. "Come on, I'll take you to see him."

Nathan and Ellie followed the Doctor as he opened the door to a side room. The sight that met Nathan's eyes was overwhelming. He could hardly recognise David as he lay there with tubes and wires all over him disappearing into the vast amount of machines and monitors. "He's stable but unconscious at the moment. The equipment is doing all the work for him and keeping him alive," said Mark as he examined the clipboard at the bottom of the bed.

Nathan pulled up a chair a long side the bed and sat down with his head in his hands. "I'll leave you alone for a while," said Mark as he left the room.

"There must be something we can do to help them?" asked Nathan rubbing his hands over his face.

"What do you suggest?" asked Ellie as she pulled up a chair a long side his and sat down. "Well unless you're willing to commit murder I don't know what else to do."

Ellie just looked at him and held his hand. "I'll do whatever it takes to help you" she said in a low voice.

Startled Nathan looked at her and knew she was telling the truth but his only concern at this moment in time was how to save David and Diana.

"There's always eBay?" asked Ellie trying to ease the tension.

"That's not funny," said Nathan starting to laugh.

"Come on, let's go and get a drink. There's not much that we can do here at the moment," said Ellie standing up.

Leaving the room, Nathan quietly closed the door behind them.

"Where can we get a drink?" Ellie asked one of the Nurses.

"There's a common room at the end of the corridor on the right."

"Thank you," said Ellie as they both made their way over.

Ellie took hold of Nathan's hand as they slowly walked up the corridor. "Hey I recognise her," said Ellie pointing to a woman lying in the bed opposite. "She was on the plane with us." Ellie began to make her way over when the woman recognised her and sat up in bed. "It's Sarah isn't it?" asked Ellie with a huge smile.

"Yes we were on the plane together."

"I'm Ellie and this is Nathan."

"Pleased to meet you," said Nathan has he shook her hand. "Aren't you Josh's mum?" ask Nathan inquisitively.

"Yes, yes I am, here he is now," said Sarah has Josh came walking round the corner holding his dads hand.

"Hi Josh," said Ellie as she picked him up, "I see you have a new teddy Josh?"

"Yes I lost my other teddy on the aeroplane and Scribbles and Fluffy are at home asleep, daddy told me they are," said Josh in a cute voice.

Ellie and Sarah continued chatting for a while Nathan was talking to Josh's dad. "We'd better let you get on," said Nathan after a while.

Ellie gave Josh another hug and sat him on the bed next to his mum.

"I hope you get well soon," said Nathan.

Ellie then said goodbye to them as well. They both left and made their way up the corridor to the common room.

The room was warm and empty as they both sat down on the sofa with a coffee. Nathan took a sip from his mug and turned to Ellie. "Did you mean it when you said you would do anything to help David and Diana?"

"Yes, yes I would," said Ellie as she looked him straight in the eye.

"Even commit murder?" asked Nathan.

Ellie paused for a few seconds. "Yes if that's what it takes, but not in the literal sense" "What do you mean?" asked Nathan looking perplexed.

Ellie took a drink from her mug and twisted round slightly to face him. "It's hard to explain without coming across wrong but life is a gift that not everyone deserves. Take for instance serial killers, why should they live but someone like David or Diana who has done well all their lives and done well in the community die? What about those who try to commit suicide and no longer want the gift of life? But thousands of pounds are spent on saving them in hospital costs and rehabilitation. Don't get me wrong, I don't mean that everyone who has done bad things should deserve to die but some people do deserve to live more than others. I couldn't use my hands and just walk up to someone and kill them for no reason but I would take a life to save another."

Nathan took a drink from his mug and pondered for a few minutes on what she had said. "I understand where you're coming from and do agree with you. I couldn't kill someone myself but maybe I could get someone else to do it for me though."

"You know someone who would do it for you don't you?" asked Ellie looking surprised. "I do know someone that would help us but he's not what you would call a normal person"

"Who would do the operations? I mean you can't just walk into a hospital with a box of human organs and not expect someone to say something," said Ellie. She picked up both hers and Nathan's mug and wandered over to the kettle to make another drink while Nathan started to think long and hard about what they had talked about.

"You know, we could go to Prison for even discussing this? Conspiring to commit murder?" asked Nathan.

"I know we could, but I will do anything for you," said Ellie.

Nathan just sat there stunned for words. Ellie perched herself on Nathan's lap and put her arms around his neck. "Get in touch with whoever it is that can help you. Make the call," said Ellie and gave him a kiss.

"What about a surgeon? We need someone that's not going to ask questions or get suspicious?" asked Nathan.

"Leave that to me," said Ellie, "I'll think of something, you just make the phone call to your friend."

"We're booked into the St Giles Hotel just down the road. I think we should say goodbye to David and make our way over?" asked Nathan, "We can make the calls and sort things out when we get there, are you sure you want to go through with this? You know the risks."

"I know the risks Nathan but I know I want you more."

Ellie wrapped her arms around him and they spent the next few minutes kissing. "Come on lover let's get going," said Ellie.

They finished their coffee and went to say their goodbyes to David.

Upon returning to leave, Nathan went over to the Nurses Station to speak to Dr Mark Sheridan.

"I'm the official next of kin to David; can I leave you my number?"

"Yes that would be useful," said Mark handing Nathan a piece of paper. "Pop down your full name, DOB, Phone number and where you're staying."

Nathan did as he was asked and handed the paper back to him.

"Thank you, we don't seem to have a next of kin for Diana yet, no one has come forward."

"I would guess that it would have been David so technically it comes back to me," said Nathan.

"In that case I will need you to sign these papers confirming you are both of their next of kin's and permit any treatment in your absence," said Mark.

Nathan glanced through the paperwork before signing them and handing them back. Both Ellie and Nathan set off back to the car.

Decisions, Decisions, Decisions
~ Chapter Four ~

The traffic was pretty light as they made their way along Regent Street towards the hotel and through the tight London streets.

"I think I'd better give me mum a ring and let her know I'm alright. I usually ring her on a Friday and if I don't she'll start to worry," said Ellie.

"Here use the mobile," said Nathan as he reached into his pocket and passed her the mobile phone that Ron had given him.

While Ellie was chatting away to her mum Nathan started to go over in his mind the thought of someone else *maybe they will find a donor in time* he thought to himself, *but then again what if they don't.*

He thought about an old mate he used to know. He was arrested back in the 80's on suspicion of murdering eight people at a holiday village near Ingoldmells but was released do to an issue with the evidence and his record cleared. *If anyone would help me it would be him.*

Thinking about a surgeon he remembered when he and David used to go to the Executive Club in Nottingham that he was once introduced to a surgeon from the QMC who was setting up his own Surgery and remembered how strange he was. *I have to find him* he thought just as Ellie hung up the phone.

"How's mum?" asked Nathan.

"She's fine, her and dad are going away for the weekend and have asked me to keep an eye on the house."

"I think we should head home tomorrow," said Nathan, "I have a few things to take care of at my apartment and I'm going to get the ball rolling. I can remember when me and David used to go to the Executive Club he introduced me to a friend of his that's a surgeon. He was a proper weirdo and probably the exact person we are looking for," said Nathan with a chuckle.

"The Executive Club as the name suggests, was for really posh people if you like. There are different people ranging from Doctors, Judges, and Teachers and of course Pilots that attend the club. It is somewhere you can go and be treated like royalty and just unwind. That's where David first introduced me to him."

"Do you think he will even talk to you though?"

"Well he seemed like he was really interested in me when David introduced us, so I think he will yes," said Nathan.

"If I remember rightly his name was Gunter Fleischer."

"That's a weird name," said Ellie.

"German," said Nathan, "He was a German surgeon at the Ludwigshafen Hospital in Germany. The last I can remember he had come over to England to set up a private theatre and Surgery."

"He sounds like just the person we're looking for," said Ellie looking really interested.

A few moments later they arrived at the St Giles Hotel and parked up before making their way to the reception.

"Good afternoon?" asked the receptionist with a friendly smile.

"Hi, Nathan Taylor and Ellie Fox," said Nathan.

Scrolling down the list of names on the computer she said "Yes, I have you here, how long will you be staying with us Sir?"

"We will be leaving tomorrow lunch time," said Nathan.

She then handed him a room key with a large yellow plastic key ring inscribed *St Giles Hotel Room 222.*

"Go across the road and through the double doors, and there's a lift to your right. Take the lift to the second floor and you're in room 222 enjoy your stay with us."

Nathan and Ellie then set off to their room across the road.

Upon arriving Nathan put the kettle on while Ellie started to unpack the suitcases. After they had finished Nathan flicked on the television and they both sat on the sofa together. "How you feeling?" asked Ellie.

"Nervous as hell, I can't believe what we're about to do but I can't let David or Diana die, it just keeps going over and over in my mind."

"Maybe they will find a donor in time Nathan but what I'm struggling with is if David is AB Negative blood group then how will we know which person will have the same blood group as him," said Ellie looking confused.

Nathan thought for a while then said "All hospitals keep patient records on a database that would have their name and address and also their blood group. If we could get access to that database we could filter out the people in the area that has the same blood group."

"That's genius!" said Ellie. "You're so clever sweetheart, what would be even better is if the list of names could be crossed matched to the Police National Computer to produce a list of convicted murderers paedophiles and rapists."

"I like that idea," said Nathan enthusiastically.

"I have an old mate from back in University Vernon Cooper; he's an absolute whiz on computers. This would be right up his street," said Ellie.

"Can you trust him though, I mean not to go to the Police or anything?" asked Nathan. "He's totally anti government and would love the challenge. I used to help him with his course work most of the time so he does owe me a few favours." Ellie picked up the mobile phone off the side table "I'll see if I can get hold of him," she said as she tried to remember his number.

Finally getting through to Vernon, they spoke for a short while remembering the days at Uni and having a laugh before Ellie got to the point.

"Vernon, I have a favour to ask of you if you think you can do it."

"Anything for you Ellie you know that, what can I do for you?"

"I need a complete list of people from the QMC hospital database with the blood group AB Negative and to cross match that list from the Police Nation Computer database for murderers, paedophiles and rapists and possibly terrorism."

"Wow what are you up to Ellie?"

"It's what you might call a case study if you like, don't worry no one will ever see the list, it's for my use only."

"You always was a bit of a genius, when do you need it by?"

"You're pretty smart too Vernon, that's why I called you, after the weekend would be great, maybe you could email me the list?"

"I'll see what I can do for you and give you a ring."

"Thank you so much Vernon, I have to go now but hope to speak to you soon."

"Take care Ellie and stay in touch," said Vernon

"You too," said Ellie.

They then both hung up the phone. Ellie turned to Nathan who just sat there with his mouth open in astonishment.

"That was unbelievable," said Nathan, "When did he say he will be able to do it?" "Knowing Vernon he'll be thinking about it now. He really does love a challenge," said Ellie smiling away.

Old Friends

~ Chapter Five ~

Vernon put the phone down, got up and walked over to his computers and switched them on one by one. He lived in a small one bedroom flat which was pretty clean and tidy apart from the odd computer magazine here and there and the three computers tucked together in an alcove at the end of the room. The computer screens burst into life. Vernon lit a cigarette and sat down in his leather recliner, grabbed an ash tray and opened a can of Red Bull. He quickly logged onto the computers and waited a few minutes for the desktops to appear. He already had mainframe access to the PNC so just needed to access the hospital database.

A piece of cake he thought to himself. He opened up a browser and navigated his way to the Queens Medical Centre's website and clicked on the *Contact Us* link at the top of the page. Quickly looking down the list he could see the hospitals' domain was qmc.org. He took a long drag from his cigarette and then stubbed it out. After logging into an acquired Hotmail account via Windows Live Mail he sent a blank email to anonymous at the qmc. org domain. After a minute or so he received an email from Mailer Daemon with the subject 'Failure Notice'. He selected the email and right clicked on it followed by clicking on 'Message Options'.

He scanned his way down the Internet Headers Information and read the line X-Originating-IP: [209.11.164.163]. *Here we go* he said to himself making a note of the IP Address. After taking a gulp from his Red Bull he opened a command prompt and connected to the IP Address by FTP as Guest. He spent a few minutes looking around and downloading random files to conceal what he was really doing until he downloaded the htaccess file and closed the connection. Next he opened *John the Ripper* and fed in the htaccess file. The htaccess file contains a list of usernames and passwords in an encrypted format. Once fed into *John the Ripper* it will attempt to decrypt the passwords, but this can take a while. He took another gulp of his Red Bull and sat back in his chair feeling pleased.

Sitting waiting for the software to finish he started to wonder what Ellie was up to. *It must have been nearly a year since the last time I saw her at Uni and she just calls me out the blue. There must be something with one of the names* he though which was now making him more determined to get hold of the list and examine it. Just as he lit up another cigarette his computer started bleeping indicating a success.

He sat upright with the cigarette in the corner of his mouth and opened the pass.txt from *John the*

Ripper. He then went back to the command prompt and issued a telnet command and logged in using the decrypted username and password. He knew that a large Organisation like this would use a backend database managed by Oracle or SQL Server. After a minute or two he had located the database file. It was huge at over 1 GB in size. So as not to reveal his identity he issued a FTP command on the remote computer and sent the database to an anonymous FTP Site to download later. Knowing it would take a few hours to upload the data; he wiped the logs clean and logged off.

All he had to do now was wait a while the database was being uploaded so he could then download it to his computer. The curiosity was really starting to get the better of him trying to figure out the link between a rare blood group and someone who had done time in Prison.

Perfect Relationship
~ Chapter Six ~

"Do you fancy going down to the restaurant for dinner?" asked Ellie looking at Nathan.

"Yes that sounds good. What do you fancy?"

"You my darling, of course," said Ellie as she leant over and gave him a kiss on the lips. "You are sweet Ellie, come on let's go and have a look at what today's special is." Nathan picked up the mobile phone and the room key and they both left.

Once they were seated they ordered a few drinks while they looked over the menu. "I'm glad we're not paying for this, have you seen the prices?" asked Ellie, "fifteen quid for a Cromer Crab and Prawn Parcel starter"

"Actually that does sound nice, I think I'm going to have the Cromer Crab and Prawn Parcel for starter and the Char grilled English Sirloin Steak," said Nathan.

"I must admit, that does sound nice. I think I'll have the same."

After the waiter had taken their order they chatted for a while sipping their drinks.

"If I know Vernon I bet he is not far off getting that list for us."

"I've been thinking about that for a while now. I'm going to need the list before I meet up with my old mate," said Nathan.

"Will you tell me a bit about him?" asked Ellie curiously, "What's his name and how come you're so sure he will commit murder?"

"His name's Shiva Lawman. He's a security guard for a bus company. We spent many nights chatting and talking about his past. He had been in Prison for eight months for murder. He was out drinking with a few of his mates when four youths came over and started to cause trouble. Shiva had remembered who they were and spent the next few days finding them one by one and slit their throats with a knife. He was sentenced to life imprisonment but due to incorrect evidence he was acquitted. It never even made it to the news papers. He was then arrested on suspicion of murdering eight people but was released again due to an issue with the evidence and his record was cleared. The truth is he did kill the four youths and the eight people in Ingoldmells. He does look like a bit of a weirdo but he confided in me, he is a misanthropist with no respect for life. He physically can't show or feel emotions and is unable to love, be loved or even be sympathetic."

Ellie just sat there in utter amazement. "It's a bit sad in one way. Not being able to feel anything and something inside making you hate people. That would explain why he could kill without emotion or regret. Didn't you feel scared being with him?" asked Ellie.

Nathan took a sip from his drink as the waiter brought over their starter. Ellie ordered two more drinks which the waiter brought over while Nathan started to tuck in.

"To be honest" said Nathan, "I was young and didn't really understand, but he saw something in me that made him open up and tell me about himself. I've kept in touch since. He's not changed at all and still makes me laugh."

"What does he look like?" asked Ellie with her mouth full.

"He's well over six feet tall and has long dark brown wavy hair and a long gaunt face with a pale completion and dark sunken eyes. Also he doesn't stand up right. It's like he used to work down the pit all his life like his head is slouching forward pulling his shoulders."

The waiter took away their plates while they carried on chatting and having a drink. "He sounds really scary looking and a bit weird," said Ellie as she took a long drink from her glass.

"Yet to talk to him, once he's accepted you he's extremely intelligent," said Nathan as he called over the waiter. "Do you fancy a bottle of wine sweetheart?" asked Nathan has he peered through the wine list.

"Ooo yes, whatever you fancy my darling," said Ellie energetically.

"Waiter, a bottle of Nostros Carmenère Reserva please," said Nathan

"An excellent choice," said the waiter as he returned with their main course and wine. He popped the cork and poured a small amount into a glass and handed it to Nathan. He took a swig and after a few seconds nodded his head and said "Yes."

The waiter then topped up both their glasses while they started to eat their main course.

"The food is excellent," said Ellie, "It's cooked to perfection and the presentation is great. I vote we move in here permanently," said Ellie laughing.

After they had finished their main course and finished their wine they made their way back to their room. Ellie locked the door behind them as Nathan chucked off his coat.

"It's a long drive back to Nottingham so I think I'm going to get ready for bed," said Nathan.

"No worries sweetheart. I will help you with the driving tomorrow," said Ellie sweetly. "That would help a lot, thank you," said Nathan as he disappeared into the bathroom.

"Do you want your back scrubbing?" shouted Ellie as she heard the shower come on. "Why not join me?" shouted Nathan.

Ellie made her way to the bathroom where they both took a shower together. When they had finished Ellie dried herself off while Nathan dried her hair. He then started to dry off himself while Ellie dried his back. When she had finished Nathan turned round to face her as she wrapped her arms around him and they kissed for several minutes. Both naked and stood in the bathroom Nathan picked her up as she wrapped her legs around him. He carried her into the bedroom, sat down and lay back on the bed. With water still dripping from her hair she sat on him with her legs either side. Smiling, she slowly bent forward to kiss his chest has her breast brushed over him. She kissed his chest moving up to his neck and cheek and kissed him passionately on the lips. He cupped his hands over her hard nipples and breasts before he carefully lifted her up and pulled her forward as they began to make love.

Ellie lay naked next to Nathan with her head on his chest and one leg over his. He had wrapped his arms around her and was holding her tight has they both drifted off to sleep.

The following morning they both woke up early. "Morning gorgeous," said Nathan. Ellie yawned and said "Morning baby, how did you sleep?"

"I slept perfect sweetheart dreaming of you."

They cuddled and kissed for a while before they both showered together.

"Do you want to talk about last night?" asked Nathan.

"Talk about it? No way I want to do it again!" said Ellie has she pulled her knickers on and fastened her bra.

"Last night you was perfect," said Ellie has she put her arms around him and buried her head in his chest.

After they had got dressed they went down for breakfast. Upon their return they were packed up and ready to go.

"I think we should hold the room," said Nathan. "Ron said we had a reservation as long as we needed one. I was just thinking in case we need to return back to London for another meeting or anything."

"Yes that's a good idea darling," said Ellie smiling sweetly.

Easy but Tricky
~ Chapter Seven ~

Vernon sat down rubbing his eyes and took a long drink of his coffee and logged onto his computer. Knowing the transfer would have finished by now he opened a command prompt and logged into the remote anonymous FTP Server and initiated the database to download. With his 50mb internet connection he knew it would take a long time to download so he lit a cigarette leant back in his chair and waited.

The curiosity was really getting to him, he could hardly wait. Just over an hour later the transfer was complete and he had the entire *Patient Medical Database* sat on his computer ready to be inspected. He quickly opened the database and started to check out the table names. TblPatient, TblHistory, TblLogins, TblAddress. After quickly decrypting the *Police National Database* he already had, he linked the two databases together and issued the command to select all patients that exist in each database and had a NG postcode and a blood group of AB Negative.

After a matter of seconds 81 records were returned. *Not bad* he thought. He then issued a command to filter the records even further to only show patients that were charged with murder, Rape, and terrorism or were convicted paedophiles and currently on release. Within an instant two records were returned.

Feeling apprehensive he clicked on the first record. Darren Moss age 42 served 7 years for rape currently living in Lenton. "Nothing strange there" he thought as he clicked on the next record. Marcus Truman aged 58 served 15 years for murder. Nothing really struck him as strange either but then he wondered *who did he murder?*

He opened a web browser and started to search the news archive around the late 80's. It didn't take him long to find the news article. Marcus Truman jailed for 15 years for the murder of his ex wife Lyn Truman. *What would Ellie want with these two people?* He thought. *Maybe she is really doing research.* He saved the two records to his desktop and emailed them through to Ellie.

The Silver Astra
~ Chapter Eight ~

"Thank you so much," said Ellie "I'll be in touch" she then hung up the phone and placed it in the glove box. "That was Vernon; he managed to get the list for us and has emailed it to me. He said there are two people's names on the list that live in the area; one was sent down for rape and the other for murder."

"I'm surprised there's not more," said Nathan as he concentrated on his driving. They were about ten to fifteen miles outside Nottingham when Nathan pulled into the Services. "Come on lets grab a coffee and have a stretch," said Nathan.

Sitting outside having a drink, Nathan noticed a Silver Vauxhall Astra slow down, pull into the car park and then reverse backup out the way.

"You see that Silver Astra, that's been following us since we got off the M25," said Nathan.

"Are you sure?" asked Ellie as she drank her coffee. "We must have passed thousands of cars on the way up. It's probably just your mind playing tricks on you."

"Probably," said Nathan.

Nathan finished his coffee while Ellie disappearing off to the bathroom. After he had finished he went back to the car to wait for Ellie. He couldn't stop thinking about the Astra as Ellie returned and got in the car, it just seemed weird.

"Were we going first?" asked Ellie as she looked at Nathan.

"Why don't you come and stay at mine?" asked Nathan. "It's not much but it's home." "That would be great," said Ellie with a beaming smile. I need to collect a few things from my flat first though if that's okay?"

"Yes no problem," said Nathan smiling.

"So you really do have a yellow Volkswagen beetle?" asked Nathan as they pulled up outside Ellie's flat.

"Yes, I told you I did," said Ellie as she laughed and elbowed him in the ribs. "Come on you can give me a hand," said Ellie as she got out the car.

After they had gone inside Ellie got her suitcase from off the top of the wardrobe and started to fill it.

"Not bad," said Nathan as he wondered around looking in the rooms. "I take it these are your designs?" he said looking at the racks of clothes.

"Yes they arc the new line that I'm trying to sell over in Europe," said Ellie as she fastened her suitcase shut.

"Right, I just need to print out the list that Vernon sent me."

She made her way into the living room and switched on her laptop as Nathan sat down on the sofa beside her. Moments later the printer on the computer desk started buzzing away as it started to print.

Nathan stood up and grabbed the print out. "There's one from Lenton and the other is from Loscoe, that's just down the road from the bus depot," said Nathan.

"Do you want a drink or anything," said Ellie as she packed away the laptop.

"No I'm okay, I'll wait until we get back to my place, I want to ring the hospital and see if there's been any change since I last rang."

"Okay sweetheart I'm ready when you are. Could you just grab the suitcase off my bed?"

"Yes no problem," said Nathan is he handed Ellie the sheet of paper.

Ellie locked the flat door while Nathan placed the two suitcases and her laptop in the boot and then climbed into the car.

"Have you got everything?" asked Nathan as she got in the car.

"Yes, all sorted."

Nathan started the car and began to make his way over town to his house while Ellie studied the names and details on the sheet of paper.

"The guy from Loscoe received 15 years for murdering his ex wife and was suspected of murdering her new husband too," said Ellie looking disgusted. "The other one was sent down for raping a woman on her way home from a night club. Well I don't think either of these would be missed in today's society do you?"

Nathan just nodded his head in agreement.

"Here we go," said Nathan as he turned into his driveway and pulled up outside his house.

"Wow," said Ellie as she opened the car door and stepped outside. "It's huge. Is this all yours?"

"Yes, all bought and paid for," said Nathan as he started to lift her suitcases and laptop out the boot.

"This is amazing," said Ellie as she grabbed a suitcase and started to walk up to the house.

The front garden was mainly *block paved* with enough room for about six cars. A small walled section in the middle, housed a few shrubs and flowers. The front of the garden was home to a few trees over hanging the garden. The house looked clean like it had been recently re-pointed with dark brown wooden lattice style windows, a dark brown square glass front door with gold handles and a brown double garage door. The sides of the house were set back along with the garage giving the whole house a Victorian look.

Nathan shut the boot and locked the car before picking up the laptop and putting it over his shoulder and then grabbing hold of the last suitcase. He chucked the house keys to Ellie who unlocked the front door and went straight in. Nathan followed right behind and disabled the house alarm and shut the door behind him.

"Let me show you round," said Nathan as he left the suitcase and laptop in the hallway. "Firstly this is the front room."

The front room was painted pure white with thick set dark wooden beams and crystal glass wall lights.

The floor was dark wood flooring complimented with a large patterned woven rug. In the corner there was a massive LCD TV and a low thick wooden coffee table in the middle of the room. Three dark brown Winchester sofas occupied the sides of the room showing style and space. The large front windows let in ample light giving the whole room a shimmering glow.

"This is the kitchen," said Nathan as he took Ellie's hand and led her into the kitchen. The kitchen was very spacious with an island at one end and a six seater table at the other end. The kitchen was expertly decorated white with cream and gold cupboards.

The sink was one of the old fashioned pot sinks under the window leaving a breath taking view of the garden. After he had shown her the rest of the downstairs they grabbed the suitcases and went up stairs.

"This is my room," said Nathan "The end drawers are all empty and you can share my wardrobe."

Ellie put the suitcase down and flopped on the bed as Nathan sat down beside her.

The bedroom was painted white and cream with a white quilt-cover over the bed and cream carpet. The wall opposite the windows was decorated with a tapestry in blue and gold thread. A large wicker chair sat in one corner of the room adjacent to the on suite bathroom. There were three large, dark wooden sets of draws and a dark wood double wardrobe around the edge of the room.

"I'm going to leave you to unpack," said Nathan.

He gave her a kiss then made his way downstairs to the front room, picked up the phone and sat on the sofa.

"ICU, nurse Carter Speaking"

"Hi, it's Nathan Taylor again. I'm enquiring about David Benson and Diana Burton?" "There's been no real change Nathan, both are still in critical condition but are stable. David did have a bit of a turn during the night but it's to be expected."

"Okay thank you, you have my number in case anything happens."

"Yes I have your number here."

Nathan said goodbye and then hung up the phone as Ellie came walking in.

"Is there any news?"

"No nothing, they are both still in a critical way but they are in a stable condition," said Nathan.

"That's good news in one way. What's the plan now?" asked Ellie as she sat down beside him.

"I'm going to send Shiva a text and let him know I will be dropping by to see him later. If all goes well then tomorrow evening we will be visiting the Executive Club to see if our surgeon friend is as weird as he looks. I think it's better if you wait her tonight though if you know what I mean?"

"Yes no problem," said Ellie, "I've got a bit of work to catch up on."

It didn't take long for Shiva to reply to Nathan which was unusual as he hardly ever replied. The text read *yes working tonight. Start at 9pm.* Nathan looked at his watch it was 5.20pm. For the rest of the evening Ellie and Nathan prepared dinner and spent time chatting and going over the details of the plan.

"I'd better get going," said Nathan as he yawned looking at is watch.

"How long will you be?" asked Ellie.

"To be honest I'm not sure so if you want to watch telly in bed or get an early night I don't mind."

He picked up his car keys gave Ellie a kiss and left. Ellie took her laptop upstairs and plugged it in, in the bedroom and then went and ran a bath.

Shiva's Hobby
~ Chapter Nine ~

Nathan originally met Shiva at University. While Nathan was studying his Ph. D. in Avionics Shiva was studying advanced biology. Although Shiva came across being scary and weird he was in fact extremely smart. From an early age he was always interested in how the human body worked. He would occasionally find a dead animal and cut it open to see how it worked. With time pushing on his fascination for body parts grew as he started to amount a collection of animal organs. His obsession grew with him as he got older until he started using human bodies and even dug up a corpse from a grave yard. Nathan kept in touch after university and became a good friend which is where he discovered Shiva's secret pastime.

Indicating left; Nathan slowed down and turned into the bus depot. He drove though a short tunnel section past the on site diesel fitter's work shop and pumps before making his way over to the traffic office portacabin. He could see Shiva's car a black Jaguar X type hidden inside the shutters. It always reminded him of a hearse. It was cold outside and had dropped dark really quick. The lights in the yard lit up with a whitish blue glow for easy access to the fifty odd buses parked up. Nathan locked the car and walked a short distance over to the portacabin. He tapped on the door and walked in to find Shiva listening to the radio and reading a magazine.

Shiva was wearing a dark blue single breast jacket with a dark blue company anorak rain coat. His face was long, gaunt and pale with long dark brown wavy hair down to his shoulders.

"Evening," said Shiva in a deep slow voice. "How's David?"

Nathan sat down and took a deep breath and explained about the crash and what happened along with the predicament David and Diana were now in. He explained his plans to get the organs needed and the rare blood group.

Shiva agreed straight away to help them.

"Our secret is still safe?" asked Shiva leaning forward and speaking in a low voice. "Very safe," said Nathan.

Shiva put down his Take a Break and removed his glasses.

"Where are you going to store the bodies and the organs until they are transferred out and what about the blood and the mess?" asked Nathan.

"Come with me," said Shiva as he pulled a packet of cigarettes from his pocket and lit one with a match.

It was very dark outside now as Shiva led him over to the shutters. Slowly approaching, the shutters sprang into life and started to clatter open. Shiva picked up two dust masks from the side and gave one to Nathan as they walked over to the paint booth.

"You crafty bastard, that will certainly hide the smell of the decomposing bodies." Shiva unlocked the booth door and they both stepped in. The room was massive with enough space to fit two double deckers side by side. It was obvious the room hadn't been used for some time but still stunk of paint and thinners.

"Surely you not just going to set up shop in here, anyone could walk in during the day?"

Shiva carried on walking so Nathan followed close to his side. They were about half way across the room when they came to an iron grate in the floor that looked like it had been there centuries. Shiva bent down and removed a small lock that was hidden out of sight to secure the grate. Nathan's eyes lit up as he was now interested and intrigued. Shiva then lifted the grate up from one side on its hinges. The grate slowly fully opened and began to reveal a startling surprise.

Ellie's Dilemma
~ Chapter Ten ~

Ellie stepped out of the bath and started to dry herself off. She spent a few minutes in front of the mirror brushing her long blonde hair and then slipped on her negligee. Feeling tired she climbed into bed but had already decided she was going to reply to her emails and catch up.

She grabbed a hold of the laptop, opened the lid and switched it on. While she was waiting for the computer to load up, she started thinking about the accident and those that didn't survive. Her shoulder still twinged a little as a reminder of what happened although she felt lucky to be alive but felt even luckier that she had found someone like Nathan.

The butterflies in her tummy made her realise she was already missing him as she started thinking of their first kiss on the plane. *I wonder how Nathan is doing, and if he has managed to convince Shiva to help us* she thought. She was kind of glad that

Nathan had asked her to wait at home, although she desperately wanted help in any way she could, sitting talking to a stranger about killing someone just didn't sit well with her. Although she hadn't known Nathan very long she could tell when they kissed and held each other that they were meant to be.

The laptop beeped as it loaded up the password screen. Ellie entered her password waited a few seconds and opened her emails. 281 unread emails, "Not too bad" she thought as she started to wade through them. It took her a while to go through all 281 emails and delete the junk and spam until she was left with just 93 emails. One by one she went back through the emails, read and replied to those that were necessary.

Happily typing away, the computer pinged to indicate a new email had arrived. She clicked on the email to open it and saw that it was from Vernon. *I wonder what he wants* she thought as she started to read through it. *Hi Ellie I was just reading the on-line news of a plane crash in Keflavik in Iceland. It stated that most people had died with only a hand full of survivors. They even printed a list of the survivors names, one being Ellie Fox aged 23. Ellie was this you on the plane? Is this anything to do with the two names I gave you? Ellie if you're in trouble you can talk to me. Please reply Ellie I'm worried. Vernon.*

Ellie was stunned, *Shit, shit, shit, shit, shitting shit and bugger. He's going to piece this together and find out,* she thought. *I know, maybe I could just lie to him and say it wasn't me, I mean there's no way he could find out that David is AB Negative, could he?* She was starting to feel a bit anxious but thought *No,*

I'll wait till Nathan gets home and discuss it with him. She closed the email and continued to read the others and reply to them.

I hope every-things going okay she said to herself as she looked at the clock. *22:10 he's been gone a while so that must be good news, because if Shiva had said no then he would have come straight back home.* Replying to the last email she hit the send button, waited until it had sent and then shut down the computer. The screen eventually dimmed down for a few seconds and then switched off. She closed the lid and placed it on the cupboard at the side. After yawning a few times she picked the telly remote and started to flick through the channels. She settled on an old film and pulled the quilt up tight, lay back and relaxed.

Secret War Theatre
~ Chapter Eleven ~

Peering down Nathan was startled to see there were steps and a light at the bottom.

"Go on," said Shiva as he nodded towards the hole.

"What's down there?" asked Nathan looking a bit nervous.

"You'll find out when your down there won't you?" asked Shiva in his usually sarcastic manner.

Nathan spun round and lowered himself onto the first step and then started to climb down.

The further down he climbed the more he could smell the damp air until he finally reached the bottom. It took a few seconds for his eyes to adjust to the dim light. Shortly after, Shiva came climbing down the steps and stood beside him. Shiva leaned in front of him and flicked a switch. The whole room lit up revealing an astonishing sight.

The ceiling was arched like a tunnel and painted in a creamy yellow colour. The walls were painted the same colour and were shiny clean whereas the floor was made of a black rubber material and although it was worn it was pretty clean. There were several pipes and cables running across the ceiling that disappeared through the walls with huge old fashioned dome lights hanging from the ceiling emitting a soft white glow. Although the room smelt damp it was particularly clean like it had been looked after.

In front of them was a mortuary gurney with green sheets neatly folded on one side and a trolley next to it with what looked like surgical instruments. Nearby a computer sat silently with its screen saver active. In the corner were several large canisters marked oxygen and a weird looking one with Entonox written down the side. Over to the right were rows of clear draws filled with medical instruments, bandages and some strange looking equipment. To the left were large containers like coolers that were plugged into a bank of sockets. Around the corner Nathan was stunned to what appeared to be a surgical table with a cluster of lights above it. Just next to it was a large trolley full of strange electrical tools all neatly placed side by side. Nathan just stood in awe and amazement.

"What the hell's all this for? What have you been doing down here?" asked Nathan feeling stunned.

Shiva reached into his pocket pulled out his cigarettes and lit one. "It was originally used during world war two as an operating theatre but later abandoned after the war. Over the past few years I've been making a few quid on the side selling organs to medical students and a few people over the internet. I've got all the cleaners that chip in and help, out getting the animal bodies and disposing of the remains. I also still get hold of the odd corpse or two to practise on and sometimes a fresh live body."

This is exactly what Nathan was looking for. "How do you get the bodies in the first place? Are they already dead or are you killing them?"

Shiva took a drag on his cigarette and blew out the smoke. "It's simple really, on the odd occasion we have to pick up temporary bus stops or go out and set them up. We usually go round the long way in the early hours of the morning. There's always someone that's had a few too many to drink and put their hand out to stop the bus. Once on board the cleaners get to work. My favourite is the knife but sometimes just a good smack on the back of the head does the trick" he said with a chilling grin.

Although he felt a little sick to his stomach, Nathan had to admit he was impressed with the set up.

"How many as there been and what about the Police? Surely someone must be getting suspicious?"

Shiva took another drag from his cigarette then stubbed it out on the floor. "There have been a few bodies through here in the past two years I guess. The Police are appealing for witnesses and asking the public to be extra vigilant but most of the time the Police think they have just moved on. Detective Neil Curtis was heading up the investigations; although it appears he's persistent he hasn't come up with anything. We keep track of the local news and newspapers on the internet."

Nathan reached into his back pocket and pulled out the list that Vernon gave them and handed it to Shiva. "How are you going to find these people?" asked Nathan.

Shiva walked over to the computer and started to search the news archives for the first name on the list. After a few seconds the article appeared on screen with his photograph. Shiva hit the print button and printed out a copy of the photograph. "I'll have the cleaner's stake out the address over the next few days and plot out his movements. We'll have him by the end of the week if we need to," Shiva said with a sadistic grin.

"Just one other thing, can you really take a heart and prepare it for re transplant?" asked Nathan.

"Yes, it's a lot simpler than it looks. Once the heart is removed it is then placed in cold storage and injected with epinephrine to increase the life of the organ during transplant. The container over there takes care of it as too much cold will burn the organ and too little will damage it."

"How the hell did you learn all this? I mean it looks so complicated?" asked Nathan looking puzzled.

"Well as you know there's not much to do on nights so I studied and read up over the years and taught myself. I learnt an awful lot when we were at university. The first few were the hardiest but it got much easier the more we did."

"We?" asked Nathan.

"Yes the cleaners, they assist me pretty well."

Shiva flicked off the light and they both made their way back up the steps. Once they were out Shiva closed the grate and applied the lock hiding it out of sight. The smell of paint was overwhelming as they pulled their dust masks back on. Shiva closed the booth door behind them and discarded his dust mask as did Nathan.

They were walking back to the portacabin when Shiva reached in his pocket took out a cigarette and lit it.

"I can't believe what a set up you have here, I would never have guessed. I must admit I am impressed," said Nathan.

Whilst they stood talking, one of the cleaners came scurrying over like a rat. Nathan jumped as he saw him.

"Hello Nay fun," said Lenny. Lenny was about 5' 1" tall; slim with dark, greasy curly hair. He was wearing a pair of really old fashioned glasses with triple thick lenses that were dirty. His face was dark and really dirty as were his jeans and florescent yellow jacket. His shoes were obviously too big and really worn out.

"Have you got a smoke I can have Shiva?" asked Lenny in a croaky voice.

Unbelievably Shiva offered him a cigarette and handed him the print out of the photograph and the address. Lenny looked at the papers, nodded to Shiva and then placed them in his inside pocket. He finished his smoke and then disappeared off between the buses in the yard.

Nathan stayed a little longer talking to Shiva and catching up while talking about the old days when he used to stay overnight with him. He was amazed that not much had changed over the years apart from the odd new bus here and there.

"Phone me when you have found your surgeon friend and I will make the necessary preparations," said Shiva.

Nathan shook his hand and thanked him before saying his goodbyes.

Executive Club
~ Chapter Twelve ~

Ellie must still be awake he thought as he saw the telly lights flickering in the bedroom window. He parked the car on the driveway and made his way to the front door. Once inside he slipped off his shoes and hung up his jacket. Yawning he wandered into the kitchen and grabbed a drink before climbing upstairs to bed. He opened the bedroom door slowly and crept inside. Ellie was sound asleep with the telly remote still in her hand. Trying not to disturb her he got washed up and changed in the bathroom and carefully slid into bed beside her. Sensing he had got into bed, Ellie rolled over and put her arm around him as Nathan snuggled up to her.

The following morning they both woke up fairly late. Sitting down at the breakfast table Nathan told Ellie all about his time with Shiva and the cleaners and how he had shown him the underground theatre. Ellie was pretty amazed and stunned as well.

After making a coffee they carefully went over their plans for the day and evening. First on the agenda Ellie disappeared off to do some shopping and visit her mum and dad while Nathan contacted the hospital again to check for any changes. After he'd hung up he decided to ring his Manager Ben Brooks and update him on the situation with David and to find out if he knew anything.

"Hi Nathan, I've been meaning to call you. How you both been holding up?"

"I've been better Sir, there's no word on David or Diana yet either. Is there any news on the ransom note Sir?"

"That's the reason I was going to call you Nathan. We have had another note claiming responsibility for the LA 1872 crash with threats of more sabotage unless payment is met. The Police have no clues or leads at present. I know we have been over this but we still believe this is an inside job Nathan. If you remember anything that seemed suspicious or different we need to know straight away, you may be the key to catching whoever is doing this," said Ben sounding concerned.

"There was one thing Sir, it might be nothing but on our way back to Nottingham from the St Giles Hotel, I think we were followed by a Silver Vauxhall Astra. Ellie thought I was just tired but I'm not sure. Like I said though, it might be nothing."

"I'll look into it Nathan and come back to you if I find anything. Meanwhile if you remember anything please contact us."

"Thank you Sir, I will" Nathan said good bye and then hung up the phone.

One last phone calls to make he said to himself. *Gunter Fleischer our surgeon friend, I might be able to find him on-line* he thought.

He got up and walked over to his computer and sat down. He switched on the computer and waited for it to load up before logging on and opening a web browser. His initial search of Gunter Fleischer bought back several results so to narrow the results he tried Gunter Fleischer Surgeon, Gunter Fleischer Doctor until he tried Gunter Fleischer Private Surgeon which gave him the result he was after.

The web page read: *Mr Gunter Fleischer MBBS, FRCS is a Consultant, Private Surgeon and Anaesthetist in Carlton, Nottinghamshire offering medical diagnosis, specialist treatment and private Surgery. Mr Fleischer specialises in private Surgery and medical treatment of cosmetic Surgery and re constructive Surgery. He was born in Germany. Mr Fleischer worked as a surgeon at the Ludwigshafen Hospital in Germany for the past twelve years.*

That's him said Nathan as he picked up his phone and dialled the number on screen. "Hello, Gunter Fleischer's Surgery how may I help you?" came the reply.

"Good morning, could I speak to Mr Gunter Fleischer please?"

"Who can I say is calling?"

"Nathan, Nathan Taylor," "Just one moment I'll check if he is available," said the receptionist.

"Hello Mr Gunter Fleischer speaking?" asked Gunter in a thick German accent.

"Hi Gunter, I'm not sure if you can remember me but I met you at the Executive Club in Nottingham with David Benson," said Nathan trembling slightly.

The line went quiet for a few seconds and then "Nathan? It's Nathan isn't it?"

"Yes it is. You remembered me."

"How could I forget, we spent hours together that night talking and drinking. How is David? I haven't seen him for a while," said Gunter.

"Well that's what I'm phoning about. He has been critically injured in a plane crash and is on life support at The London Royal Trauma Hospital. Can we meet up tonight?"

"That's terrible, yes, yes we can meet. 7:30pm at the Executive Club?"

"Yes I'll be there with my partner," said Nathan. "Thank you Gunter, I'll see you tonight" Nathan hung up the phone and breathed a sigh of relief.

It didn't take long for them to unpack the shopping and put it away. Afterwards Ellie told Nathan about the new dress, shoes and handbag she'd bought for the meeting they'd anticipated tonight.

"It's a long red evening dress with black stilettos and matching bag. You can't see it until later though when I wear it," said Ellie excitedly.

Nathan finished tidying up the kitchen and made some coffee while Ellie took her clothes and stuff upstairs.

They spent the next few hours chatting and going over what Nathan had seen and discussed with Shiva.

"That's unbelievable!" said Ellie sounding shocked.

Nathan took a sip from his mug of coffee. "Believe me I was just as shocked. To think I had been visiting him there all these years and had no idea that there was some sort of pre-war shelter underneath the offices."

"Come on," said Ellie. "We'd better get ready it's half six."

Nathan was ready first and back downstairs wearing a black pinstripe suit, white shirt, dark blue tie with grey flecks and polished black shoes. Not long afterwards, Ellie came walking down the stairs. She paused half way down.

"Wow!" said Nathan as he stood staring at her.

She was wearing an elegant long red evening dress that came up just above her chest leaving the tops of her shoulders bare. It flowed down hugging her tummy and hips before resting on the top of her black high heels. Her make-up fell in contrast with her blonde hair that was expertly fastened back into a cute side ponytail.

"You look absolutely gorgeous. Do we have to go out?" asked Nathan in a cheeky tone. "Ooo you mucky bugger," said Ellie playfully

"Come on" she said "We'll be late" as she picked up her black clutch bag and made her way to the door. She locked the front door behind them as Nathan held the car door open for her.

"After you Ma lady," said Nathan in posh accent trying not to laugh. Ellie smiled sweetly also trying not to laugh as she carefully climbed in to the car. Nathan went round the other side climbed in and they both set off for the Executive Club.

"What's the food like?" asked Ellie rubbing her tummy "I'm starving."

"I do remember the food here is pretty good especially the rib eye steak," said Nathan licking his lips.

"You are a tease," said Ellie giggling and still rubbing her tummy.

"Don't worry we're nearly there, just a few more minutes."

No Reaction
~ Chapter Thirteen ~

"What do you fancy to drink?" asked Nathan as they walked up to the bar.

"Malibu Pineapple please," said Ellie as she made herself comfortable at a nearby table. Nathan ordered the drinks and bought them over. "Here you go, one Malibu Pineapple," said Nathan as he placed the drinks on the table.

"Mmm that's nice," said Ellie as she took a sip from her drink. "Do you think he will turn up?"

"I do yes. He's fairly good friends with David so I'm sure he will want to help."

The place felt more like a country restaurant than an Executive Club. It felt cosy and homely with the plush burgundy pile carpet that complimented the dark wood furniture, tables and chairs. On the opposite side of the bar was a coal fire burning with a few logs that had been thrown on. In front of the fire were several black sofas in an arch separated by small wooden tables. Along the top of the fireplace were a few Toby Jugs and two old Indian Beheading swords crossed and securely fastened to the chimney breast. The walls were old and cracked in places, painted cream with oak beams along the ceiling. Apart from the low hum from the ceiling fans it was pretty quiet with only a few people seated and one or two stood at the bar. There was a separate eating area situated next door or the choice to eat in the main bar area.

"Gunter," said Nathan as he stood up and held out his hand to greet him. "Ellie this is Gunter, Gunter this is Ellie my partner" he said as he shook Gunter's hand.

"Hi Gunter," said Ellie smiling.

Gunter Fleischer was about 5' 7" tall and slim with black short sweptback hair slightly grey above the ears with an unusually long forehead leading down to his black medium bushy eyebrows. He had jet black penetrating eyes with bags beneath and an average nose that was slightly pointed. The bottoms of his cheeks were sunken and pulled inwards giving the impression of gritting his teeth. He also had a very wide mouth but thin lips in the middle. His jaw was very square leading down from the corner of his mouth and under his chin with clean shaven pale skin.

At first sight of him, Ellie felt uneasy as he took a seat and joined them.

"Can I get you a drink?" asked Nathan.

"Yes please I'll have tonic water and then you can tell me all about David."

While Nathan had gone to the bar Gunter and Ellie started chatting.

"How long you have known Nathan for?" asked Gunter.

"I've known him a few weeks now but it feels like a lifetime."

"Love at first sight then?" asked Gunter.

"You could say that yes. I met Nathan on the flight over to Denver. Although not in the best circumstances, I knew when I met him that he was the one. It was weird really, I kept getting butterflies in my tummy when I saw him and just felt I had to be with him all the time."

"I don't think you could do any worse than Nathan. He's a good lad and will take care of you. David would always speak very highly of him, they are like soul mates, inseparable," said Gunter speaking energetically.

Ellie wasn't surprised to hear that. She knew David and Nathan were close and hoped that one day she would be as close to Nathan's heart as David was.

Nathan returned with a tray of drinks and set them down on the table. "Here we go" he said as he handed the drinks around.

"Thank you Nathan. Shall we order some food?" asked Gunter.

"Ooo yes," said Ellie as she grabbed a menu from the table.

Nathan just laughed as he grabbed some menus and handed one to Gunter. Upon placing their order they all decided to sit on the sofas by the fire.

"So, tell me Nathan, how is David, what's been happening and how can I help?"

Nathan leant back and got comfortable before taking a sip from his drink. "We were on a routine flight from Germany to Denver when we started to experience multiple system failures. A small explosion in one of the engines ripped off the outer cover which in turn smashed into the side and underside of the fuselage. We tried everything we could to continue on route but had no choice but to divert to Iceland and attempt an emergency landing. Three quarters of the people on board were killed while David was thrown through the wind shield. He landed on a piece debris that punctured his lung and pierced his heart slicing through what I think is called the Superior Vena Cava and part of his Aortic Valve. He was initially pronounced dead at the scene but a trauma surgeon cut him open and restarted his heart and helped stabilise him. The two valves are beyond repair with the only hope of a heart transplant. However, to complicate matters further David's blood group is AB Negative."

"Which hospital is he in at the moment?" asked Gunter.

"He is at The London Royal Trauma Hospital along with Diana."

"Diana? What happened to her?"

"She was severely crushed damaging her spleen, Liver and Kidney and needs a transplant urgently. She also has a fractured skull."

"I imagine they are receiving the finest care possible where they are, but as for David if he doesn't receive a replacement heart soon, well I wouldn't like to say, but how can I help?" asked Gunter.

Nathan felt nervous for the first time. He felt very tense and his palms were sweating as he took a sip from his drink. He was just about to speak as the waitress appeared with their food. Ellie starting tucking into her food straight away but Nathan paused for a while trying to find the right words. "I don't really know how to put this but I'll try to come to the point."

"Go on," said Gunter sounding interested.

"If we can get the transplant organs will you do the Surgery?"

"Yes, yes of course I will, but where are you intending to locate an AB Negative heart and the other organs?"

"Well, it's like this," Nathan took a deep breath and was about to speak when Ellie spoke, "We have a list with two names on it, they are released convicted murders and rapists that are AB Negative. Nathan has a friend that is willing to take them out of society and deliver their organs to you to transplant." Nathan just stared at Ellie and then looked at Gunter expecting the worst. Gunter's expression didn't change as he carried on eating his lunch. "Your friend Nathan, does he know what he's doing and know what's involved?" asked Gunter as he took a drink of his tonic water and carried on eating.

Nathan couldn't believe what he was hearing. Stuttering to speak Nathan said "Yes, yes he does. He is highly fascinated with biology. When he was a child he would dissect animals and collect their body parts. Growing older he then got hold of several corpses to experiment."

"Tell me a bit about him," said Gunter sounding interested.

"His name's Shiva Lawman. I met him at the university while I was studying avionics he was next door studying biology. He actually works as a security guard for a bus company. One night he was out drinking with his mates when some youths came over starting trouble. Shiva spent the next few days finding them one by one and slit their throats. He was sentenced to life imprisonment but due to incorrect and tampered evidence and procedures he was acquitted. He was then arrested on suspicion of murdering eight people but was released due to a lack of evidence and his record cleared. The truth is he did kill the four youths and the eight people in Ingoldmells. He is smart, intelligent and has spent several years studying and practising organ removals. I was privy to see his set up, where he performs the operations and must admit, for an amateur set up I was impressed."

"And what is the turnaround from a request for an organ to killing the person shall we say to the actual delivery?" asked Gunter like he'd just asked for directions or another drink. *He's going to help us* thought Nathan. "To be honest I'm not too sure at the moment but I would imagine maybe a few days."

Meanwhile Ellie was just finishing off her food "Can I get you Gentleman another drink?" asked Ellie

"Yes that would be good," said Gunter.

Ellie returned a few minutes later with a tray of drinks and placed them on the table.

Gunter finished eating and wiped his fingers and mouth on a napkin. He took a drink of his tonic water, turned to Nathan and said "I can help David and Diana. My usual fee would be £60,000 per transplant."

Jonathan G Rigley

Nathan just looked at Ellie as if to say "Where are we going to get £180,000 from?" "However I think we can discuss some kind of arrangement," said Gunter as he took another sip from his drink.

"What do you have in mind?" asked Ellie sounding inquisitive.

"I can have David and Diana transferred to my Surgery by tomorrow afternoon and placed under my care. The minute your friend Shiva has the organs ready to transplant I can proceed. In return, you and Shiva will supply on demand any such organs that I might require in the future. The transplant donor list takes time, weeks or even months. Most of my patience's are very wealthy and would not care or even know where the transplants came from."

"I think I get the picture," said Nathan feeling a bit nervous.

"I understand you both are taking a great risk in supplying organs so I suggest a little compensation, say £5000 per organ?"

"Wow," said Ellie, "I think we have a deal but need to propose the idea to Shiva"

"He'll do it," said Nathan without hesitation.

"Good," said Gunter. "May I suggest another drink to celebrate a long and happy working relationship?"

Nathan stood up and made his way to the bar as the waitress started to take away the empty trays, glasses and plates.

Everybody was feeling happy as they raised their glass "Cheers," said Ellie as they all clinked their glasses together, but something was bothering Nathan. Something wasn't right.

"I'll authorise the transfer straight away," said Gunter as he started to place a call on his mobile. Meanwhile Nathan was sending Shiva a text message. *Me and Ellie need to meet you with a business proposal but it's good to go ASAP,* Shiva replied almost straight away. *Meet any time, will deliver by Friday.*

Today was Tuesday giving them just a few days to get sorted. *Excellent* Nathan thought *it's all beginning to come together. If David can hang on just a little while longer.* "Right we're all sorted," said Gunter as he hung up the phone. "Come and see me at the Surgery tomorrow afternoon about 4pm. David and Diana should be there by then and we can sort out the fine details. Until then I must now leave."

Both Nathan and Ellie stood up and shook his hand, thanked him and said their goodbyes.

After he had left, they sat down to finish their drinks. Nathan just sat staring at the fireplace listening to the crackling noise of the burning logs.

"What's wrong sweetheart?" asked Ellie sensing something was amiss.

"Something just doesn't feel right."

"What do you mean?" asked Ellie leaning forward on her seat.

"Well in effect I've just told a complete stranger that me and my mate are planning on killing someone and then using their organs to save the lives of two people that I hold dear to my heart and he didn't move a muscle. He just carried on eating his shrimp salad as though we were discussing work or something. I mean, why didn't he even look shocked or anything, what if he was an undercover cop or something?"

Ellie just burst out laughing at him, "You numpty, of course he's not a Policeman, you contacted him from his website and you've met him before," she said still giggling. "You don't become a surgeon by being thick as two short planks do you? So my best guess is that he already had a feeling you were going to say something like that."

"Yes you're probably right. It just seemed too easy," said Nathan. "Well we'll find out for sure tomorrow if he is for real if David and Diana get transferred."

Transfer
~ Chapter Fourteen ~

"Nurse Bagnall," said Dr Mark Sheridan. "David Benson and Diana Burton are being transferred up to Nottingham tomorrow afternoon. I need you to make the necessary arrangements and ensure they are both stable."

"Yes Doctor," said nurse Bagnall.

Following protocol, she made her way back to the Nurses' station and picked up the Patient Transfer Procedure handbook and had a quick read through it to refresh her memory. The first step was to ensure that the patient was capable of being transferred so off she went to check on David first. She quietly and carefully opened the door to his room and stepped inside. Reaching down she took hold of the patient record, attached to the clipboard, at the end of his bed and began to study it. David's punctured lung had been repaired but he was currently on a heart bypass and dialysis.

This wasn't a problem as the units were mobile and easy to move. She set the transfer for twelve, midday, tomorrow and marked it down on his record. Tomorrow, the day shift staff will prepare him for moving and secure the mobile units to the bed. She then made her way next door to Diana. Looking at her records, she saw she had a ruptured spleen, broken pelvis but the damage to her Liver and Kidney were beyond repair. Suffering from a fractured skull she was currently in a head and neck brace. Again she marked down on the patient record to prepare the patient for transportation at twelve, midday. She replaced the clipboard and made her way back to the Nurses' station. Due to the nature of the injuries she decided the best method of transport would be by ambulance with blues and two's.

Looking down the telephone list she sorted out the number for the Ambulance Control Centre and gave them a call.

"Hi this is Nurse Grace Bagnall from The London Royal Trauma Hospital. I have two patients that need to be transferred to Nottingham at midday tomorrow."

"Okay, what department is it and what are the patient's names?"

"It's the ICU department and it is David Benson and Diana Burton, they will need to be transferred *Code One*," said Grace.

"What's the reason for transfer?" asked the Operator.

"They are in need of specialist care due to the need for organ transplants. They are being transferred to Dr Gunter's Health Complex in Nottinghamshire for one to one treatment and care."

"Do you have your Authorisation Code?" asked the Operator.

"Yes," said Grace, "514423."

"Okay all received. Confirming two patients to be transferred tomorrow 28th September 2011 at 12:00pm to an address in Nottingham by *Code One* Blues and Two's?" "Yes that's correct. Thank you," said Grace as she hung up the phone.

The last job was to contact the Surgery in Nottingham to confirm the address and an estimated time of arrival. Reading the telephone number off the information sheet, that Dr Sheridan had given her; she proceeded to dial the number.

"Dr Gunter Fleischer, how can I help you?"

"Good evening Dr Fleischer, this is Nurse Grace Bagnall from The London Royal Trauma Centre. I'm calling with regards to David Benson and Diana Burton. I'm confirming that they will be transferred at twelve midday tomorrow, code 1 and should be with you by half one."

"Excellent, can you update me on their injuries and progress?" asked Gunter.

After updating him and confirming the address she hung up the phone and updated the procedures record.

Marcus's Routine
~ Chapter Fifteen ~

10pm as always, Marcus Truman locked the front door, walked down the weed infested path of his overgrown garden and made his way to the pub for last orders. Since being release from Prison, Marcus had lived on his own with his dog Jake and he had pretty much kept himself to himself. Some people might have called him a cantankerous miserable old git because of his moody ways and recluse life style. It would take him about fifteen minutes to walk the short distance to *The Man in Space* public house. He'd order his usual pint of bitter and a hamlet cigar and then go sit over near the bay window. After 7 or 8 pints he'd light his cigar outside and stagger home. He was disowned by his family and friends, so had little much to care about in his life which is why he probably spent each night at the pub. Hearing the key in the door Jake, Marcus's 4 year old grey lurcher, bolted into the living room, hid behind the sofa, amongst the piles of newspapers and lay shaking.

"Jake! Come here you little shit," said Marcus in a slurred voice as he fell through the front door.

The hallway was disgusting with an old push bike leant against the side of the radiator. All shoes scattered on the floor amongst a few letters, leaflets and newspapers. The carpet was threaded and worn like it had never been hovered since it was first laid down. The bottom of the walls were mouldy and the wallpaper was ripped and peeling off. He staggered into the front room knocking over a refuse sack full of rubbish, cans and takeaway boxes.

"You little, shit, where are you? Don't you dare hide from me!" he said in slow slurred voice.

Figuring Jake was behind the sofa he pulled the sofa out and grabbed him by the scruff. Jake yelped in pain as Marcus picked him up and threw him across the front room. Although he landed on a pile of dirty washing he just lay there motionless with his eyes closed. Marcus stood swaying just looking at him with an evil grin on his face before falling flat out on the sofa.

Every time Marcus got drunk and came home he would take his anger and frustration out on Jake. However, the following morning he wouldn't remember what he had done but Jake would. After a few moments Jake managed to get up on to his feet. He shook several times and slowly crept into the kitchen and lay down in his bed trembling. The following morning when Marcus woke, his head was pounding and sore. He made his way into the kitchen to make a coffee. Waiting for the kettle to boil he opened the back door to let Jake out. The back garden was fairly big but all fenced in so he couldn't escape.

The garden was overgrown with brambles and nettles all covered in rubbish that had blown over from other gardens, unsecured bins and was just generally a real mess. Jake wearily climbed out of his bed, went under the table and trotted along to the back garden. "Morning Jake," said Marcus having no idea what he had done to him the previous night.

Jake raised his head slowly and looked up at him but still carried on walking out to the garden. Marcus sat down at the table drinking his coffee. He heard a small noise coming from the front door. Wandering over to investigate he saw that it was only the morning post and newspaper. He put the newspaper under his arm, as he walked back to the kitchen, examining the several letters that had been delivered. He could see one of them was from the council that would be threatening legal action if he didn't sort out his gardens. He'd had one before and wrote back to the council telling them if they wanted it neat and tidy to come and do it themselves. He didn't really care and just threw the letter on the floor amongst the other letters and newspapers. Finishing his coffee he put the cup in the sink and went upstairs to take a shower and get changed.

He would sometimes help out at the local market putting out the stalls and assisting in unpacking the produce to earn a few extra quid, but mostly his bills and rent were paid for by benefits. Returning from his shower he sat on the sofa switched on the telly and started browsing through the channels.

Disaster Strikes
~ Chapter Sixteen ~

Although they were both still unconscious David and Diana were stabilised and ready to be transferred. Two Specialist Paramedics Bill Stone and Amanda Shaw arrived to transfer David and Diana the short distance from the Intensive Care Unit to the waiting ambulance down on the first floor. The ambulance was an advanced ambulance equipped for two patients with full trauma support, emergency medicine and equipment. Once both on board they were securely fastened in and their life support equipment was connected to the on board power supply system and checked.

Exiting the hospital grounds the driver activated the blue lights and sirens and began the dash through London to Nottingham. The sirens reverberated off the nearby buildings; they were lit up by the intense blue flashing lights as they manoeuvred their way through the busy traffic. Ten minutes later they arrived at the tip of the A1, which as usual was at a near standstill. With the blue lights blazing and sirens wailing they navigated their way through the traffic up to the M1 connection. Having joined the M1 it was then none stop all the way to Nottingham. Passing Luton and heading towards Milton Keynes they were making good time and were on schedule.

"Something doesn't feel right," said Bill as the steering wheel started shaking.

Within a split second the front offside tyre exploded sending bits of rubber flying up in the air hitting cars behind. The ambulance spun out of control as it swerved into the central reservation. The bonnet crushed inwards as the radiator burst spraying hot liquid over the road. Bill was fighting to gain control of the ambulance while Amanda hung on for dear life. Several of the cars behind managed to stop in time or swerve out the way but the articulated lorry following was unable to stop in time.

The lorry hit the ambulance square on in the side flipping it over. The sound of scraping metal was deafening as they slid down the motorway and came to rest on the hard shoulder. A few people had stopped and came running over to the ambulance to check the driver and passengers.

"Are you okay Bill?" asked Amanda as she unclipped her seatbelt.

"Yes I'm okay but I can smell the electrics burning we need to get out."

Bill unclipped his seatbelt, lent back and kicked out the windscreen. They were both helped out the ambulance by the people who stopped to help.

"Get the patients out while I contact control," said Bill trembling.

Several of the helpers, along with Amanda, managed to force open the back doors. Bill pulled out his mobile and dialled the Ambulance Control Room. Amanda managed to pull David and Diana from the ambulance and keep them safe and stable.

"Bill, the batteries are showing fifteen minutes remaining!"

"Hello control this is ambulance 416 making the patient transfer to Nottingham. We have crashed with two patients on board. The patients are safe but the life support battery's are showing fifteen minutes remaining. The ambulance power has burnt out."

"Standby," said the controller on the other end of the phone line.

Bill could see Amanda was okay managing David and Diana but he could see the concern on her face. If the battery runs out David and Diana would die right here on the motorway. *Come on* Bill said to himself as he started to get agitated.

"Bill, the Air Ambulance has just been dispatched and will be at your location within ten minutes. The pilot as been notified of the battery situation and the Police and Fire Brigade are on route," said the controller.

"Thank you," said Bill feeling a little better.

"Amanda, the Air Ambulance is on its way."

Moments later the Police arrived. There were four; T5 Volvo's which surrounded the scene, while two whizzed past to close the opposite carriageway. Behind them, he could see a rolling road block, until the Police had completely stopped the traffic about a mile behind. Upon hearing the Air Ambulance had been deployed, Amanda steered David and Diana well away from the ambulance and close to a potential landing spot, before being joined by Bill. A minute or two later the Fire Brigade arrived. Three fire engines pulled up close to the ambulance, which was now smouldering with smoke billowing out the back doors and from under the crushed bonnet.

The firemen unwound the hoses just in front of the ambulance as it burst into flames sending plumes of black smoke into the air.

"What's the battery's reading?" asked Bill as he kept an eye out for the helicopter. "Seven minutes remaining. I hope they make it, there's no sign of them yet though," said Amanda nervously.

Bill pulled the covers up over David and checked the vitals on the monitor. *All is well* he said to himself. He too was feeling nervous as he kept checking his watch.

The firemen did their level best to bring the fire under control but black smoke was still billowing into the afternoon air, which would create difficulties for the pilot to land.

"Five minutes remaining," said Amanda as she started shifting on her feet. The alarms on the equipment activated with an intermittent beep and wailing siren, indicating a critical condition.

The flames were extinguished completely and the smoke started to clear when the ground started to vibrate. Out of nowhere a red MD902 Explorer Helicopter thundered past overhead banked round and flew round in an arch before coming to a hover above. Bill just looked at Amanda. His heart was beating so fast with only a few minutes battery life left. Two Police Officers cleared the road as the helicopter began to descend. With the skill and precision of a surgeon, the pilot expertly landed the helicopter just a few metres away. A paramedic and Doctor leap out the helicopter as the rotor blades began to wind down.

"How long do we have?" shout the Doctor over all the noise.

"Two minutes," said Amanda trying to speak over the noise of the rotor blades.

David and Diana were quickly transferred to the helicopter that was specially adapted to carry stretches and patients. Once strapped in safely the life supports were connected to the on board power system and activated. Bill handed over the paperwork with the patient's records and Dr Gunter's Surgery address that he'd managed to grab from the ambulance. The alarms on the life supports silenced as the batteries began recharging. It was decided that Bill and Amanda would travel in the helicopter and accompany David and Diana.

Shutting the doors the pilot was given the go ahead to proceed. The co pilot logged the address into the air GPS as the pilot increased the power and pulled the helicopter up into a hover. The emergency services on the ground were acknowledged by the co pilot with a wave as the pilot lifted off from the hover. Climbing to around two hundred feet, the nose dipped down as they accelerated off in to the distance.

Unexpected Entrance
~ Chapter Seventeen ~

"I've arranged for us to meet up with Shiva tonight?" asked Nathan.

Ellie and Nathan were both sat on the sofa watching the news and discussing the fine details of their plan to save the lives of David and Diana.

"Do you think he will do it? I mean will he take someone's life and remove their organs to sell for money?" asked Ellie.

Nathan shuddered at the thought of it. "I have a strong feeling he will. Between you and me I think he has killed more people in his lifetime than what we know about. I know the right thing is to go to the Police but Shiva is a friend and the chances are David and Diana won't make it without his help," said Nathan with a grim look on his face.

Ellie took hold of his hand and leant her head on his shoulder. "Well, we're in this together sweetheart. You have to do, what you have to do.

David is so important to you and you should do what you can to save his life, even if it does mean removing some of the scum out of society to get it done. Vernon has emailed me again about the list of names he sent me. He's been fishing for information but I'm trying to put him off," said Ellie as she snuggled up closer to Nathan.

"The thing is Ellie; I think we could use Vernon and his skills. If Gunter is wanting regular donors then surely targeting people who don't want to live or don't deserve to live would make better sense. Who better to supply that list on a regular basis than Vernon?"

Ellie pondered over what he had said for a while. It did make perfect sense but would Vernon do it? He didn't know about Nathan and might be a little jealous. *What about the prospect of the people on the list being killed. How would he react, what if he calls the Police thought* she thought.

"Let's bring Vernon in on this," said Nathan.

"Yes but I'm a little bit scared if I'm to be honest with you. I mean what if he calls the Police, how would he react to the people on the list being targeted to have their organs removed by the psycho from hell?"

Nathan laughed, "The psycho from hell, that's funny. He's not going to call the Police I can assure you of that. He's just hacked into the hospital database and Police National Computer. At this moment in time he has more to hide than us. Don't forget everybody has a price. We could offer him a thousand pounds each time he sends the list?" asked Nathan.

"I tell you what," said Ellie, "Let's wait and see what Shiva says. We could tell him about Vernon and see if he would be willing to work with him directly. If he agrees then we can approach Vernon. I suppose if it goes wrong then he could be Shiva's next victim?"

"You can be really scary sometimes," said Nathan jokingly.

"David and Diana should be arriving soon. I think we should get ready and take a slow ride over to Gunter's Surgery," said Nathan

"Okay sweetheart, I'll just get me shoes on and I'll be ready."

Nathan went outside, started the car and waited for Ellie. Ellie came out a couple of moments later and locked the front door behind her and climbed into the car.

"Seat belt," said Nathan chuckling.

Arriving at the Surgery, Nathan parked the car and they both stepped out.

"Wow this place is massive. It looks like brand new Nathan."

"Yes it is; he had it specially built when he came over from Germany. It has two theatres and room for about twenty patients. He is fully staffed with his own people he bought over from Germany. Occasionally in an emergency, patients are bought here from the hospitals because it is so well equipped and maintained."

"Nathan, Ellie. Good to see you," said Gunter as he came out to greet them. "You're just in time. I've just had word that David and Diana will be landing any second now."

"Landing?" asked Nathan.

"It's a long story. Come with me, the helipad is round the other side."

Nathan locked the car and joined Ellie and Gunter as they made their way round the other side of the complex.

"How many staff do you have working here?" asked Ellie as she walked along by his side.

"My medical team consists of twenty surgeon's Nurses and general staff. I also have two surgeons and three Nurses on emergency standby. If you like I'll show around the next time you visit and give you the grand tour?"

"That sounds brilliant," said Ellie enthusiastically.

"Looks like they are here now," said Nathan pointing to a red helicopter in the distance.

Gunter took out his mobile phone placed a call and spoke to someone in German. Moments later several of the medical team appeared out of a side door and joined Gunter.

The ground began to vibrate and shake beneath their feet as the Air Ambulance approached overhead. The helipad was clearly marked out and visible to the pilot as he skilfully approached and slowly began to descend. The skids touched down. The pilot powered down the helicopter and the rotor blades began to slow down and eventually came to a stop. The medical team rushed over to meet the Dr and paramedics. David and Diana were carefully lowered from the helicopter, transferred along the concourse and into the building. Gunter spoke briefly to the Dr and collected the paperwork before leaving and being joined inside by Nathan and Ellie. The Air Ambulance powered back up then lifted off gracefully, banked round and accelerated off into the distance and headed back to The London Royal Trauma Centre.

David and Diana were already on the ward and being transferred over to the on site life support equipment as they were joined by Gunter, Nathan and Ellie. David was stable but still in a serious condition while Diana's ECG readout showing that she was in pain. One of the Medical Staff injected her with a shot of morphine and placed her on a morphine drip to control the pain.

Gunter signed off some paperwork and started to examine David's medical records. "David's condition is deteriorating slowly. I estimate he as only a few days left before there is permanent damage." He replaced David's medical records at the feet of his bed and stepped over to Diana and picked up her medical records. "Diana has a fractured skull which is causing pressure on the brain. This is giving her some slight pain and needs to be operated on. I will schedule the Surgery in the next few hours. I'm going to be blunt with you Nathan. You need to contact Shiva as soon as possible. David needs to receive the transplant in the next few days or he will die."

Nathan just looked at Ellie not sure as what to say. "We have a meeting with Shiva in a few hours. He should be able to update us on the progress," said Nathan.

"Contact me or any one of my Medical Staff as soon as you can confirm delivery." Nathan shook Gunter's hand and thanked him before he and Ellie left.

"I feel a bit nervous," said Ellie as they both stepped out of the car into the bus car park. Ellie jumped as one of the cleaners darted past her. "This place gives me the creeps," said Ellie as she grabbed hold of Nathan's hand.

"Don't worry; no one will hurt you here." Nathan could see Shiva outside the portacabin having a smoke as they walked across the car park. Ellie squeezed Nathan's hand even tighter. Nathan just looked at her and smiled. "Shiva this is Ellie, Ellie this is Shiva Lawman" Shiva just grunted as Ellie shook his hand and smiled at him.

"You'd better come inside," said Shiva as he took the last drag from his cigarette and stubbed it out on the floor. He walked round the side of the portacabin with his head down and his hair slightly hanging down and blowing in the breeze as he opened the door. Nathan made everybody a drink as they discussed the proposal with Shiva.

"And I get to choose how they are killed?" asked Shiva with a really scary grin.

"Erm, yes I suppose so," said Nathan.

"We have been watching Marcus for a few days now learning his movements. He goes to the pub every night at ten then returns home a little while later drunk. That's when we will take him," said Shiva.

"When can you do it?"

"Tomorrow I will have Gunter prepare David at midnight for Surgery. I will use my car to transfer the organ to Gunter's Surgery so have him look out for me."

"Thank you," said Nathan.

"What do you do with the rest of the body when you have done with it?" asked Ellie inquisitively.

"You don't want to know," said Shiva with a slight smile and a quiet chuckle.

Ellie looked at Nathan bewildered.

"I think we should be going now," said Nathan standing up, "Gunter will discuss the money transfer details with you and how he will communicate his donor requests to you when you see him tomorrow night."

Ellie finished her coffee and they both left.

It was pretty late when Ellie and Nathan got home so they both decided to go straight to bed. Ellie was last out of the bathroom as Nathan was already in bed. Ellie pulled back the covers and slid over to him. She kissed him on the lips and then lay her head down on his chest. Nathan wrapped his arm around her and pulled the covers up over the both of them.

"I hope it all goes well tomorrow night," said Ellie.

"Are you going to speak to Vernon tomorrow?" asked Nathan.

"Yes, I'm going to ring him in the morning and arrange to meet him."

"Do you want me to come with you for support?" asked Nathan as he cuddled her tight. "Yes if you would sweetheart."

The following morning Nathan was up and about as Ellie woke up with a yawn and a long stretch. After going to the bathroom and having a wash she wandered downstairs in just her bra and knickers.

"Morning gorgeous," said Nathan.

"Morning sweetheart," said Ellie as she threw her arms around him and kissed him.

Ellie jumped up and wrapped her legs around him. Nathan fell backwards onto the sofa with Ellie on top of him. They both started laughing as Nathan began to tickle her until she was hysterical.

"I need a drink," said Ellie as she sat up with her legs either side of him. "Come on I'll make you breakfast sweetheart," said Ellie. Nathan picked her up and gave her a kiss and then gently lowered her down to the floor.

The rest of the morning flew by really quickly. Ellie had rung Vernon and briefly spoke to him on the phone. She explained that she was with Nathan and they would be interested in receiving a list updated to be sent on a regular basis. Nathan was right. Everyone has a price including Vernon. He took it very well when he learnt about Nathan but he was more interested in the money for the list of names.

"Do you fancy driving? You know where we are going," said Nathan.

"Yes sweetheart, make sure you lock the front door," said Ellie as she climbed into the driver's seat.

Vernon lived at the other end of the city towards Top Valley, so it would only take about fifteen to twenty minutes to get there.

Five minutes or so into the journey Ellie said "I could do with a drink. I'm going to pull in at this petrol station. Do you want anything?"

"Go on then yes I'll have a can of Red Bull."

While Ellie popped into the petrol station, Nathan noticed a Silver Vauxhall Astra slow down, pull in and stop across the road for a few minutes.

Catching view of part of the number plate, he remembered it was the same one that he thought had followed him from London. He decided to go and speak to the driver but as he opened the door to get out, the car sped off. "What's wrong?" asked Ellie as she returned with some drinks.

"That Silver Astra, I've just seen it again"

"Are you sure? There must be thousands of Astra's, they all look the same," said Ellie as she passed Nathan his Red Bull

"Yes I think I'm sure. I recognised the last bit of the registration plate"

"How can you *think* you're sure?" asked Ellie laughing, "Come on get in."

Ellie was still teasing Nathan as they arrived at Vernon's house.

"Alright, alright I get it!" said Nathan.

She took hold of his hand as they walked up the path and knocked on Vernon's door. A few minutes later Vernon answered.

"Ellie, come in, how are you?"

"I'm fine thank you, this is Nathan, Nathan this is Vernon."

Nathan and Vernon shook hands as they stepped inside and Vernon shut the door behind them.

"Make yourselves at home" he said as he sat down on his leather recliner. Nathan sat down on the sofa next to Ellie as she started to speak. "The list that you created for us was very useful, very useful indeed, to the point where we would like you to supply the list updated and on a regular basis. We would be willing to generously compensate you for your time."

"Why is this list of names so important to you? What's it for?"

Ellie looked at Nathan to see any changes on his face as to indicate do not tell him or yes go ahead, but he just sat there.

"You've known me a long time Ellie, you can trust me. You know you can."

Ellie took a deep breath and sat back. "You're right, I was on the flight that crashed in Iceland. Nathan was the First Officer flying the plane with Captain David Benson."

"I knew it, I knew it was you!" said Vernon energetically.

"That's where me and Nathan first met," said Ellie as she smiled and looked at Nathan. "But what's this got to do with the list of names?" asked Vernon.

Ellie was looking really nervous now. "When the plane crashed, David was thrown through the wind shield and was critically injured. So badly that he needs to have a heart transplant."

Vernon sat with his mouth wide open just staring at her. *Say something then* she thought to herself.

After what seemed like hours Ellie said "Penny dropped?"

Vernon cleared his voice and said "Yes. Penny dropped. You are one crafty sod. I am impressed. I take it David's blood group is AB Negative?"

"Yes, yes it is."

"You wanted the list of names as they are bad people. You don't just want to do it to any old person but only those that have done bad things. What I don't get though is after David's transplant why do you need me to update the list and send it regularly?"

Ellie had made her mind up now that Vernon would help them rather than turn them in, so she decided to just come out with everything. "We found a surgeon that was willing to do the Surgery free of charge. Dr Gunter Fleischer is really good friends with David and Nathan and have known each other for several years. He agreed to do the transplant in return for mores organs as and when he needs them."

"Wow, this is incredible. Are you actually going to kill these people yourselves? Where are you going to do it and how the hell do you know what you're doing. I mean it's not just a matter of cutting someone open, reaching in and pulling out a lung or something?"

"No, neither of us will be killing anyone. We already have that side dealt with. Shiva Lawman, one of Nathan's friends has agreed to help. He will be collecting the organs and dealing with the transportation. All you will have to do is, once he contacts you with the relevant information, on the type of person he is looking for, simply update the list, send it to him and you will then be reimbursed for you time."

"Erm how much are we talking about exactly and how often do you think he'll want the list updating?"

"I'm not sure about the frequency of the list but Gunter owns his own Surgery and carries out quite a few transplants. We were thinking about £500 each time you supply the list?" Nathan nudged her in the side.

They originally decided on £1000 but she was playing hard ball with him. She looked at Nathan as if to say *shut up and behave yourself.*

"£500 each time I update the list and send it to Shiva." Vernon thought about it for a little while. "There is a huge risk involved in getting the list, the passwords could change or I could be tracked."

"I doubt it Vernon, you're too smart to get caught. I tell you what, £750? Do we have a deal? You could end up supplying the list several times a week in some cases I reckon."

The thought of all that money was too tempting for Vernon. "Yep you got a deal." "Brilliant," said Ellie.

"Well done mate," said Nathan as he got up and shook his hand. "Any chance of a drink now?" asked Nathan laughing.

"Yes I'll pop the kettle on," said Vernon getting up and walking into the kitchen. *Who says crime doesn't pay* he thought to himself.

Victim Number One

~ Chapter Eighteen ~

Jake would have no idea that this was the last time he would see Marcus or have to suffer any more violence when he was drunk. Marcus shut the door and left for the pub making the same trip he made every night. He was already tipsy as he had been drinking earlier in the day. Arriving at the pub, he ordered his usual pint of bitter and cigar and went and sat over by the window.

Shiva was sat in the driver's seat of bus 426, a red solo, as he waited for his two cleaners to accompany him. Lenny hopped on board first, followed by Uncle Fester. Uncle Fester was 5' 11" tall with an extremely exceeding forehead a chubby face and was slightly overweight. He wore round rimmed glasses that were hanging off the end of his nose. He also wore a yellow reflective vest and dirty jeans the same as Lenny.

Shiva lit a cigarette, "Have you got everything and you both know what you're doing?" he said with the cigarette hanging out the corner of his mouth.

They both nodded at him.

"Time to slice and dice!" said Shiva grinning.

Having done this many times before, they all knew what they were doing and knew what treat lay ahead of them.

Shiva slowly drove past the pub to confirm Marcus was sat in his usual spot by the window. He drove a little way down the road and parked up. The road wasn't too well lit which would make things a little easier. Shiva took out his newspaper and started to read as they waited.

Marcus drank up his last pint, got up and made his way to the door. Stepping outside, he then lit his cigar and took a long drag and blew the smoke out. He started to stagger his way home still smoking his cigar.

"Hey mister?" asked Lenny as Marcus walked past.

Marcus turned round and stepped on the bus. With a flash of a blade Shiva expertly slit his throat spraying blood all over the bus. He pulled on Marcus's shoulder and spun him around as he made a gurgling noise and held his hands to his throat. The knife sank all the way up to the handle as Shiva pierced the knife upwards into his lung preventing him from making a noise. Shiva pulled the knife out and wiped it on Marcus's shirt before returning to the driving seat. Checking nobody saw what had happened Shiva started the bus and drove back to the depot.

He carefully backed the bus in through the shutters, after silencing the reverse alarm. Uncle Fester jumped down, unlocked the paint booth doors and pulled them open. While Shiva continued to reverse into the paint booth, Uncle Fester removed the lock from the grate in the floor while Lenny closed and locked the doors behind them. Lenny climbed into the underground Surgery and turned on the lights. Uncle Fester took hold of Marcus and lowered him down to Lenny. Uncle Fester then followed Lenny down to the Surgery as they both placed him on to the theatre trolley.

Shiva joined them shortly afterwards, as he left a few of the other cleaners to clean the blood out the bus and any traces of Marcus. He first activated the cooling boxes that would be used for the transfer. He then put on his green gown, his hat and latex gloves. Lenny and Fester had already stripped the body and was starting to wash it down.

Shiva took a scalpel and made an incision just above the left breast and a straight line down to just below the breast. Peeling the skin back he carefully sliced open the pectoral muscle and tissue until he was in the chest cavity. He clamped several forceps onto the skin either side to open the cavity. He placed an expansion device inside, which opened the cavity to about four inches wide. Lenny placed a metal dish on top over the body as Shiva carefully cut two of the ribs and through the arteries and vessels until the heart was free. He carefully lifted the heart out as blood began to drain from it. Gently lowering the heart into the metal dish, Lenny swiftly packed in ice and placed it in the donor transfer cooling box ready. Shiva handed Lenny his car keys so he could go and place the organ in his car boot while he cleaned himself up.

The bus had been scrubbed clean and returned to the bus park after being refuelled. Walking through the paint booth Lenny was returning and handed Shiva his keys back.

"It's all yours now," said Shiva with an evil grin.

Lenny's eyes lit up as he quickly made his way back downstairs. He was soon followed by Uncle Fester. Shiva got in his car started it up and hit the air con. He carefully pulled out from under the shutter doors and sped off through the bus park and made his way to Gunter's Surgery. Using the built in hands free he dialled Gunter's mobile number Nathan had given him.

"Yes I can confirm the heart is now on route, is David prepared for Surgery?" asked Shiva.

"Yes David is ready. Come through the car park and drive round to the rear entrance. My Medical Staff will be waiting for you. Derek will take your account details and discuss the encryption and email communications."

"Excellent," said Shiva, "I'm ten minutes away."

Shiva hung up the phone and continued his way to the Surgery. The heart only has a life span of a few hours once it has stopped beating so time was critical.

Uncle Fester was named because of his near bold, egg-shaped head and black rings around his eyes. His real name was Paul Baker, 26 years old and lived in Aldercar. He came across as being really slow and backwards but anybody who thought this was wrong. He enjoyed his job as a cleaner for the bus company but he loved the perks even more.

Paul had nearly removed both legs while Lenny was still sawing through the left arm. The front of his gown was covered in blood has he picked up the legs one by one and placed them on the trolley behind him. Carefully but accurately he separated the leg by removing the knee cap and foot leaving the leg in two pieces. After removing all the skin he then did the same to the other leg separating it in to two pieces. When he had finished, he took the first arm and removed the hand and elbow also leaving the arm in two pieces. Lenny did the same to the other arm. They placed the knee caps hands, elbows and feet inside the body cavity and then stapled it closed.

The pieces of arms and legs were all skinless and carefully rinsed clean. Paul and Lenny then wrapped the rest of the body in brown wrapping paper, being careful not to rip the paper. Both ends of the body were tied closed as they lifted it off the trolley and into a large metal bin at the end of the corridor. Paul pulled on a pair of heavy duty rubber gloves knelt down and removed the lock from the cupboard. He pulled out a container labelled Calciumdimetracid. Lenny came over to him with a bucket of water and placed it by his side. Paul poured two capfuls of Calciumdimetracid into the bucket of water, which started to fizz violently. He carefully placed the container back in the cupboard and replaced the lock. Taking hold of the bucket, Paul carefully poured the liquid all over the body that they had placed in the metal bin. Instantly the body started to melt and dissolve away like melting ice cream.

Paul and Lenny just stood staring as the Calciumdimetracid went to work dissolving the bones, skin and head. Lenny always found it fascinating how the bones went all mushy before dissolving and disappearing altogether.

Calciumdimetracid was invented in Russia in the late 1940's to sell to Germany for the mass disposal of bodies. It was so effective at completely dissolving a body that it was declared illegal in most countries. How Shiva came by the liquid is not fully known. He may have connections on the other side of the water or he could have discovered it by chance when he learnt about the underground Surgery. But one thing was for sure, it was his and he knew how to use it. Stored at room temperature in a metal container, Calciumdimetracid is safe, but as soon as it is mixed with water and exposed to the air it becomes volatile.

Remembering Marcus had a dog, Paul sent Shiva a text to see if he would want to do anything about it, but Shiva was too busy at the moment. He had just pulled into the car park at Gunter's Surgery and pulled round to the back entrance where he was then met by Derek and Simon from Gunter's medical team. Shiva opened the boot and passed the transplant cooler to Simon who instantly took it inside and into theatre one.

Shiva stayed a short time while exchanging details with Derek. Having read Paul's message he decided to pay Jake a visit at Marcus's house. He shook hands with Derek and left heading off towards

Marcus's house. He boldly walked up the path and round the back of the house before quietly forcing the door open. When Jake heard the door open he ran and hid behind the sofa again, expecting Marcus to come in drunk and start beating him.

Shiva moved the sofa and was greeted by a dog lying on the floor shaking and whimpering. Jake looked up at Shiva with is long floppy ears and big puppy dog eyes as if to say *please don't hurt me*.

Unusual Disappearance
~ Chapter Nineteen ~

"999 Emergency; which service do you require?"

"The Police, quick someone is breaking into next door. There's an old man that lives there with his dog."

"Okay madam just calm down a moment. Now what's your name?"

"My name, it's Doris, I'm Marcus's neighbour."

"My names Shirley, what's Marcus's address Doris?"

"He lives at 38 Stanley Avenue in Lenton. I live at 36 next door to him. He's such a nice man. He always smiles at me."

"The Police are travelling to you as we speak Doris. Can you tell me what else you saw?"

"There was a tall man with long dark hair. He had a bit of a stoop, bent over like he had been down the pit all his life. He was wearing a long dark blue anorak and dark trousers."

"Okay, what else did you see Doris?" asked the Operator.

"Well I was in the back kitchen getting a glass of water as I couldn't sleep. You know how it is at my age. Anyway when I leant forward to turn the tap on I noticed him walking around the back yard. He pulled some sort of large device from under his coat and got into the door within seconds. That's when I rang you or just after I'd drunk my water. But I did see him leave about five minutes later with Marcus's dog Jake. Did I tell you I'm 86 years old? I can still get about on my own you know."

Doris's front room had lit up from the powerful blue flashing lights from the two Police cars that had just arrived.

"The Police have just arrived Doris if you want to go and let them in. Thank you for calling us Doris and take care of yourself."

Doris hung up the phone and made her way to the front door. She was greeted by two Police Officers while two more went next door to Marcus's house. The two officers took a brief statement from Doris before leaving her and joining the other two offices next door.

Marcus was well known to the Police due to his prior conviction. He'd been in trouble a few times before, for brawling in the street and being drunk and disorderly. There was no sign of Marcus or his dog Jake which was unusual. The Police knew he had little friends and no family to speak of so decided to treat the incident as suspicious.

Listening to *Relight My Fire* Shiva backed his car inside the garage behind the shutters and stepped out. Lenny and Paul were waiting for him when Jake jumped out the car and sat proud beside Shiva.

"I think he's took a shine to you," said Paul.

"He'll be staying here with us from now on. Make sure he's looked after," said Shiva. "We're having a bit of a barbecue; he can come and join us." said Paul.

They all walked over to the waste ground just behind the bus park where nearly all the cleaners were chatting and tucking in. Lenny cut a large piece of meat off the bone and gave it to Jake. Jake looked really thankful as he sat down and started to chew his way through it. Jake stood up licking his lips as one of the cleaners chucked him a bone. He lay down and put his paw over it and started to have a little chew. He looked up at Shiva who had just lit a cigarette as if to say thank you. If only Jake knew what he was eating!

Gunter Operates

~ Chapter Twenty ~

"More suction please. Okay, pass me the sutures and increase ten degrees on the dialysis flow."

Gunter had successfully removed David's heart and was now transplanting the new heart. Even though all blood is bypassing the heart valves and being pumped through a life support machine, the cavity where the heart sits still fills with blood hampering the stitching of the arteries and valves. He carefully sutured the three valves above the Aortic Valve inserting one stitch at a time. It would only take a matter of days for the valves and arteries to knit together fully. This is the critical time where the patient must remain laying down and as still as possible. Any stress could cause the heart to beat faster with the onset of Ventricular Tachycardia increasing pressure and eventually blowing out the sutures.

Next, he reconnected the Superior Vena Cava, adjacent to the Aorta and applied several sutures.

"Suction Please?" asked Gunter as he reconnected the remaining arteries and replaced the third and fourth rib.

"Atropine 1 mg IV push," said Gunter as he picked up the defibrillator paddles.

This was a tense moment as it was now time to start David's new heart. The Atropine would help suppress the low heart beat while the defibrillator would assist in starting it. "Disengage the Dialysis," said Gunter as he placed the paddles either side of the heart. "Charging 50," said Gunter.

The Defibrillator started to make a whining noise increasing in pitch until it was a steady tone. "Clear!"

The Anaesthetist removed the oxygen mask and the medical team stepped backwards. "No change, charge 100, and clear." Gunter shocked the heart a second time as it slowly started to beat.

The Anaesthetist replaced the oxygen mask on David and checked his vitals and said "BP 100 over 60."

Gunter observed as the heart gradually start to beat faster and pick up into a normal rhythm.

"BP 125 over 84 and stabilised," said the Anaesthetist.

"Good job everybody," said Gunter. "Let's start and sow him back up."

The assistant to Gunter's left released the clamps and forceps to allow the cavity to close in on itself. To keep scaring to a minimum the muscle just below the skin is sutured together pulling the skin together, this in turn would soon knit together and heal nicely.

After the skin was cleaned, David was transferred to a trolley and wheeled into the recovery room. The next twenty four hours would tell if the heart would be rejected by the body or not.

Ellie and Nathan were in bed watching telly and talking while waiting for any news on David and Diana.

"David should be having his operation by now," said Nathan yawning.

He had just received a text message from Shiva confirming he had delivered the heart to Gunter's Surgery.

"He'll be fine sweetheart," said Ellie as she cuddled up to him.

They had just finished watching titanic when Ellie turned to Nathan "How come she says she'll never let go but then let's go and watches him disappear under the water. He might have just been asleep or something?"

Nathan started to laugh "It's only a film but if it was me I wouldn't have let go."

"Me neither. What other films have you got?" asked Ellie.

"There are loads in the rack, go and see what takes your fancy."

Ellie pulled her dressing gown on and got out of bed just as the phone rang.

"Hello, Nathan speaking."

"Nathan its Gunter I'm ringing you with an update."

"Who is it?" asked Ellie.

"Its Gunter," said Nathan.

"Diana's operation was a success relieving pressure on the brain. The fracture in her skull has been pinned and she is no longer in pain."

"That's excellent news," said Nathan.

"What about David?"

"David's transplant went smoothly without any problems. He is now breathing on his own and is currently off the life support equipment. He's now resting in the recovery room." Gunter could hear the sigh of relief from Nathan as he said "Come tomorrow afternoon and you can see him. Meanwhile I'll keep you up to date with any problems." "Thank you Gunter, thank you so much."

Nathan hung up and turned to Ellie. "Both David and Diana are fine and doing well. Diana is no longer in pain and David's transplant went perfect. We can go and see them tomorrow."

Ellie and Nathan continued chatting for a while before falling asleep.

Operation Abyss
~ Chapter Twenty One ~

It was approaching lunch time as the Police had tapped off Marcus's house while the Scene of Crimes Officers was searching the house. Several finger prints were taken from the back door and the kitchen door. Although the house was in a mess everything was organised and in order except a pile of CD's pulled from the rack and scattered across the floor. On top of the pile was an empty case from *Take That's Greatest Hits*. This was dusted for prints along with some of the other CD's.

The Police had quickly built up a profile of Marcus to try to anticipate what may have happened to him. Speaking to the Landlord at the 'Man in Space' Pub, he confirmed that Marcus had been in as usual at ten o'clock and ordered his usual pint of bitter and a cigar. He had sat by the window all night reading the newspapers before leaving at quarter past eleven. Obtaining a description of the clothes he was wearing, the grey coat was nowhere to be found in the house. Fearful that he may have been drunk and wandered off, the Police helicopter was bought in to search the area but nothing turned up. Several more officers were drafted in to help search the area and perform a door to door inquiry.

Neil Curtis had just started his shift when he logged on to his computer to check the latest incidents. Straight away the Marcus incident stood out at him. He was investigating a rising amount of missing persons in and around Derbyshire and Nottinghamshire with no apparent reason or link to one another. It wasn't unusual for people to go missing without trace, but the past few months had seen a massive increase with as many 120 people missing in a 3 month period compared to the usual 20-30 people that had been reported missing in the previous months.

Neil was 42 years old, divorced with no children. He had light brown hair and a rugged completion, he stood at 5' 10" tall with a bit of a pot belly. He'd been in the force a long time making his way up to Chief Inspector. He had solved hundreds of cases and won many awards but he had to admit to himself that this case was getting the better of him.

He was convinced that there was a link between the missing persons but just couldn't put his finger on what it was. With about forty officers working with him the case had been code named *Operation Abyss*. Within the operations room was a huge map of Nottingham and Derby with push pins indicating the missing persons. There were huge piles of records detailing information on each missing person. The opposite wall was decked out with every missing persons photograph and name from over the last six months. The range was from as young as 23 to as old as 67 both men and women and mixed races. He logged out of his computer having decided to visit the scene at Marcus's house.

Detective Claire Sheppard had been Neil's colleague since his promotion and had been working *Operation Abyss* with him from the beginning. They both stepped out the car having arrived at Marcus's house.

There were Police Officers everywhere and Scene of Crimes Officers going in and out of the house. Neil was well known and respected in the Police Force and didn't need to identify himself. They were met by the Officer in Charge (OIC) who showed them around and filled them in on the details. Claire was making notes throughout even the smallest detail. Neil noticed from the statements that Marcus was wearing a grey jacket when he left the pub but there was no sign of it in the house. Whoever had broken into the house had used a crowbar to open the back door. Nothing else appeared to be missing from the house apart from Jake, indicating it wasn't a robbery. Why would someone break in and take a dog, was there something hidden in the CD's that they were looking for?

Claire wanted to believe that he had simply wandered off drunk but it was becoming obvious he had been abducted and they had come back for the dog. Claire collected up all the statements from the door to door enquiries in hope of spotting some small details. Neil took several photographs inside and outside the house to use in the investigation. He spoke briefly to the OIC and then left with Claire heading back to the Police Headquarters.

GPS Tracker
~ Chapter Twenty Two ~

"What? What is it" shrieked Ellie as Nathan ran past her down the stairs and out into the front garden.

Ellie ran after him wondering what the hell was going on.

Out of breath Nathan said "Somebody was messing underneath the car then ran off and got into the Silver Astra that has been following us, I know this time I didn't imagine it." "What did they do to the car?" asked Ellie looking gob smacked.

Nathan paused a moment to catch his breath and gather his thoughts. "I'm not sure what he did. It could be a bomb or anything."

"We need to phone the Police," said Ellie.

"No! What if it's something to do with you know what," said Nathan.

"It can't be; no one could have found out or link anything back to us. Phone the garage and have them pick up the car immediately."

"That's a good idea," said Nathan as he picked up his mobile phone.

It had been about two hours since the garage had taken Nathan's car when there was a knock on the door. It was the mechanic from the garage, he had bought Nathan's car back. "That was quick, come in, come in," said Nathan.

The mechanic handed the keys to Nathan and a small black and grey box before taking a seat in the kitchen. Ellie just looked at Nathan with a confused look.

"What's this?" asked Nathan spinning the box over in his hands and looking at it.

"That is a GPS & GSM Tracking receiver," said the mechanic.

Being a pilot Nathan was familiar with GPS. GPS or Global Positioning System is capable of tracking your location anywhere on earth. In this case the GPS position was gained and then sent back as a text message through the GSM Mobile network.

"It looks like someone wanted to track where you were going mate," said the mechanic.

Nathan paid the mechanic and he left.

"What's going off?" asked Ellie.

"I have no idea but I sure would like to know who it is in that Astra and why they are following us. Why would anyone want to track where we are going? It doesn't make any sense," said Nathan as he sat back down at the table.

Ellie boiled the kettle and made two coffees as Nathan sat down trying to get his head round what was happening.

"This has got to have something to do with the company. It's the only thing I can think of," said Nathan as he took a sip from his coffee.

Nathan decided to ring his Manager Ben, and update him on David's progress and see what he could find out. He took another sip from his coffee and started to dial his number. Ellie sat down opposite him as the line started ringing.

"Hello, Ben speaking."

"Ben, it's Nathan."

"Nathan, how are you?"

"I'm good; I just wanted to update you on David and Diana's progress. Diana is doing well but still waiting for a donor. David has had the heart transplant and is set to make a full recovery."

"Thanks so good to hear Nathan. I was planning on ringing you soon. The NTSB has confirmed the crash was in fact deliberate. We received another phone call claiming responsibility for the crash. The good news is, the Police had tapped the line and traced the call leading to an arrest. The person they arrested is a known terrorist cell operating in London."

"Terrorists, that's unbelievable," said Nathan.

Nathan pulled the phone away from his mouth to tell Ellie what was happening as she sat forward listening. Nathan proceeded to tell Ben about the sightings of the mysterious Silver Astra and the GPS tracker found under his car. Ben agreed it was really suspicious and that it could be linked to the terrorist's but, why?

"It's time we went to see David and Diana," said Ellie as Nathan hung up the phone. "Hopefully he has come round now and might be able to tell us what is going off," said Nathan.

"Do you think he as something to do with this?" asked Ellie.

"To be honest I don't know what to think anymore. There's so much happening, it could be anyone or anything."

They both drank their coffee and left to go and visit David and Diana.

Arriving at Gunter's Surgery, they were both greeted by the Medical Staff.

"Put these on please," said the Nurse as she handed them a green surgical gown and cap.

They both placed on the gowns and caps as the Nurse took them to see David. He had been transferred from the recovery room to the side ward and was semi conscious.

"David," said Nathan has he took hold of his hand.

"Can he hear me?" asked Nathan to the nurse.

"He might be able to hear you. He's been drifting in and out of consciousness since the operation. Don't worry its perfectly normal."

David started to groan a little as he squeezed Nathan's hand.

"He's trying to say something," said Ellie.

Nathan moved closer to try to hear what he was saying but it was mumbled.

"Would you like to see Diana?" asked the nurse.

Nathan and Ellie followed the nurse past a few other patients and over to where Diana was.

"She's still unconscious but she's not in any pain. Diana is still on the transplant list for a Kidney and Liver. The machine at the side of her is doing the work of the organs and keeping her alive. She is in a stable condition but desperately needs the transplant."

"I'm sure something will come up soon," said Ellie sounding sympathetic.

The Nurse left and Nathan picked up the patient clipboard from the end of the bed and studied it.

"B positive blood group," said Nathan quietly.

He pulled out his mobile and sent a text message to Shiva. *B Positive, Kidney and Liver* and then put the phone back in his pocket. Soon Shiva would contact Vernon for an updated list and then Shiva and the cleaners would collect their next victim. Nathan went back over to David in hope that he had come round but he was still unconscious.

"Come on, there's not much you can do here. You'll be more comfortable at home and I need to stop by my place and collect my mail."

Nathan sighed, he wanted to be there when David woke up but it could still be days yet before he was fully conscious.

"Okay, come on lets go. Do you mind driving?" asked Nathan

"Of course not," said Ellie as she reached in his pocket and pulled out his car keys. "Careful," said Nathan smiling.

Ellie gave him a peck on the cheek and took hold of his hand. Gunter promised to call them if there were any significant changes as Nathan and Ellie left.

"It's there again, the Astra, look!" said Nathan pointing over towards the road.

This time Ellie saw the car and turned to Nathan. "Who is it? What do you think they want?"

"I have no idea but I'm about to find out," said Nathan as he started sprinting towards the car which was about three to four hundred yards away.

Nathan was in good shape and very fit as he continued running across the car park. "Wait" shouted Ellie. "Wait, you don't know who it is, they could have guns or anything!"

Seeing Nathan running over, the Silver Astra started up and wheel spun off. Nathan stopped running and bent over with his hands on his knees catching his breath. Ellie soon caught up with him as she came running over.

"You tool, that could have been anyone in that car," said Ellie.

"I know, I know but I just want to know who it is and why they following us and watching us?"

"Come on let's get going," said Ellie.

They made their way to the car, climbed inside and set off towards Ellie's house.

They were only a few miles away when Ellie noticed blue lights flashing in her rear view mirror. Drawing closer she pulled over to the side to let them pass. A Fire Engine whizzed past them sirens wailing and blue lights flashing. Thinking nothing of it they continued on their way until several more, blue flashing lights appeared behind them. Pulling over, two more fire engines and several Police cars shot past.

"Bloody heck," said Ellie, "That doesn't look good."

"Look," said Nathan. "The black smoke over there, look there is shit loads of it. It looks like a house fire or something."

They continued driving and chatting about the smoke and fire engines for a while, when Ellie realised they were getting closer to the fire, the closer they got to her house. She indicated to turn down her street and waited for a gap in the traffic. Turning into the street she slowed down to a stop, staring with her mouth open. She couldn't believe the horrific sight that met her eyes.

Unusual Sightings
~ Chapter Twenty Three ~

"Sir."

"Yes Claire."

"Sir, did you know Marcus had a blood group of AB Negative? I've just been reading the Prison admittance forms. Each prisoner has to have a blood sample taken to test for HIV and other diseases, the test flagged up his blood group."

"So what difference does that make?" asked Neil looking a bit confused.

"AB Negative is extremely rare. Look the PNC shows there are only three people in the whole of the valley with this blood group, two of which have a criminal record."

"So we have a missing murderer with a rare blood group. This just gets better. Who is the other one with the record?"

"Darren Moss a 42 year old rapist from Lenton Sir."

Neil paused for a few seconds thinking about what she had said. Maybe she had stumbled on something here. They had no real leads to go on so it wouldn't hurt to follow the lead on this one. His gut instinct was telling him to follow this up but he wasn't sure where to start.

"Okay people can I have your attention?" asked Neil as he stood up at the front of the room. "Marcus as well as being a convicted murderer has a rare blood group of AB Negative, this could be something or nothing but I want all the existing missing persons checked for previous convictions and order by their blood group."

There was a shuffle of papers and talking has everyone got to work straight away. "Bring the car round Claire, I think we'll pay Darren Moss a visit and see if anything strange as been going off with him."

"Yes Sir."

Claire was programming the address into the GPS as Neil climbed into the passenger seat.

"That's good work Claire, spotting the blood group."

"Thank you Sir."

Neil sat reading through the Police record of Darren; it listed his crimes, current address, family, friends and several other details. Darren had been out night clubbing in town, as he was making his way home he came across a young girl who was a little worse for wear having had too much to drink.

Instead of being a gentleman and helping her to get home he dragged her behind some skips at the back of the petrol station and repeatedly raped her.

She was too drunk to fight back but knew what he was doing and that he was hurting her. Once she had managed to escape from him she ran into the petrol station screaming with her clothes ripped and torn. The Police were called and picked him up within a matter of minutes having caught him on the petrol station CCTV walking past.

The Judge sentenced him to twenty years imprisonment as it was the most horrific and violent rape he had ever dealt with. He concluded that Darren although only eighteen at the time, was a danger to society and would not only be locked up to protect the public but to protect himself. After his release he applied for a new identity but was refused by the court of appeal saying it was in the public's interest to know who he was and what he had done.

Arriving at Darren's house, Neil placed the records back in his briefcase and stepped out the car. Claire followed him after locking the car and knocked on the front door. They were greeted by a clean shaven well dressed man.

"Can I help you?"

"Are you Darren Moss?" asked Claire.

"Erm yes who's asking?"

"Detective Sergeant Claire Sheppard and this is Chief Inspector Neil Curtis. May we come in and ask you a few questions?"

"Yes sure come in."

Darren was very polite as he then took them into the lounge. The house was clean and well looked after. The wooden floors were polished and clean with all the shoes and coats in the hallway neatly stacked and hung up.

"You have a nice house," said Claire looking around.

"Thank you, can I get either of you a drink?" asked Darren.

"No thanks," said Claire.

"No I'm good," said Neil.

Neil sat down next to Claire. "We're investigating a missing person in Loscoe; you might have read about it in the newspaper or seen it on the news. At present we don't have any leads to go on except that he is a convicted murderer and has an AB Negative blood group the same as you."

Darren sat with his mouth open not sure what to think or say.

"I don't understand, you don't think I had anything to do with it do you?" asked Darren looking worried.

"No," said Neil. "Have you seen anything different in the past week? Has anybody been to visit or phone, emailed written or anything like that?"

Darren thought for a while but couldn't think of anything out of the ordinary.

Just then the front door opened as Darren's wife and young son came in.

"Hi," said Karen.

Darren proceeded to fill her in why the Police were there. She too was shocked.

"So you're assuming that this Marcus as been abducted because he his AB Negative which means you're under the impression that he has been killed? If you're not suspecting Darren then you must be assuming that they may be attempting to take him or might even still take him?"

Neil just looked at Claire. Claire spoke out and said "That's pretty much it yes. So it's important to remember any detail that was out of the ordinary or didn't seem right, however small it may seem it could be important."

Karen thought hard while Darren was taking Jamie's coat off.

"The only thing I can think of is, a few days ago I was awoke by something noisy driving up and down. It was about 11:45pm. It's normally very quiet along this road which is why I got out of bed to have a look. I saw a red bus drive by. The driver looked like something out of a heavy metal rock band with a short scruffy looking guy in a yellow coat stood next to him. I was so tired that I thought no more of it, closed the curtains and went back to sleep."

Claire was busy writing notes on what Karen had just told her.

"Would you recognise either of them again?" asked Neil.

"I think so yes, although it was dark."

"What bus company was it?" asked Neil.

"I'm not sure, the bus had out of service on the front. It was a smallish red one like on the 32 service that runs from along the boulevard."

"You've been very helpful," said Neil as both he and Claire stood up.

"If you can think of anything else please don't hesitate to call me on this number," said Neil as he passed Karen a card.

Karen closed the door behind them as they both left walking up the pathway. Claire unlocked the car and they both climbed in.

"What do you think Sir?" asked Claire.

"There could be something in it. A bus would be a great way of transporting a body. I'm betting that one of the statements from the door to door enquires mentions a red bus. How many bus companies are in the area?"

"There are three companies to my knowledge Sir."

"Okay, take me over to Loscoe, Marcus's house."

There were still Police Officers standing guard at the front and the back of the house as they drove up the street. A Police Officer who was taking a statement from someone lifted the blue *Police Do Not Cross* tape as they drove underneath it. Claire parked up outside the house as Neil stepped out. He walked over to the Officer who had lifted the tape over the car and asked him if there had been any developments.

"No Sir, not as yet."

"Can you tell me if this road is on a bus route or not?"

The person whom the Officer was taking a statement from chirped up and said "No it's not Officer. The 72 runs past the end of the road but it's been about eight years since a bus service last came through here. There wasn't enough call for it."

"Thank you," said Neil, "Have there been any reports of any buses driving along this street at any point?" asked Neil.

"Not that I can remember Sir, but I would have to check the statements."

The woman next to him shook her head as well.

Neil got back in the car as Claire was filling in her notes in her notebook.

"They didn't see anything nor is this road on a bus route, so if anyone did see a bus I want to know what it was doing up here. Head back to force headquarters; I want you to check through those statements."

Dangerous Driving
~ Chapter Twenty Four ~

Shiva had received the text message from Nathan and had printed off a photo of his next victim. He had been watching her most of the day coming and going. Margaret was in her mid 40's and lived with her husband. It appeared that she was looking after her grandchildren as she was taking them and fetching them from the local school. She lived local in West Hallam which was a quiet village just on the outskirts of Ilkeston.

She had been in Prison for six years for death by dangerous driving. While coming home from the pub she mounted the pavement killing a young mum to be. It was the third time that she had been caught drink driving but this time it had disastrous consequences.

Ten years on she still receiving hate mail and would come home to the occasional bag of rubbish chucked over the garden or a window smashed. The Police did very little to help by stating that there was no witnesses. There never would be. She was disliked by most people not just for the fact that she had killed a young woman and her unborn baby but the fact that she had been caught before and the time before that drinking and driving. She had moved house time after time but in the end decided to just stay put. Her family supported her but if the truth was known they would probably despise her.

Shiva began to prepare the two cleaners, rechecked the paperwork and the route. Tonight Shiva would collect his next victim. He smiled slightly out the corner of his mouth at the thought of what lay ahead. Paul could hardly contain the excitement as he told Lenny the good news. Lenny had just returned, carrying a plastic bag, from taking Jake for a walk.

Jake loved his new owner, he was well cared for, clean, brushed and well fed. He felt like a puppy all over again with so much life and energy. He absolutely adored Shiva and would follow him everywhere. Everybody at the depot loved Jake not for the fact they were scared of Shiva but the fact he was such a loving dog. Lenny would spend hours playing with him throwing his ball while Jake ran off to find it. He was now considered part of the family.

Deliberate
~ Chapter Twenty Five ~

Ellie had tears rolling down her cheeks as she stood watching her home go up in smoke. She held onto Nathan tightly and buried her head in his chest sobbing. The Police had taken a statement from her while the Fire Brigade confirmed with her that no one else was in the building. Her car that was parked outside was completely gutted black and smouldering. The black smoke was still pummelling out the top of the house as the Fire Brigade did their best to bring the fire under control.

Moments later a small explosion blew out the front windows sending slivers of glass flying through the air and landing on the street below. Tiles began sliding off the roof as the searing heat cracked and dislodged them. Within moments the entire roof collapsed inwards sending bright orange sparks and flames shooting into the night air. Twenty minutes or so had passed when the Fire Brigade had bought the fire under control and virtually extinguished it. Officers could be seen through the windows searching the remains of the house and damping down any remaining flames.

A nearby neighbour seeing Ellie stood across the road with Nathan bought them a cup of tea to help comfort them. The Police came back over to talk to Ellie and confirm an address where she would be staying.

"Miss Fox, I'm sorry to say this, but the Fire Chief has confirmed that the fire was started deliberately. Traces of an accelerant have just been found in the kitchen area. There is glass on the work surfaces indicating the window had been smashed from the outside."

Ellie started to sob. It was her first house and her independence since she had left home. Although most of her possessions and important things were at Nathan's house it didn't help much.

Nathan gave her a hug and a kiss. "Don't worry sweetheart, you're living with me now. I'm here for you, my home is your home you know that sweetheart."

"Who would do something like this and why? I've no enemies nor do I hate anyone enough for them to do this. This has something to do with that device what was put under your car. It's the same people isn't it?" asked Ellie with tears still rolling down her cheeks. "They are teaching us a lesson aren't they? What have we done to deserve this though?"

She took a sip from her tea as Nathan took out a tissue and gently wiped her eyes. He kissed her on the forehead and then on the lips and said "Come on lets go home." Nathan and Ellie turned around and started to slowly walk back to the car.

Heart Attack
~ Chapter Twenty Six ~

Shiva was reading the newspaper as his phone started to beep. It was Gunter wanting confirmation of the delivery of the two organs tonight. *60 minutes* replied Shiva.

Paul bought the bus round to the entrance as Lenny jumped on board. Shiva walked out the portacabin lit a cigarette and started to walk over to the bus. Tonight Shiva would collect his next victim personally.

Still smoking his cigarette Shiva stepped onboard the bus and sat down. At the back of the bus were several temporary bus stops that they would use as an excuse if they were pulled over. The temporary bus stops were basically the sign attached to a pole that had been welded to a bus wheel. They were extremely heavy so they stayed in place on the bus.

They arrived at Ilkeston in no time as they continued driving out towards West Hallam. Paul slowly drove pass the house to confirm they were asleep. There were no lights on in the house or any of the neighbouring houses. Paul parked the bus in the next street and turned off the engine. All three of them quietly stepped off the bus as the doors hissed as they closed behind them. They would usually collect their victims as they were out and about but Shiva made an exception this time. It wasn't the first time they had collected their victims from home but Shiva had to admit to himself that this was one of his favourite methods. A sly grin appeared at the corner of his mouth as he thought about the terror that his victims would feel in the next few minutes.

They casually walked up the driveway of the house, four doors down and walked round onto the back garden. Making their way, quietly, they climbed over the fences and through a few hedges until they came to Margaret's house. Kneeling down behind the house they quietly pulled on their latex gloves and prepared to go in. Paul took out a knife from his inside jacket pocket and stood up. He placed the knife in the rubber seal around the window and slit the rubber all the way around. Lenny helped him pull off the rubber seal as he then gently popped off the plastic coving. Paul was just about to snap out the spacers when he heard a noise behind them. They both quickly knelt down. It was a huge ginger cat strolling up the garden path meowing. Shiva bent down, picked the cat up and gave it a fuss.

Paul stood up and continued to quietly snap out the spacers. With the last spacer removed, the window fell towards him. Lenny helped Paul as they both lifted the window down and lay it on the grass on the garden. Shiva stopped stroking the cat and put it down as he stood up. One by one they all climbed through the window and into the kitchen.

Shiva took a long steak knife out the kitchen draw and checked with his thumb to make sure it was sharp and then started to make his way upstairs. The stairway and landing was fairly dark as they crept along the landing. Carefully opening the first door led them to the bathroom. Paul brushed past Shiva and opened the next door which started to creak. He continued to open the door to let Lenny and Shiva slip inside.

Both Margaret and her husband were sound asleep over the other side of the room. Shiva nodded to Paul and towards the husband. Paul quietly walked round to him placed his hand on his mouth and slit his throat. The blood splattered out in a spray over the sheets and up the wall. After a few seconds the spray slowed down to a trickle running down and off the bed. A pool of blood had started to form underneath the bed as the blood dripped off. Shiva stood looking at Margaret as she slept having no idea what had just happened. Lenny turned on the bedroom light when Shiva poked her several times with the tip of knife. She slowly opened her eyes and then sat bolt upright. She looked at Lenny and Paul then turned and looked at her husband. Seeing his throat gaping open and the blood covered sheets she looked straight at Shiva who stood at the side of her holding a steak knife up glistening in the light.

She started to make a groaning noise and began to gasp for air as she clutched her chest. Her face began to turn red then purple as sweat started to pour down her face. She continued staring at Shiva as her eyes bulged and the veins started to show on her forehead and temples. Making one finale gasp for air she made a choking noise, flopped onto her side and went limp. She was dead.

Shiva was absolutely gutted having wanted to kill her himself but now she was already dead. He just couldn't believe how rotten his luck was so left Paul and Lenny to bring her body downstairs as he went into the front room to rifle through their CD collection. Lenny returned from the spare bedroom with a large blanket and laid it out on the floor next to the bed. Paul gave Margaret a shove and she fell out of bed and flat on the floor on top of the blanket. Both Lenny and Paul each took hold of a corner of the blanket and dragged her along the bedroom floor, across the landing and down the stairs. Shiva joined them in the kitchen and unlocked the back door. Margaret was dragged outside and onto the back garden. Once outside they wrapped her tight in the blanket while Shiva cut down the washing line and wrapped it around the body.

Paul took hold of one end of the blanket while Lenny took hold of the other. Shiva assisted, holding the middle with his left hand while clutching a Tesco carry-a-bag containing an assortment of CD's in his other. They managed to carry her through the hedges and over the fences until they came back to the driveway they came down. Lenny casually walked up the driveway and over to the bus before opening the doors. Checking no one was around or looking out the windows, Lenny signalled to Shiva and Paul, whom then hurried up the driveway with the body, on to the bus and set her down on the back seats. Shiva quickly climbed into the driver's seat, started the bus and slowly drove away. Fifteen minutes later Shiva arrived back at the depot and backed into the garage.

Lenny took the keys off Shiva unlocked the paint booth as Shiva backed in the bus. Moments later Lenny had unlocked the grate and climbed down the steps as Shiva and Paul lowered the body down to him.

Paul cleaned out the bus, refuelled it and drove it back into the bus lane. Walking briskly back to the paint booth he locked the door behind him and climbed down the steps to meet Lenny and Shiva.

Shiva had already lifted the body onto the trolley and was fastening his green surgical gown. Lenny who was already wearing his, started to cut away the clothes line and blanket. He then removed the top half of her clothes and placed them in a black bag, with the clothes line and blanket. Shiva turned on the transportation coolers and then casually walked over to the trolley pulling on his latex gloves.

He picked up a number 23 scalpel from the instrument tray and made an incision across her chest and below her breasts. He then made a second incision, from the first one, down to the bottom of her stomach. Shiva pulled back the flaps of skin and muscle and held them in place with forceps. The miniature surgical circular saw spun into to life, as Shiva pressed the on button. Lenny and Paul watched as he removed all the ribs one by one placing them in the tray on the side.

Once all the ribs were removed this gave access to the Liver and Kidney. He swapped his number 23 scalpels for a number 10 general purpose one then cut through the renal vein and arteries then cut through the urethra and lifted out the kidney. Paul took hold of it and packed it in ice before placing it in the transportation cooler. A few minutes later Shiva lifted out the liver dripping with blood and passed it to Paul. With both organs packed in ice and ready to transport Shiva removed his gloves and gown and set off with the organs to Gunter's Surgery.

It was dark and cold as Shiva pulled out the garage with Jake on the back seat of his car. Jake had got used to being in the car and enjoyed it. He was very obedient and well behaved and in return was well cared for and fed. Shiva turned off the main road and onto the dual carriageway and accelerated hard. His car, a black Jaguar leapt in to life and shot down the road like a scolded cat. Continuing his way down the dual carriageway listening to his recently acquired Hits of the 60's CD, Shiva noticed in his rear view mirror blue lights approaching.

Easing up off the accelerator he started to slow down as the blue lights were gaining on him. Remaining cool and in control he prepared to pull over as the blue lights that appeared behind him was a Police car. He was just about to reach for the indicators when the Police car overtook him and disappeared into the distant night. The streets were deserted as Shiva pulled into the Surgery car park. He switched off the engine and popped the boot. Stepping out the car he was quickly met by a Nurse who took the transportation cooler from his boot and thanked him. She quickly left as Shiva opened the back door to let Jake out to stretch his legs.

Watching Jake run around lifting his leg to every tree, Shiva reached in his pocket and pulled out his cigarette. He stood for a while smoking and thinking how good life was when he decided he wanted to overlook the operation. *I could always learn something new* he thought to himself as he whistled Jake over and put him back in the car. Activating the central locking and stubbing his cigarette out on the floor then he made his way over to the rear entrance where the Nurse appeared from.

Smooth Operation
~ Chapter Twenty Seven ~

Considering the time of night, the Surgery was fairly busy with Medical Staff buzzing around all over the place.

"Hi, can I help you?" asked one of the Nurses.

"Yes I'm looking for the observation area for Diana Burton's Liver and Kidney transplant."

"Yes Sir, follow me. Can I get you a coffee?"

"Yes that would be great," said Shiva sounding polite and thoughtful.

The nurse past him a coffee from the Klix machine and took him through a side door. The room was fairly small and dimly lit. It was similar to a mini cinema the way the seats were laid out and the huge glass partition at the front.

Shiva took a sip of his coffee and sat down. The view of the operation and theatre was crystal clear with everything that was said, by the Doctors and Nurses, played through the internal speaker system.

Shiva was impressed and sat back in the leather seat and got comfortable.

Gunter was pleased with the speed and accuracy of Shiva's work as he first pulled out the liver from the transportation cooler followed by the kidney. Diana had been intravenously injected with 7mg of Sodium Thiopental and was out cold unconscious.

"Vitals please?" asked Gunter.

"BP 127 over 85, Pulse 87, 02 Saturation 97% all within norms."

Looking at the 52 inch plasma TV in the observation room, Shiva could see every detail of the operation as Gunter performed a perfect T Section incision. He placed an incision across her chest below her breasts and down the middle to the bottom of her stomach. Gunter chose to work under the ribs. The dialysis machines were in full flow as he snipped away at the liver and carefully removed it. While the medical team prepared the new Liver and Kidney Gunter reconnected the liver connections and proceeded to remove the left kidney. The new liver was refitted under the ribcage and expertly reconnected while the renal artery and vein were reconnected.

Gunter took a few moments to examine all the connections testing they were secure with no leakage. Each valve was pressure tested and cleaned before the ribs were repositioned back into place. While Gunter was performing the checks the Medical Staff fitted a catheter to detect any bleeding in the next few days. Each clamp was carefully removed and the muscle and skin pulled back over into place over the chest.

Shiva was impressed at the speed at which Gunter worked and how methodical he was.

He decided to try a different method to stitch up to remove all possible scars. An assistant handed him a silver tray with several needles and several heaps of sutures. Starting at the groin using dissolvable sutures he began to stitch the muscle together from the inside. After about thirty minutes he was reaching the last stitch. One of the assistants began to clean the entire stomach and chest area as the laser torch was being prepared. The following procedure in a way melts the skin back together instead of using sutures. The result is fairly messy to begin with but it forces the skin to graft leaving no visible scars.

The laser looked a little bit like a dentist's anaesthetic needle. Holding it in his right hand he activated the laser which shone a bright red light onto the skin. Moving slowly and carefully he made his way from her groin to her chest and along the top of the T section. The procedures were a complete success as he nodded to the anaesthetists to start to bring her around. Having seen enough but learnt plenty Shiva got up and left making his way back to the garage.

Diana was wheeled out into the recovery room and was hooked up to a monitor. With an oxygen mask on her face she was slowly starting to come round trying to remove the mask. Knocking the mask off her face, one of the observation Nurses slid it back over her mouth. "How you feeling love?" asked the Nurse but Diana was too incoherent to understand.

Gunter finished scrubbing up then came out to check on Diana's progress and vitals. He took the patients sheet from the clipboard, filled in a few details and signed off the sheet, then replaced the clipboard at the end of her bed. Happy that all had gone well, he reached in his pocket, took out his mobile phone and sent a text message to Nathan letting him know the operation was a success. Before retiring for the night Gunter decided to check on David's progress. The monitor was indicating a steady pulse of 78 but his blood pressure was low at 98 over 53. Gunter was a little concerned with this.

Normally by now the patient would be conscious but David was still out cold. He walked over to the store room and unlocked one of the medical cabinets. He took out a syringe and a vial marked Ephedrine (low blood pressure). He walked back over to David and removed the patient clipboard from the end of his bed. He spent a moment checking the statistics and vitals. The staff too had spotted the low blood pressure and had been monitoring it every fifteen minutes. Gunter decided to go ahead with the Ephedrine injection. Pulling the top of the syringe with his teeth he pushed the needle into the rubber top of the vial and half filled the syringe. He placed the vial on the side and held the syringe upwards and pushed out the air until only two CC's of Ephedrine remained. Taking hold of the intravenous drip, he opened the valve and injected the Ephedrine straight into the tube which would continue down into his veins.

He carefully disposed of the syringe in the sharps box and returned the vial to the medical cabinet. Washing his hands in the sink at the side of David, he could see his Blood Pressure had already started to rise slightly. After he washed his hands, he dried them off with a bunch of paper towels and then sat on his bed to fill out the medication section on his patient's record. Sitting down he noticed David's feet sticking out the bottom of the bed were swollen along with his ankles. He instantly felt them but they were warm. He pulled the sheet back and tested the reflex in his legs. The left leg was fine but the right leg was sluggish to respond. This was a sign of fluid retention. Fluid retention and low blood pressure were bad signs with a possible meaning the new heart was being rejected.

Acute organ rejection is not uncommon after an initial transplant and can usually be managed using medication. Gunter replaced the patient sheet at the end of the bed having requested continued fifteen minute observations. He decided he would wait until the morning to check on David before making any decisions. Feeling tired, Gunter decided to call it a day and returned to his office to collect his coat and car keys before heading off home.

Mysterious Sightings
~ Chapter Twenty Eight ~

Nathan woke up rubbing his eyes as he sat up in bed. Noticing his phone flashing, he reached over and took hold of it. The front of his phone read *2 New Messages*. They were both from Gunter. The first one was confirming the operation had gone ahead and Diana was doing fine. The second message stated that although David was well, he was still unconscious with a small chance that the heart was showing signs of rejection. He recommended that Nathan come in for a chat today to discuss the possibilities. Trying not to wake Ellie, Nathan slipped out of bed and into the bathroom. Having taken a shower he brushed his teeth before finishing off drying his hair. He quietly got dressed and went down stairs to the kitchen. He decided he would make Ellie some breakfast in bed, hoping that it might cheer her up after the house fire.

Carefully and quietly he crept upstairs with the tray trying not to slop coffee everywhere. He opened the bedroom door as Ellie was just waking.

"Morning Gorgeous," said Ellie.

"Morning sweetheart, breakfast in bed this morning."

"Ooo that looks perfect," said Ellie as she sat upright in bed.

They sat chatting in bed for a while drinking their coffee and nibbling on some toast. "I received a text from Gunter last night. We need to go in and see David this morning. It seems the new heart is possibly being rejected by his body."

"What's going to happen if does?" asked Ellie as she nibbled on her toast.

"In the text it said that acute rejection is normal and can be dealt with, so I assume there's nothing to worry about but I thought he might be conscious by now though."

"More to the point," said Ellie. "How did Diana's operation go?"

"I completely forgot about her," said Nathan as he took his mobile phone out his trouser pocket. He quickly read through the text again and said "Yes Diana's operation was a complete success."

"At least that's good news," said Ellie.

Nathan sat down on the bed beside Ellie while drinking his coffee.

"What do you think the chances are that David's heart could be completely rejected?" asked Ellie.

"To be honest I'm not totally sure. Do you think we should tell Shiva? I mean he does have another name on the list."

"I think we should wait and go and see David and see what Gunter has to say first." Ellie handed the tray back to Nathan and climbed out of bed.

"I'll get ready and we'll go and see him," said Ellie eating her last bit of toast.

Nathan took the tray and cups downstairs to the kitchen while Ellie got washed up and dressed. He was finishing drying the cups when Ellie joined him in the kitchen.

"Thank you for the breakfast in bed sweetheart," said Ellie as she put her arms around him and gave him a kiss.

"You look really gorgeous," said Nathan smiling.

Ellie was wearing her long sleeve purplish red silky blouse, black tight fitting jeans and black shoes. "Thank you," said Ellie "I'm ready when you are."

Nathan finished drying the cups and returned them to the cupboard and hung up the tea towel. Nathan then grabbed the car keys out the fruit bowl and they both left to go and see David and Diana.

"That's unusual," said Nathan.

"What is?" asked Ellie as she turned to face him.

"Did you notice the council van as we pulled out?"

"The green escort type van, yes I did but why is that unusual?" asked Ellie.

"Well this is a private road all the way down to Darwin Close. None of these houses are council owned."

"Maybe it's just someone visiting?" suggested Ellie.

Nathan indicated right and pulled into the Surgery car park. Stepping out of the car, Nathan didn't notice the same council van pull up opposite on the main road behind him. Inside the van Mason and Nolan were loading their weapons, checking their intercom devices and pulling on their balaclavas. This was it, this was the moment. They had their orders and knew what they had to do. They were preparing to go in hard and ruthless.

Mason stood at 6' 4" broad, very stocky and muscular were as Nolan was a slightly shorter 6' 1". Weapons at the ready and balaclavas pulled down, Nolan drove the council van into the Surgery car park.

There were already four or five people waiting for morning Surgery as the receptionist recognised Ellie and Nathan and beckoned them through to the side door.

"Come through, Gunter is expecting you," said the receptionist.

Ellie and Nathan followed her through the corridors and on to Gunter's office. She paused for a moment and then knocked on his door.

"Come in," Came a voice from the other side of the door.

She opened the door and said "Nathan and Ellie are here Sir."

"Send them in," said Gunter.

Nathan and Ellie were shown into Gunter's office as the receptionist then left and headed back to the reception.

Gunter stood up from behind his desk and shook hands with Nathan and then Ellie. "Good morning, take a seat both of you," said Gunter as he gestured to the two chairs in front of his desk. "First of all let me tell you that Diana's operation was a success however this is not really easy to say but last night David's blood pressure had dropped a fair amount. After running a few simple tests it appears that the heart is being rejected by his body. Acute rejection is not uncommon after a transplant and it can be treated with medication. We are keeping a close eye on David and we are treating him accordingly. It's unusual for him to be unconscious for so long so I've ordered an MRI scan of his brain to check all is in order. I'm sure there's nothing to be worried about but I would look at any opportunities of obtaining a new heart."

"Wow that's straight to the point," said Nathan feeling a little bit shocked.

"There was another name on the original list that Vernon sent," said Ellie looking at Nathan.

"Yes, yes there was. How soon will we know if he will need another heart?" asked Nathan.

"It's a bit hard to say at the moment but if his blood pressure continues to drop and he is still unconscious over the next five to seven days then I would recommend a second heart transplant."

"I think I'll speak to Shiva and have him prepared just in case. Can we see David and Diana now?" asked Nathan.

"Yes of course you can, come on we'll go now."

Gunter stood up and they all left his office and walked along the corridor towards the end of the complex, where David and Diana were staying on a private ward. The corridor was well lit with pure white walls and light green floor. The smell in the air was fresh and cool but with the usual disinfectant smell. Before making their way through the double doors to the ward, they all scrubbed their hands with the hand sanitizer from the hand pump on the wall. "Ooo that smells gorgeous," said Ellie as she rubbed her hands together.

The smell of the sanitizer was sharp but with a pleasant fragrance of apple.

"It looks like Diana is coming round," said Gunter as they approached her bed. Nathan's walked round the bed and took hold of her hand, "Diana? It's Nathan." Diana croaked slightly as she opened her eyes and tried to clear her throat.

"Nathan," she said in a very quiet voice.

"How are you feeling?" asked Nathan still holding her hand.

"I feel a bit sore. What's happened Nathan? Where are we?"

Diana's heartbeat began to rise suddenly, from 56 bpm to 97 bpm.

"It's okay Diana, you're safe and you're going to be just fine. You remember the Denver flight and that we was experiencing several severe difficulties, well things got a little worse and we attempted an emergency landing up in Iceland but it went horribly wrong. You were thrown around a little bit and suffered a serious crush injury which left you in a critical condition. You are well and doing fine now.

You're in a private Surgery in Nottingham under the care of Dr Gunter Fleischer."

"What's wrong with David?" asked Diana in a croaky voice as she gestured her head towards the next bed.

Ellie looked at Nathan as if to say *careful what you say to her.*

"Erm David is Erm, well he's not very well," said Nathan stuttering slightly.

"What do you mean he's not well?"

"Hi Diana, my names Ellie I'm a friend of Nathan's. What he is trying to say is David wasn't very well but he underwent an operation and is now recovering."

"I'm pleased to meet you Ellie. Is David awake? I'd like to speak to him."

"He's still unconscious at the moment." Gunter chirped. "You need to get some rest Diana you're still weak. Nathan and Ellie can come back tomorrow and see you."

Diana nodded in agreement as she was starting to drift off. Nathan gave her a peck on the cheek turned sharply and looked at David. It took a moment to register what was happening as Ellie was shouting his name. The alarm coming from the heart rate monitor was deafening indicating David had flat lined and was dying.

Blood Group
~ Chapter Twenty Nine ~

Jenny was sobbing badly as she was being comforted by a paramedic. The undertakers bought out Alan's body and placed him in the back of their silver van as Jenny watched from the back of the ambulance.

"There's no sign of Margaret Sir," said Claire as she walked into the bedroom.

Neil was talking to the Scenes of Crime Officer when Claire walked in.

"Thank you," said Neil to Claire. "Have we got any witness statements or did anybody see anything?"

"No Sir, I can't find anything, although uniformed officers are still speaking to the neighbours so I'm going to go back and check with them."

The bedroom was still dark with only a beam of light shining from between the curtains. It was a very warm sunny day with the temperature rising in the bedroom. Neil carefully made his way over to the window trying not to disturb any evidence, gently pulling open the curtains and then opened the windows.

"Sir?" asked one of the Scenes of Crimes Officers.

"Yes?"

"Sir, look at the blood spray pattern on the bed. The spray on the right hand side of the bed is over the pillow and wall which would indicate a jugular arterial spray."

"You mean his throat was cut?" asked Neil.

"Yes, but the spray of blood started to pool on the bed and ran underneath him. The odd thing is that the blood stopped towards the middle of the bed. I would have expected to see the trail of blood to go all the way across the bed and some of the arterial spray on the adjacent pillow but there's very little, if any in fact. This would indicate that someone was in bed at the side of him when he was killed."

So where is Margaret now Neil thought to himself. *Was this just some random killing or an abduction or ransom? Why murder Alan but take Margaret. Is she alive or dead?*

Neil was trying to figure out a motive or what the intentions were as he left the bedroom to check the rest of the house. Walking into the kitchen it was obvious how they had gained entry to the house but it was more impressive that they'd managed to remove an entire kitchen window without making any noise or anybody seeing what had happened.

Leaving the kitchen he wandered outside to see if there was anything obvious that was a miss.

Noticing that the pine trees had been disturbed, he shouted up to one of the Scenes of Crimes Officers. "I want the entire back garden photographed paying attention to the pine trees. Check for any evidence near the trees and along the edge of the garden next door." Peering through the trees the Scenes of Crimes Officer and Neil could see part of the fence missing from next door but one's garden. Neil started to get the idea that Margaret didn't walk out the house but was in fact carried. *So why would she be taken but Alan was left behind,* he thought to himself. *What did she have that he didn't?*

Neil took out his mobile and dialled the number for the Organised Crime Unit. "Hi, it's Neil. I want one of you to access the medical records of Margaret Hanson and her husband Alan and find out what blood group they both are. Go down to the morgue to get Alan's blood group if you have to." Neil then hung up the phone.

If Neil's hunch paid off then Margaret's blood group would be AB Negative. The Scenes of Crimes Officer continued taking photos as Neil left him and walked back to the house. He took a few moments to examine the kitchen window and door from the outside before making his way to the lounge. Straight away he saw the pile of CD's scattered on the floor next to the television. Alarm bells started ringing in his head as he remembered the same situation at Marcus's house. He knelt down and moved the CD's around using a pen from his pocket so as not to contaminate any evidence. The case from Hits of the 60's was lying open with the CD missing.

"There's not much in the statements from the neighbouring houses except one odd one. The lady three doors down has a ginger cat, she said he came back this morning with part of his tail cut off. She took him to the vet first thing and they said although it had been cut off the cat was in fact fine and doing well," said Claire.

Neil couldn't help but smile slightly. "Who would cut off part of a cat's tail? What the hell for?"

"Beats me Sir, I'm not sure that it's linked in any way though," said Claire.

"So nobody saw anything," said Neil sounding a little bit annoyed.

"No not a thing."

"Okay collect all the statements up from the officers. I'm nearly done here, although I've learnt from the blood patterns, the arterial spray and the fact that the hedges and trees have been disturbed that, along with the neighbours fence, Margaret was at the side of Alan when he was murdered and was more than likely carried out of the house and through the back gardens."

Claire thought about this for a moment and came up with the same conclusion as Neil. *What did Margaret have that Alan didn't.* Then she saw the pile of scattered CD's on the floor with one missing.

"I bet she is AB Negative Sir," said Claire eagerly.

"Funny you should say that Claire, I said exactly the same thing. I've ordered a check on Margaret and Alan's blood group. Were there any signs of a bus or a mention of any noise in the night?" asked Neil.

"Not that I've seen Sir. I'm going to co-ordinated the efforts of the uniformed Officer to expand their efforts further afield. If they carried her over the back gardens then they must have walked up one of the driveways further up. How many Scenes of Crimes Officers are on site Sir?"

"At the moment, there are only three officers."

"I'm going to contact control and see if we can get anyone else to check out the back gardens and driveways."

Claire left the front room and went outside to contact the control room. Moments later she returned to inform Neil that four more officers would be joining them within the hour to assist, in collecting evidence along the back gardens and driveways.

"That was Sheila on the phone," said Neil, returning the mobile phone to his jacket pocket. "Neither Margaret's or Alan's blood group were AB Negative."

"Dam, I was so sure that they would be," said Claire looking very annoyed. Claire Sheppard who was in her late twenties was wearing a white blouse and dark grey pinstriped suit trousers. She had dark red hair which came just past her shoulders with a silky glow. She'd always been interested in becoming a Detective with Sherlock Holmes being her idol. Until recently she had been a uniformed Officer still on probation but after her passing out parade she put in for an immediate transfer to CID. Although it had only been a few months, she did enjoy working with Detective Chief Inspector Neil Curtis but occasionally found him to be a bit irrational sometimes and not make much sense.

Neil had been in the force for over twenty years starting out as a uniformed Officer, passing his exams and working his way up the ladder. He had only been a Detective Chief Inspector for two years and was still keen to impress his superiors. It wasn't exactly his ambition to work in the Police Force but felt the pressure to follow in his fathers and grandfathers footsteps, who both worked for the metropolitan Police. He found working with Claire a pleasure, with her being intelligent and fast thinking. She wasn't scared to show her thoughts or feelings so he always knew where he stood with her.

Hostage
~ Chapter Thirty ~

"Call the code!" shouted Gunter as more alarms and beeping filled the air. He ran over to David's bed and smacked the red call button on the wall above his bed. He then lowered the top of the bed so it lay flat. "I need a crash cart in here stat!"

Several Nurses came running in from all directions as an announcement came over the tannoy. "Code Blue on East Wing 4, Code Blue on East Wing 4."

An Anaesthetist and two surgeons came running in followed by two more Nurses. A crash cart containing life saving drugs and equipment had been brought in from the next ward.

"What's happening?" sobbed Ellie as she stood trembling by Nathan's side.

"It's David. I think he's dead," said Nathan just staring at him. He took hold of Ellie to comfort her amongst all the commotion.

"Injecting 2mg of Atropine," said one of the surgeons.

The long steady tone from the heart monitor indicated that David's heart was still not beating.

"Get the defibrillator!" said Gunter.

A Nurse gelled up the paddles and handed them to Gunter. "Charge 200," shouted Gunter.

The Nurse turned the dial on the defibrillator to 200 and hit the charge button. The machine started making a whining noise that rapidly increased in pitch and then stopped. "Clear!" shouted Gunter as he then held the paddles, one on David's left part of his chest and one on his right side.

Pressing the paddle buttons, David's body jolted upwards as the heart rate monitor made several short rapid beeps then fell to a continuous tone.

"Charge 250," said Gunter.

The Nurse rotated the dial to 250 and hit the charge button. Again the machine started charging until the charge tone stopped.

"Clear!" shouted Gunter again.

Gunter rubbed the paddles together, placed one on either side of David's heart and hit the button. David's body instantly jolted upwards and stayed there for a second until Gunter released the button on the paddles. The heart rate monitor start to beep slowly at first then started to get a little faster until it showed a pulse rate of 64bpm.

"He's back with us," said Gunter. "Get him prepared for emergency Surgery! He needs a temporary pace maker to stabilise his heartbeat."

"I think there is a good chance his heart is being rejected by his body," said the surgeon.

Before Gunter could reply and agree with him, the air was filled with the sound of an almighty cracking noise like thunder as the building shook. Several canisters rolled across the floor as smoke started to pour out of them.

"Down on the floor" Came a voice from behind the smoke.

The air echoed again with the sound of gunshots, as several bullets sprayed through the air killing two of the surgeons by David's bed. Without thinking Nathan pushed Ellie down under Diana's bed out the way.

"Nathan, NATHAN!" screamed Ellie, but he ignored her as he tried to figure out what was happening. Ellie reached out from under the bed grabbing Nathan's leg pulling him to the floor.

Appearing from the adjacent wards, through the smoke stood Mason and Nolan. They were dressed in black from head to toe holding M-16 Rifles across their chests and a Sig Sauer P229 pistol on their belts. Wearing breathing masks over their balaclavas they looked very intimidating, like SAS soldiers.

Nathan got the feeling they weren't here to help as one of them pointed a rifle at his head. "GET UP!" said Mason to Nathan.

Nathan stood up in front of Mason followed by Ellie. Mason was considerably taller than Nathan and scary looking.

Ellie felt a sharp searing pain in her head. Losing grip of Nathan she flew backwards hitting the wall; she slid down the wall and landed on the floor. Everything started to go quiet and become peaceful as her vision slowly started to fade away.

Dead End
~ Chapter Thirty One ~

Having received a phone call informing him that both Margaret's and Alan's blood group were not AB Negative. Neil felt like he had hit a dead end. He was so sure that this particular case was related to that of Marcus's but now he was not sure how. The CD's on the floor could have been a coincidence after all. What about the bus being seen at Marcus's house? Was this also just incidental?

"Claire I want the door to door enquires extending into the next street. Get the statements we have and send them straight back to the incident room. I want every word checked and re checked for any signs of a bus or any other vehicle. Margaret didn't just walk out of this house and pop to the shops, she was carried out."

Claire left Neil in the living room as she went outside to talk to the Sergeant. Having instructed him to co-ordinate efforts into the adjacent streets, she took the statements and made her way back to the car.

All in all there were around 40 statements with some of them simply saying they saw nothing and some in more detail. Claire sat in the car for a while thumbing through the statements until something caught her eye. A single mum in her late thirties had got up in the night to feed her baby. She remembered hearing a hissing noise outside and for a moment I thought the dustbin men were outside emptying the bins. When she had come to her senses she took a brief look outside but couldn't see anything so carried on feeding her baby. *A hissing noise* thought Claire. *A bus could make a hissing noise as the doors open and close at the front of the platform;* she secured the other statements in the glove box and locked it while keeping hold of the women's statement.

Stepping out the car, she closed the door behind her and locked the car. Feeling pleased with her findings, she made her way down the path, round the back of the house where she met up with Neil. "Sir, Sir I have something. Take a look at this," said Claire as she handed him the statement.

Neil took the statement off Claire as they stood in the back garden with the afternoon sun bearing down on them. "You might have something here," said Neil as he turned the page over. "Come on, I want to go and see Ms Heather Delaney and see if she can tell us anything else. Well done Claire." Neil and Claire both left the house and started to walk up the street towards Heathers house.

"Ms Delaney?" asked Neil as young women answered the door.

"Yes. Can I help you?"

"Detective Chief Inspector Curtis," said Neil as he showed her his warrant ID Card. "And this is Detective Sheppard. I wonder if we could have a chat about the statement you gave to one of our officers? Maybe you could help us further?"

"Erm yes of course, sorry do come in the both of you."

"You have a lovely house Ms Delaney," said Claire.

"Please call me Heather and do take a seat." Neil and Claire sat down on the sofa next to each other as Claire instinctively took out her note book. "We have your statement however, in your own words and your own time, if you could tell us again what you saw and heard," said Claire.

Heather bent down and picked up baby Archie out of his play pen and gave him his bottle. "It was about ten past one in the morning when Archie woke up for his feed. I've been absolutely drained over the past few days so it took me a moment to come to my senses. I said to the other Officer I heard a hissing type noise, like the dustbin men were outside emptying the bins. I got out of bed, put my dressing gown on and went over to the window. It was still really dark outside but there were no sign of the bin men. The strange thing is, well I feel a bit stupid really."

"No," said Claire "Please tell us"

"Well as I looked down the end of the street, I thought I saw the back of a bus going round the corner but this road isn't on a bus route though, so it couldn't have been one could it?"

"We're not sure at the moment but will be looking into it. Could you tell me Heather, what colour was the bus?"

"Well it was dark but I think it was red. It wasn't one of those full size buses but one of those 40 seater city hopper buses if you know what I mean."

"Can you tell me more about the hissing noise?" asked Neil.

"Erm well it made like a Shhhhhh sound like the dustbin men. Do you think it could have been that bus?" asked Heather feeling a bit embarrassed.

"Yes, it is more than likely. Tell me did you only hear the hissing noise once or is it possible you might have heard it before?" asked Claire.

Heather took the bottle from Archie and put it on top of the fireplace and then started to slowly rub his back. "Thinking about it, about half an hour before I woke up to feed Archie something did briefly wake me up although I'm not really sure what it was." Suddenly Archie burped as she finished rubbing his back. She then popped him back down in the play pen.

"I don't think there's much more I can tell you Officer."

"You've been very helpful Heather," said Claire as she was jotting down some notes. "You didn't happen to catch the company name on the bus at all?" asked Neil.

"No I'm sorry I didn't," said Heather with a frown on her face.

Neil and Claire said their goodbyes and left. Claire unlocked the car and they both climbed inside.

"What do you think Sir?" asked Claire.

"I think that bloody bus as something to do with it. What I'm struggling with is the blood groups. Marcus was AB Negative and there was sights of a small bus however both Margaret's and Alan's blood group weren't AB Negative and yet there was still a possible sighting of a bus."

"Sir, a bus would be a perfect getaway vehicle. What I mean is you could easily walk straight on board with a body and dump it down the back of the bus with minimal effort. It wouldn't be my vehicle of choice Sir but a bus driving along the streets at night time is not really suspicious either."

"You sound like you've actually done this before Claire," said Neil laughing. "But you do have a point."

They back at the force headquarters, signed into the log book and took the short walk down to the incident room.

"Jackie, I want the list of the bus companies from the local area and surrounding areas if you will?"

"Yes Sir," said Jackie as she disappeared over to her desk to get them. She grabbed a beige folder and took it over to Neil who was now sat down in his office.

"Thank you Jackie," said Neil as he took the folder and opened it.

"There's only three, I thought there would be more to be honest with you Claire. The closest depot to Margaret and Marcus's is Brenton Buses with the next nearest company being NTC," said Neil

"Does it say who runs Brenton Buses Sir?" asked Claire.

Neil checked over the paperwork but couldn't find any reference to the owners. "No, it just states Brenton Buses. I'm thinking the best course of action now would be to pay them a visit and take a look at their night shift procedures."

Neil jotted down the companies address, on a post it note and handed it to Claire. Closing the folder and placing it in his out tray, he stood up and left his office followed by Claire. They both signed out, in the log book and walked out across the car park to their car. Claire climbed into the drives seat and programmed the address into the cars satellite navigation system.

It didn't take long to find the address as they pulled up outside the main building just off the main road. Adjacent to the main entrance was a sign that read *All Enquires.* Claire carefully opened her door, as to not get it knocked off by passing vehicles and slipped out of the car. Neil had already got out and was stood waiting for her on the short pavement.

Inside the main entrance was very small with another door a few feet away leading into what looked like the drivers rest area, as there were several drivers sat drinking and chatting away. To the right there was a reception window. It led into the main traffic office where two people were seated.

"Can I help you?" asked a polite woman.

"Detective Chief Inspector Curtis and this is Detective Sheppard," said Neil as he held up his warrant card. "Is your general manager or site manager around?"

"Yes. Keith Black our Operations Manager." She picked up the phone and spoke briefly before saying, "Come through."

Keith was middle aged dressed in a casual suit and tie. He stood up from behind his desk to greet Neil and Claire as they entered his office.

"What can I do for you?" asked Keith.

"We are just making general enquires with the local bus operators with regards to the night shift operational procedures," said Neil.

"Sure that's not a problem. What would you like to know?"

"How many staff approximately do you have on the night shift and what are their responsibilities?"

"We have a Shift Supervisor, one night man and two garage staff. There's about eight cleaners also employed to clean the buses while the garage staff catch up from the day shift. The main job of the night men is to ferry the driver's home and to pick them up in a morning along with the late night service on a Friday and Saturday. They are ultimately responsible for the security of the buses, premises and ensuring that all the buses are organised in the correct manor."

"Are they permitted to take any of the buses out at night time?" asked Claire as she was scribbling down some notes.

"Erm to be honest I don't see why not but it would depend on the reason. If there are road works then they are required to site temporary bus stops and then recover them when the work is complete. If they wanted to nip to the late night petrol station or supermarket then I don't foresee any problem."

"That should be all except I'd like a copy of the night shifts personnel records," said Neil.

Keith stood up and walked round his desk to a filing cabinet and flicked through several of the records before removing some of them. "I'll just get these photocopied," said Keith as he left his office. Claire continued writing out her notes as they both waited for him to return.

"Here we go," said Keith as he returned and passed the photo copies to Claire.

"Thank you," said Claire as both her and Neil stood up to leave.

"If I can help with anything office please let me know," said Keith as they shook hands and left.

Neil sat looking through the personnel files as Claire drove and made her way back to the incident room at force headquarters. Neil suddenly stood in his tracks and held one of the sheets of paper up.

"What is Sir?" asked Claire.

Neil turned to look at her, "Shiva Lawman!"

Mysterious Container
~ Chapter Thirty Two ~

Ellie lay on the floor unconscious with blood dripping from her nose and down her face. She had been hit in the head with the butt of Mason's rifle. "You bastard!" screamed Nathan as he lunged forward at Mason. He quickly found himself being pushed back again as Mason's rifle was being jabbed into his throat.

With the rifle under his chin Nathan was asked, "Where is it?" Mason spoke with a thick English accent whereas Nolan, who was moving the Doctors and Medical staff into the corner, had more of a different accent.

"Where's WHAT!" shouted Nathan.

"Where are the containers that were on the plane?" asked Mason in a slow calm authoritative tone.

One of the Nurses ignoring what was being said walked over to Ellie and placed a cushion under her head.

Everybody screamed as the back of the Nurses head exploded and blew out on to the wall sending blood splattering all over Ellie and up the bed were Diana lay unconscious. Mason never moved or flinched as Nolan had fired his pistol with pin point accuracy from across the room shooting her twice in the head. This time all the Nurses and Doctors did as they were ordered. Several of the Medical Staff were sobbing in tears and being comforted by one another as they just looked on unable to do anything.

"Where are the containers from flight 1872?" asked Mason again.

"I swear I don't know what fucking containers you're talking about! I swear on my life I don't know!"

"You might just have to do that," said Mason in low deep voice as he smacked Nathan around the head with his rifle.

"Him," said Mason pointing his rifle at David. "What's wrong with him?"

Nolan bought over one of the surgeons nudging him in the back with his gun.

"Move," said Nolan.

"He needs Surgery," said the surgeon "He recently had a heart transplant but it is being rejected by his body. He needs a temporary pace maker fitting to regulate his heartbeat. We need to act now or he will die"

"He was the Captain of Flight 1872 and you the First Officer?" asked Mason looking at Nathan.

"Erm yes, yes we were," said Nathan looking puzzled.

Mason hit Nathan hard in the stomach with the end of his rifle. Nathan instantly doubled over in pain and went down onto his knees. Mason drew his pistol from its holster and pointed it straight at Nathan's head.

"There's no need to do this," said the surgeon. Mason placed the pistol in left hand swung round hard and punched the surgeon square in the face splitting his nose open and knocking him to the floor. He placed the gun back in his right hand and again pointed it a few centimetres from Nathan's forehead as if nothing had happened.

"Where are the containers?"

"I swear to you I don't know what you're talking about. The cargo manifest is the Captain and the Ground Crew's responsibility."

Mason cocked the pistol as Nathan closed his eyes and bent his head down. *This was it* thought Nathan. *This was the end, killed on the floor of a Surgery with no idea why.*

Pausing for a few seconds Mason thought to himself *if he knew anything he would have shit himself and said by now.* He re-cocked the pistol and readied the weapon safe placing it back in his holster.

"Get up!" said Mason. Nathan slowly opened his eyes and stood up. He turned to look at Ellie who was lying on the floor just behind him. The Nurse was slumped by her side with both of them covered in the Nurse's blood. Nathan started shaking and felt a burning sensation rising in the pit of his stomach as he saw Ellie laying there not knowing if she was alive or dead.

Nolan slumped to the floor as three bullets flew across the room striking him twice in the head and one in the back. He was killed instantly by the Police sniper on the roof of the adjacent building.

Outside, six Volvo V70's and four black range rovers surrounded the complex with the Police helicopter hovering nearby. With more than 25 Police Officers down in the car park the scene was buzzing with sirens and blue lights. The incident Chief Inspector was preparing the Firearms Unit and traffic unit as a small explosion inside the complex vibrated the ground. Realising he was in trouble Mason had thrown out several tear gas canisters again to stop the snipers getting a clear shot at him.

"Weapons Hot" shouted Sergeant Robin Berkeley as several officers readied their weapons. Robin was part of the Elite Special Tactical Firearms Unit and responsible for the unit and public's safety. She had worked on the unit for eight years and was proud of her job as well as taking it very seriously. None of her officers had ever been injured on any of her shifts and she was making sure that this shift would be no different.

"First strike team, you're up. Intelligence tells us he is heavily armed and dangerous. Several tear gas canisters have been deployed in the ward to shift cover but snipers have turned to infra-red vision and have a good view of the scene. It's not certain at this time but it looks like he has taken a close hostage."

Four of the firearm officers advanced forward towards the Surgery entrance. The First Officer at the door swivelled his fingers in the air and proceeded through the doors. Inside was dark as the lights had been smashed out. On the floor lay several bodies of patients and staff. Keeping low and to the sides of the room the four officers moved forward into the corridor. The corridor was about 20 metres long; it was nearly pitch black apart from the glow of the emergency lights in the side rooms.

Reaching the end of the corridor the team were joined by two other armed officers. To the right was the theatre and to the left led down to the ward. Moving slowly and quietly the six officers spread out along the walls and carefully moved down the next corridor heading for the ward. The lead Officer motioned to the officers behind that he could see movement ahead, as all officers slowly and steadily, moved in to take their positions. In a matter of moments all the officers would be putting their training and experience to the test as they planned to take down a vicious and notorious terrorist.

Nathan could hardly breathe as Mason's arm pulled tightly around his neck from behind. Nathan had now been taken hostage by Mason. He held onto Mason's arm trying to pull it away from his throat as he felt himself choking.

"What's that?" asked Mason sounding angry.

David's monitor had tripped the distress alert system as he went into Ventricular Tachycardia. His heart was beating rapidly and irregular as it was under a tremendous amount of stress. Out of second nature the crash team began to rush over to him but Mason shouted "GET BACK, NOW!" Everybody froze not daring to move. So many people were already dead with no one else wanting to join them.

The alert system continued the low-high warning beep as Mason pulled a canister from his combat jacket. "Shut that thing up!" said Mason losing his temper. He knew the building would be surrounded now and that a hostage would be of little consequence.

Mason was an active terrorist working under orders along with Nolan before his timely demise. He belonged to a terrorist cell Organisation capable of working as a team or as independent individuals. This made them a deadly Organisation to track and monitor. There was no telling when a cell would be activated or strike but this time and for the last time, Mason was on his own.

"SNR3 to all units standby, Target has an IC1 male hostage and has deployed an additional gas canister. I'm waiting for a clear shot."

The air was now filled with the continuous tone from the alert system from David's heart monitor. David had flat lined, his heart had stopped.

"We need to help him!" shouted the Doctor by his side. "He's dying for Christ sake. Let us help him!" but Mason stood firm and ignored them. He crouched down slightly to look out the window. He could see several black dots on the roof of the adjacent building and knew that the snipers were targeted on him. He furthered his grip on Nathan pushing him towards the corridor. The ward was engulfed in smoke now with poor visibility. The flashing red duress light above David's bed managed to pierce through the smoke and penetrate to the surrounding walls. The flat-line tone continued to echo through the ward and corridors as David lay dead.

Still struggling and choking Nathan tried to struggle free but Mason was too strong for him. "Whatever it is you're after, you won't get it if David is dead will you?" Nathan tripped forward and landed sprawled out on the floor as Mason pushed him away.

"It's too late for that now." Mason quickly unzipped his combat jacket to reveal eight strips of C4 plastic explosive strapped round his chest. He was about to reach into the back of his jacket for the trigger when he fell to the floor unconscious.

"SNR8, All Units, target is down, repeat target is down. All Units GO, GO, GO."

Ellie just stood with the bed pan still in front of her as Nathan scrambled to his feet. He ran towards her wrapping his arms around her. "I thought you were dead!" said Nathan.

The night light from the Police helicopter shone through the windows as the first strike team burst in and took control. Within seconds Mason was disarmed with his hands cable tied behind his back. The C4 explosive vest was deactivated and removed before Mason started to regain consciousness and come round. Before he could speak, a black cloth bag was placed over his head as he was led out the building. Seven or eight more officers joined the scene, all with two of the forces specialist paramedics.

"CHARGE 300 NOW" shouted Gunter.

The force paramedic spun the dial on the defibrillator to 300 and pressed the recharge button. The defibrillator started making the whining noise that rapidly increased in pitch and then stopped.

"CLEAR!" Shouted Gunter as he then hit the button on the paddles, David's body jolted upwards and then relaxed. The monitor was still outputting a flat-line with a continuous tone.

All the officers and Medical Staff stopped what they were doing as the room went deadly quiet.

"CHARGE 350," said Gunter.

"Charging 350," said the paramedic.

The defibrillator whined into action as Gunter shouted "Clear" and hit the discharge button on the paddles. David's body jolted upwards again and then relaxed back down.

"Jesus this isn't working," said the paramedic.

"An Intra-cardiac Injection of Adrenaline," said the paramedic.

"Yes, 2cc's stat!" said Gunter.

The Adrenaline was injected directly into David's heart and the defibrillator tried again.

David's head had been packed in ice and his jugular artery had been injected with a new ice solution. The solution which resembles a slushy ice drink travels up to the brain, where it slows down the metabolism of cells so that they need less oxygen to survive. In some cases the brain can survive up to forty minutes after the heart has stopped.

"Charge 400," said Gunter. The defibrillator started to charge as the Nurse turned the dial to 400 and hit the recharge button.

"Clear," said Gunter as he pressed the discharge button.

The distress alarm had stopped its continuous alarm and started pulsing in a patterned rhythm.

"Jesus, he's back," said the surgeon.

"Get him down to Surgery stat before we lose him for good," said Gunter.

Nathan just stood in amazement holding Ellie. He was clearly in shock as Gunter walked over to him.

"Nathan, Nathan," said Gunter shaking him. "It's okay; everything is going to be okay."

Nathan calmed his breathing down as he came to his senses. Nathan could feel his legs going weak as he started shaking again. Gunter took his arm and walked him over to an empty bed opposite and sat him down.

"Bringen Sie zwei Tassen Kaffee bitte," said Gunter very quickly to one of the Nurses. Moments later she returned with two cups of coffee.

"Here, get this down you it will help," said Gunter passing one of the cups to Nathan.

"Is there something you've not been telling me?" asked Gunter as he stood in front of Nathan drinking his coffee.

"I truly have no idea what he was on about," said Nathan still trembling.

Ellie had already been cleaned up by the Nurses having only suffered a nose bleed and a few bruises. Nathan wiped some blood off her cheek and kissed her.

"What are we going to do now?" asked Nathan.

"The Police will want to talk to you," said Gunter. "You know they are going to want to take a statement from all of us don't you?"

"Yes I do. Where has David gone?" asked Nathan as he picked his coffee back up. "He's been taken down to theatre to have a pacemaker fitted. Nathan, I know now is not the right time but you need to speak to Shiva."

"I understand," said Nathan.

Ellie was still hugging him and had rested her head on his shoulder as she perched herself on the bed to the side of him.

The sirens from the Police cars could be heard outside and wailing in the distance as more officers arrived. Four armed officers stood strategically near the exits and windows.

Two CID officers had arrived and were taking statements as Nathan felt a wave of panic.

"There's no way they can find out about Shiva or the transplants is there?" he asked Gunter.

Gunter chuckled at Nathan. "No way at all Nathan," said Gunter as he patted Nathan on the shoulder.

"Take your time and just describe in your own words what happened," said Karen speaking to Nathan.

Karen Summers had worked for *A Division* CID for nearly 7 years but she had to admit to herself this was the worst crime scene that she had ever dealt with. She flipped over a sheet on her notepad and wrote Nathan's full name and date of birth on the top right corner. "We had been here for about fifteen minutes visiting Diana and David when there was a really loud crack."

"Who is we?" asked Karen

"Sorry, I mean Ellie, Ellie Fox my partner."

"And what relation are you to Diana and David?" asked Karen.

"Erm they both friends and work colleagues, I'm an airline pilot, First Officer. David was my Captain and Diana our senior flight attendant. Both of them were injured in a plane crash in Iceland some weeks ago."

"I remember reading about that and seeing it on the news. How are they both doing?" "They are doing well. We're hoping they will be released soon," lied Nathan.

He didn't want to say too much so as not to complicate matters.

"So what happened after the loud cracking noise?"

"Oh yes. Erm after the loud crack, two tins came rolling across the floor from the corridor over there. The room filled up with smoke really quickly and started to burn my eyes."

"Yes we found the canisters. It turns out that they were in fact *tear gas* canisters."

"A few seconds later the two SAS looking guys came bursting in. One of them hit Ellie and knocked her out and then held a gun to my head."

"What did he want?" asked Karen as she continued writing out the statement.

"He kept asking 'Where is it?' Apparently there was some container on board the flight that crashed. I have no idea what he was on about. The Captain and Ground Crew are responsible for the manifest and cargo so I guess David might be able to fill us both in when he comes round?"

Nathan bit his lip realising what he just said. The Police would now want to talk to David.

"What happened next?"

"The other guy was moving the Doctors and Nurses into the corner but the one of the Nurses came over to deal with Ellie and placed a pillow under her head. She was shot dead by that other guy. Shot dead for trying to help someone and for doing her job."

"Seeing Ellie just laying there on the floor I felt so angry. How could he shoot an unarmed woman, what was he going to do next?"

Karen continued writing out Nathan's statement and then took a brief statement from Ellie. While Ellie was giving her statement Nathan went over to speak to Gunter.

"How long will David be in Surgery?" asked Nathan.

"It shouldn't be long now Nathan, about an hour or so."

"I want to see him as soon as he comes out," said Nathan sounding very eager. He then turned around and made his way back over to Ellie.

The Nurse whom had been shot was now covered over with a sheet and being transferred out by two undertakers. Nolan was still being photographed by Scenes of Crime Officers and CID officers. Nathan stopped as he saw Nolan's body laying there motionless. His stomach started to turn at the thought that Nolan was a cold blooded killer.

"I need a drink, let's go over to the canteen. We can wait for news of David over there. I'll nip and tell Gunter," said Ellie.

Within a flash she was back, taking hold of Nathan's hand they slowly walked through the corridor to the canteen.

After they had ordered their drinks and something to eat, they both sat down at a table near the window.

"I think now would be a good time to text Shiva," said Nathan. He took his phone out of his pocket and sent Shiva a text message explaining what was wrong with David and that he had spoken briefly to Diana. He quickly outlined what had happened at the Surgery with the two masked men as well.

Nathan and Ellie chattered for a while eating and drinking their drinks when Ellie's phone rang.

"Hello," said Ellie.

"Ellie its Vernon, hope I'm not disturbing anything?"

"No, No. What can I do for you mate?" asked Ellie.

"Well it's not what you can do for me but more of what I can do for you!"

"Go on," said Ellie sounding interested.

"I've just had a text from Shiva for an updated AB Negative list. Ellie your ex boyfriend is on the list."

Guess Who's Back
~ Chapter Thirty Three ~

Time to get to work thought Shiva as he read Nathan's text message again, although he wasn't thinking of his job with the bus company. Nathan had sent Shiva a text message updating him on David's progress and the need for a second transplant. In turn Shiva had requested an updated list from Vernon cross matching known criminals with an AB Negative blood group that had been released from Prison living in the Nottinghamshire postcode area.

Noticing the new name in the list, Shiva opened up the news archives on his laptop and began to search listings. Jason Fletcher aged 31 was arrested and convicted of raping a 21 year old woman he was currently living with and sentenced to six years imprisonment. The photograph taken before he was imprisoned showed him with jet black hair with a roundish face, dark complexion and dark stubble. Shiva took an instant dislike to him. Shiva sat stroking

Jake as the corner of his mouth opened slightly into an evil grin. Shiva had found his next victim and was now eager to get to work.

Jason had only been released 14 months ago and had been living in the Leicestershire area until last week when he moved up to Nottingham. Living in Radford he had found himself a fulltime job as a supermarket supervisor. The pay was good and the hours were steady which suited him. He would spend most of his evenings home alone on his Xbox battling with his on-line mates. At the weekend he would stay over at his girlfriends and go to the pictures or out drinking.

"I don't believe it!" said Ellie.

"What is it? Who was that on the phone?" asked Nathan sounding concerned.

"I need to get out of here. I feel sick. Will you take me home?" asked Ellie.

"Yes baby of course. Come on."

Nathan took hold of her hand as they left the Surgery through the reception area. Passing through, they saw the receptionist lying dead on the floor partly covered over with a blanket. Several of the other staff had been killed too with paramedics filling out paper work and removing the equipment that they had used to try and resuscitate them. Ellie looked away as they continued through the reception and out into the car park.

Outside armed officers stood outside the main entrance and were guarding the main entrance while several officers and Scenes of Crimes Officers were searching the council van for evidence. Nathan and

Ellie climbed inside Nathan's car, left the car park and started to head towards Nathan's house.

"Are you going to tell me what that was all about on the phone?" asked Nathan.

"It was Vernon on the phone. Shiva had requested an updated list. Nathan, my ex boyfriend is on the list."

"You mean Jason Fletcher? The one who . . . Well you know."

"Yes him," said Ellie wiping tears from her eyes. "I hoped he would never get out of Prison but what's harder to believe is that he's AB Negative."

"Do you want Shiva to deal with it or pick another name on the list," said Nathan. "Nathan, after what he did to me I want him dead now!"

Nathan indicated and turned to pull into his driveway.

"I'll sort it sweetheart don't worry."

"Nathan, I'm scared. He treated me bad. I never want to go through that again. Afterwards, until I reported it to the Police, he would stalk me and follow me everywhere. I ended up having a nervous mental breakdown for several years. I don't feel like I've ever got over it."

Nathan turned the car off as he removed the keys. They both stepped out the car and went inside. The weather was still warm outside as the light was starting to fade so they both sat outside on the back patio whilst Nathan poured a gin and tonic. "Get this down you," said Nathan as he passed her the drink. Ellie took a sip from the glass and wiped her eyes again.

"I'm going to ring and speak to Shiva now and set the ball rolling," said Nathan.

"No," said Ellie. "I want to speak to Shiva."

"Erm are you sure you want to do that," said Nathan sounding cautious.

She held her hand out and took the phone from Nathan. She dialled Shiva's number and held the phone to her ear as she took another sip from her drink.

"Shiva, it's Ellie."

"Yes," said Shiva.

"The new list Vernon sent you; it will contain a new name on it."

"Yes I saw that. Jason Fletcher. Served six years I think for rape and torture?"

"Erm well, it was me that he raped and tortured Shiva."

Ellie started to cry. The phone line went silent for a few seconds. Ellie couldn't do it. She passed the phone to Nathan.

"Shiva, it's Nathan."

"Do you want me to take care of him?"

"Yes, yes I think that would be for the best," said Nathan. "I want you to hurt him like the hurt he caused Ellie. The bastard deserves everything that he gets," said Nathan getting upset.

"When can he do it Nathan?" asked Ellie.

"When do you think you will be able to take care of it?" asked Nathan.

"Well Nathan, as you know that this needs to be done properly as once the organs have been removed they will only survive a few hours at most.

I'll take care of him as soon as Gunter is ready to proceed with the operation."

"Yes I understand and agree Shiva," said Nathan

"I'll see if it can be done tomorrow night. You can also tell Ellie from me that he will suffer before he dies," said Shiva.

"I will, she will be pleased to hear that. Thank you Shiva."

"What did he say Nathan?" asked Ellie as she sat biting her nails.

"He has to do this properly because the organs only have a few hours of life before they start dying off. He says that he is thinking of tomorrow night and going to confirm with Gunter."

"That's good of him," said Ellie.

"Oh and he also told me to inform you that Jason will suffer."

"Good, He deserves to suffer. Don't you think you should give Gunter a ring and see how David and Diana are doing?" asked Ellie.

"Shit, yes, yes I will." Nathan picked up the phone, dialled Gunter's mobile number and held the phone to his ear. After a few rings Gunter picked up.

"Hello Nathan. Are you ringing about David?"

"Yes I am how is he doing Gunter?"

"He's fine and doing well at the moment but he does need that second transplant and soon. The pacemaker is fitted and regulating his heart beat but it's not a permanent fix. Shiva is aware now and making his preparations for tomorrow night."

"Good Nathan, that's good. I'll keep you up to date with his progress until then."

"How are things back at the Surgery?"

"There's still a few Scenes of Crimes Officers kicking about but nearly everyone has gone. They even sent in a specialist cleaning crew to mop up the mess! How are you and Ellie feeling?"

"We're okay, still a little bit shocked though. I still can't get my head round what they meant with the container. I just hope David will be able to shed some light on what's going off."

"Well hopefully in a few days you will be able to ask him yourself."

"Thank you Gunter." Nathan hung up the phone.

"He's doing well at the moment," said Nathan to Ellie. "All being well in a few days we will be able to speak to him after the transplant and bring him up to date. He then might be able to tell us what the hell is going on and what the so called container is all about."

"Maybe they are full of treasures and gold," said Ellie smiling.

"In today's day and age you never know," said Nathan.

Escape Route

~ Chapter Thirty Four ~

Shiva found the address straight away as he drove around the estate a few times to familiarise himself with the area. Tomorrow he would be back with the cleaners to clean away this piece of rubbish for good. Wanting to get a closer look, Shiva decided it was time to take Jake for a walk. He slipped his lead on, opened his door and got out. "Come on Jake," said Shiva. Jake jumped over the seat and out the door and then had a good shake. Shiva closed the door and locked his car before taking Jake for a little walk.

Jason still had his curtains open as Shiva and Jake walked passed. Shiva could see Jason sat on the sofa with another youth sat on the chair. There were cans of lager on the floor and coffee table as they sat playing on what looked like a games console. In front of his house was a short well kept garden next to a tarmacked driveway. At the front of the garden there was a low hedge that was slightly overgrown. The drive gates were open but the garden gates were shut. On the driveway was a black Golf GTI. Shiva guessed this might have been Jason's friend's car as there were no other cars nearby, although it could have been Jason's.

Shiva kept walking past slowly looking down the driveway through to the back garden. On the rear of the garden he could see a field, although the light level had dropped in the past hour Shiva could make out horses in the field. With no one around, he was tempted to pay Jason a visit now but decided it would be best to wait for the cleaners tomorrow. At that moment, the street lights all popped on emitting a soft orange glow. Just down the road about three doors down Shiva could see an alleyway between the houses. "Come on Jake," said Shiva as he headed off towards the alleyway.

Once he had walked all the way down to the end of the alleyway there were three wooden stakes sticking out the ground in a bid to stop motorcycles and anything else unwanted. He bent down and unclipped Jakes lead to let him run off and have a play but Jake stayed by his side. "Go on if you want to," said Shiva looking at him but Jake still stayed by his side. It was fairly dark in the field as he walked down to the bottom out of sight. Looking back he could see the backs of the houses lit up. At the bottom of the field he paused to light up a cigarette. He took a drag from the cigarette and blew the smoke out of his nose. *How would he get the body out of the house and back to the bus* he thought to himself. The fence at the back of Jason's house was about chest height and looked fairly easy to climb over. Standing puffing on his cigarette he noticed another dog owner walking down the alleyway and into the field.

Shiva stubbed his cigarette out and began to walk along the bottom of the field with Jake, up towards Jason's house. The woman walking her dog left after a few minutes having not seen Shiva. Swinging Jakes lead around, he casually walked across the field to the back of Jason's house and peered over the fence. The back garden wasn't as neat and tidy as the front garden but it was still well kept. Along the back of the house were double glazing windows with a solid double glazed door. At the side of the house was the car porch that led through to the front garden. Shiva had decided that the only way he would get into the house was by *jacking* the back door.

"Come on," said Shiva to Jake as he began to head back to his car. Tomorrow night Jason would meet Shiva and Shiva would meet his next victim, Jason.

Ellie's Cheque
~ Chapter Thirty Five ~

Ellie was about to speak but the door bell rang.

"Are you expecting anyone?" asked Ellie.

"No, no one," said Nathan as he stood up from the sofa and went to the front door.

It was just past lunch time with the weather outside dimming down but still warm with the smell of freshly mown grass. Nathan reached forward and unlocked the catch. Opening the door, Nathan was greeted by a well dressed middle age man wearing a grey pinstriped suit and holding a black briefcase.

"Can I help you?" asked Nathan politely.

"Yes my names Arthur Meakin, I represent Dun & Elm Insurance. I'm looking for Ellie Fox; she gave this address as her current abode?"

"Yes, come in," said Nathan.

Spotting Ellie sat on the sofa, Arthur introduced himself to Ellie.

"I'm here about your home insurance claim," said Arthur.

"We spoke on the phone last week?"

"Is there a problem with the claim?" asked Ellie looking a bit concerned.

"No madam in fact quit the opposite. I'm here today to present you with a cheque." Ellie's face lit up as she began to smile.

"Do you have a passport and driving license?" ask Arthur.

"Yes of course I'll go and get them, sit yourself down."

"Can I get you a drink?" enquired Nathan.

"Yes I'd love a strong cup of tea please," said Arthur as he sat down on the chair opposite.

Nathan disappeared into the kitchen as Ellie swiftly came back down stairs and into the lounge. Arthur had opened up his briefcase and removed a small pile of paperwork and a sealed padded envelope as Ellie passed him her passport and driving license.

"Right I just need you to sign and date here, here, here and here," said Arthur as he passed several sheets of paper and a *Silver Parker Pen* to Ellie.

Ellie sat down and began to read through the paperwork and sign each one as instructed as Nathan came in with Arthur's tea. He placed the cup down on the table at the side of Arthur and took a seat on the sofa at the side of Ellie.

"Do you need me to do anything?" asked Nathan to Ellie.

"Ooo yes please, can you just cast your eye over these?" asked Ellie passing the signed papers to Nathan.

After they had checked and signed all the paperwork Arthur asked Nathan to sign a witness declaration document before removing the seal on the envelope. Before he went any further he took the statement from his briefcase.

"You have been awarded £184,000 for the contents and for the actual house as agreed." He then handed the cheque over to Ellie.

"Thank you," said Ellie as she reached over and took the cheque from him. They all spoke for a little while and finished their drinks before Arthur packed away the rest of his paperwork and left.

Breaking Mason
~ Chapter Thirty Six ~

The remote interview room was only about a 15 foot square, with a single dark brown table in the middle of the room and two chairs, one either side. The walls were concrete slabs with a light fitment embedded in the top whereas the floor was just bear concrete. A black swan neck type lamp was fastened to the desk and shining directly at Mason.

His black hood had been removed but his hands were still cuffed behind him. Taking security very seriously, there were two firearm officers behind him in each corner of the room with their weapons across their chest at the ready. Maggie who was sat opposite Mason was reading through several statements and some *classified* documents. Maggie Smith was the Assistant Director of Counter Terrorism at MI5. She was in her mid fifties but looked older. Her face was old and drawn with a dark complexion and wrinkled features. Her lips were thin yet still hid her yellow stained teeth. Her fingers were also stained yellow from the constant smoking year after year. Her appearance sometimes fooled people into thinking she might not know what she was doing but all in all she was as sharp as a tack, knew every single terrorism law, procedures and was still an expert in unarmed combat even at her age. Her main expertise was in body language. She could read a person like book and was using this to her advantage right now. Mason had asked for a smoke having seen the stains on her fingers. This could indicate that he was nervous. His legs were crossed with his top leg hanging over with his foot pointing towards the direction of the door indicating where he was focusing his attention.

Maggie placed the statements and documents down on the table in front of her. "We've been watching you for some time Mr McDonald," said Maggie. "What was the reason you was at Dr Gunter's Surgery?" she said in a soft low tone.

"I ain't telling you shit!" said Mason and spat in her face.

The Assistant Director just wiped the spit from her face very calmly and repeated the question. "I'll ask you once again Mr McDonald. What was the reason you was at Dr Gunter's Surgery?"

This made Mason feel nervous as he was trying to be the big hard guy yet she never moved or flinched.

"The container on board flight LA 1872, what did you want with them?" ask Maggie. "I don't know anything about no frigging container," said Mason sounding annoyed at the question and avoiding eye contact with her.

Maggie got up walked around the desk and stood at the back of Mason. With his hands cuffed behind him at the back of the chair he was unable to turn around or see her. She stood there quietly not moving for a few minutes then bent down and whispered in Mason's ear. "What were you doing at the Surgery?" Mason could feel his heart pounding as she made him jump. He was no stranger to interrogation techniques and procedures but experiencing them in real life was very different. Maggie came across as icy and remorseless. Mason began to feel like she was capable of anything.

"I don't know about any container," said Mason just looking ahead.

Maggie grabbed the back of Masons head by his hair and slammed his head hard into the table and pulled it back up. Blood began pouring from his nose down his face and began dripping from his chin as he winced and groaned in agony.

"What the fuck was that?" asked Mason, nearly choking.

The two officers behind Maggie stood firm looking straight ahead. Whatever Maggie did they would not stop her they would not speak they would not intervene, they were professionals and highly trained.

"What were you doing at Gunter Fleischer's Surgery and what did you want with the container?" asked Maggie again in her icy tone.

Mason was not prepared to give anything to Maggie but he was getting the feeling that she knew what was in the container and knew where they were.

Now Who's Suffering
~ Chapter Thirty Seven ~

Shiva had just finished taking the last driver home when he pulled into the bus park. He parked the bus next to the cabin, got out and slowly walked over to the cabin. He was wearing his usual dark blue company issue anorak on top of his blue jacket. He walked with his back slightly bent, his head down and his hair hanging down.

With his hands in his pockets he tapped the door open with his foot and jumped in through the gap. Straight away he walked over to the radio on top of the fridge and turned on the radio. He re tuned it too Easy Listening FM. He then flicked the kettle on, made a quick brew and sat in his favourite seat in the corner. He sat reading his Take a Break for a while and supping his tea. After about an hour Lenny and Paul both knocked on the door and walked in.

"Everything's in place Shiva," said Lenny.

Shiva put down his magazine and made his way to the door. "Come on you pair," said Shiva has he went outside and lit a cigarette. With the cigarette hanging out the corner of his mouth he made his way over to the bus followed by Lenny, Paul and Jake. Jake had been waiting outside the cabin door for Shiva and was now excited to see him again running round in circles and barking. Once onboard Lenny and Paul removed their high visibility jackets and then sat down. Jake ran onto the bus and sat on the seat behind the driver's cab where he would be able to see Shiva.

Shiva still hadn't made a decision yet whether he would leave the body at the scene or transfer it back to the depot. He was still gutted about Margaret having a heart attack before he could finish her off so decided he would make sure he killed Jason himself. It would be easy to cut out the organs at the scene but it would also give away the nature of what they might have been up to. He started the engine and the bus roared into life and hissed slightly as he removed the parking brake. The journey didn't take too long and was quiet, with everyone too excited to talk. Shiva pulled up just past Jason's house near the alleyway. He quickly switched the engine off and opened the doors. Having bough Jake along with him, he attached his lead and stepped off the bus as if he was taking Jake for a run down the field. Once he was out of sight Paul and Lenny waited a few minutes then quietly stepped off the bus to join him. He was down in the corner of the field chuffing on another cigarette when he was joined by the two cleaners. Jake was running round in circles getting excited like he knew what was coming. Shiva pointed towards the bus while looking at Jake. Jake did no more than trot off jumping on board the bus to wait for Shiva.

"You see the house with the hanging basket?" asked Shiva, "Well the house to the left is Jason's, come on."

All three of them walked along the bottom of the field until they were level with Jason's house. It was just gone 2am cold and very dark there was no movement or anybody in sight so they slowly advanced towards Jason's back garden over the fence and up to the kitchen window. Peering through, they could see Jason had fell asleep in the living room on the sofa with the Xbox controller still in his hand.

Lenny was carrying a short scaffolding bar and a car jack. He placed the scaffolding bar across the back door with one side touching the door frame. He placed the car jack on the other side between the scaffolding bar and the door frame and began winding the jack up. After a few turns the jack was tight. Paul held the scaffolding bar in place while Lenny began winding on.

The door frame started to creak as it was being pushed apart by the jack. Lenny could see a small gap appearing between the door and the frame, as he kept winding the jack. Shiva stood at the side of the window peering across into the living room, just in case Jason woke. After a few more turns of the jack the door popped open with a click. Lenny quickly unwound the jack and removed it as Paul took the scaffolding bar away.

Shiva took up first position pushed the door open and entered the house. He was followed by Paul as Lenny waited outside and kept watch. Quietly and carefully they both walked through the kitchen and over to the living room door. Jason sat on the sofa asleep snoring away. Shiva crept up to him and took the Xbox controller from his hand and wrapped it around his neck.

"So you like to play games do you?" asked Shiva loudly.

Jason woke abruptly with the cord of the controller wrapped around his neck. Shiva yanked hard on the cable and dragged him to the floor. Paul dropped down on to the floor with his knees on Jason's chest, preventing him from moving. Shiva tightened the cable around his neck and whispered into his ear. "This is from Ellie Fox," Shiva held the cable in his left hand as Paul passed him a knife, which he had taken from his pocket. Jason started choking as Shiva pulled even tighter on the cable.

He took the knife and held it above Jason's left eye. "Curse the day you ever pissed Ellie off? I'm going to make sure you never lay another finger on her." Jason started to shake his head from side to side choking so Shiva placed his knees either side of his head to stop him from moving. Paul had taken hold of his hands while Shiva placed a hand on Jason's forehead and then slid the knife straight into Jason's left eye.

Blood began spurting from the eye socket as the eyeball eventually burst. Jason's body started twitching violently as Shiva slid the knife in further and deeper. Bright red crimson blood gushed down over his face, down his cheeks and onto the carpet. Shiva twisted the knife and moved it from side to side when Jason stopped twitching and went rigid. He pulled the knife out which was also covered in blood and then sat staring at the hole where his eye had been. Shiva seemed mesmerized and fascinated by the gaping hole that once use to be Jason's eye. Jason didn't move. Jason didn't breath. Jason was dead.

Paul whispered over to Lenny to give him a hand with the body while Shiva started looking through Jason's CD collection. Lenny ran upstairs and grabbed some blankets off a bed and bought them down. They laid the blankets out flat on the living room floor and then rolled Jason's warm body over onto them, then wrapped his body in them. Paul took one end while Lenny took the other. They carried him outside over the fence and into the back field. They walked along the edge of the back gardens carrying Jason and trying to keep low in case anybody saw them. Shiva came sprinting up the field to meet them clutching a hand full of CD's including Depeche Mode and the Smurf's greatest hits.

Shiva tucked the CD's in his pocket as he walked passed Lenny and Paul and on towards the bus. Checking that nobody was watching or kicking about, Shiva beckoned them over. They carefully climbed on board the bus and manoeuvred their way down to the back. They lowered Jason's body to the floor as Shiva started the bus and drove back to the depot.

Minutes later they arrived at the depot complete with a dead body in the bus, the body of Jason Fletcher. Shiva backed the bus through the shutters and parked near the paint booth. Lenny jumped out, unlocked the paint booth shutters as Shiva drove in. Shiva slowly drove through the shutters and down towards the grate. Safely inside Lenny pulled down the shutters and joined Shiva.

Shiva was bent down removing the lock from the grate before pulling it open. "Give us a hand," said Paul.

Lenny jumped back on board and helped Paul carry Jason's body to the entrance of the grate. Shiva was safely down and had the lights on as a huge thumping noise echoed through the rooms. Lenny and Paul came down the steps and picked up Jason and took him over to the trolley. Shiva didn't waste any time as he buttoned up his gown and pulled on his latex surgical gloves. He had recently purchased an electronic rib cutter from eBay and was eager to try it. The ribs are really tough and hard to cut so any time saved was a bonus.

He first made an S incision from Jason's throat to his stomach and an incision across his upper chest. Paul bought a metal tray containing eight pairs of forceps and handed them to Shiva. Lenny stood nearby watching having activated and prepared the transportation cooler.

Shiva took the first pair of forceps and peeled back the top left flap of flesh and breast tissue. The weight of the forceps hanging keeps the pieces in place. He followed this by pulling back each piece of flesh until the entire chest was exposed. It took a few minutes to cut away the fat and muscle before he got to the ribcage. This was the bit he had been waiting for. The rib cutter was silver and a very odd shape, a bit like a dremel with a two inch cutting disk. It ripped into life as he flicked the on switch and stood holding it up in front of himself grinning like a cat drinking cream.

Bits of bone flicked up into the air as he cut through each rib with expert precision. Each cut was quick and clean as he reached the last rib. He placed the rib cutter down on the side and took hold of the ribs and pulled them away. Paul quickly scooped them up and took them to the metal disposal bin.

Locating the heart, Shiva took a syringe from the tray and injected 2cc's of adrenaline into the heart then squeezed the heart several times to pump the liquid injection around the inner chambers. The heart would now be good for at least another hour which would be plenty of time. It would take Shiva a few minutes to free the heart cutting through the Pulmonary Trunk and veins, Aorta and both Vena Cava's.

Once the heart was freed he then passed it to Paul. Paul then packed the heart ready for transportation and slid it into the transportation cooler. Shiva then removed his gown, scrubbed clean, took the cooler and headed for his car. While Shiva was waiting for the shutters to open he sent a text ahead to Gunter letting him know he was on his way.

"Has Shiva left?" asked Lenny as he came walking back into the theatre.

"Yes he just left. Are you ready?" asked Paul.

Lenny was wearing a gown and surgical gloves the same as Paul as he said "Yes ready when you are."

Paul had removed the rest of Jason's cloths as Lenny took a large incision blade and cut a neat line around the top of Jason's left leg. He spent a second or two cutting through the muscle all the way round until, he made contact with the bone. Paul started the same procedure on the arms cutting around the arm through the flesh and muscle until he could feel bone. They both took a surgical saw each and begin the slow process of cutting through the bones. Paul finished first as the humerus bone is much thinner than the femur. Paul removed the arm, laid it down on the side and proceeded round to the other arm. Lenny had just finished cutting the first leg off as he wiped the sweat from his forehead. Gathering a bit of momentum Paul was half way from cutting the next arm off sawing away as Lenny had finished cutting through the bone.

With both arms and legs removed, Lenny bought over the large metal bin, so they could both roll Jason's corpse in to it. The next step was to remove the hands, feet, and the elbow and knee joints. Lenny and Paul chatted away as they made several incisions and cuts. The first hand was cut off and thrown into the metal bin, with the corpse, followed by both feet. Lenny then moved on to help Paul with the knee caps as the other hand went flying into the bin.

"I'm starving Paul," said Lenny.

"It won't be long now," said Paul.

Lenny began watering down the eight pieces of arm and leg as Paul very carefully took out the Calciumdimetracid, added a little water and poured it all over the corpse and body parts. Lenny stopped what he was doing as he watched the flesh melt and the bone dissolve. He was absolutely fascinated as the bones fizzled and melted away like ice on a hot day, he just stood there staring.

Over the next half hour Lenny cleaned the rooms and floors as Paul placed the limbs in a bread box and took them outside. He walked through the spray booth and under the shutters and could see the smoke from the BBQ over in the corner of the bus park and could smell the smoke. Weaving his way through the buses he made his way over carrying the limbs. Most of the cleaners had already arrived and began cheering and clapping as he arrived. Ted was in charge of the BBQ and took the bread box from Paul. They all began chatting and talking away as their food was cooking away, they were all very excited.

Shiva too was enjoying himself, listening to the Smurf's—Oops upside your head, as he made his way to Gunter's Surgery. He had left Jake back at the bus depot, so he could join in the feast. He was only about ten minutes away from the Surgery, having pulled off the bypass and onto a local road, when he saw a traffic Police car pull out of a side street catch him up and began to follow him. He knew if they suspected anything or searched the car then it was over.

Trying to play it cool he turned the radio off and sat upright and tried not to look suspicious, but where could he say he was going at this time of the morning, it was in the very early hours with no other cars and the road and streets deserted. He had to be smart and quick thinking. He had to come up with the perfect excuse so he paused for a moment to gather his thoughts and come up with a plan. Just as he was thinking where he could say he was going the lights on the Police car came on piecing through the dark night and lit up his car. He calmly indicated to the left and pulled over to the side of the road into a bus lay by and looked in his mirror.

The Police car overtook him and shot off down the road like a scolded cat leaving a trail of blue lights reflecting of the adjacent buildings. Shiva took a deep breath and rubbed his face. He would have to be more careful in the future. Until now he never really thought what he would do if he was caught or how he would explain a human organ in his boot. After another deep breath, he selected first gear, indicated right and pulled away to finish his journey to the Surgery.

The Truth is Out
~ Chapter Thirty Eight ~

"I've just got to give mum and dad a quick ring and we can go if you want?" asked Ellie.

"Yes that sounds perfect; I'm going for a shower then while you ring them." Nathan stood up and gave Ellie a kiss.

"Shout if you want your back scrubbing" shouted Ellie in a cheeky voice.

Ellie took a sip from her coffee and grabbed the phone from the lounge.

"Hi mum."

"Ellie, how are you?" asked Linda.

"Mum, I've got some really good news. The insurance company has paid up."

"You're kidding?"

"Nope, straight up, £184 thousand pounds."

"What are you going to do with it?" asked Linda.

"Well for now I'm going to ask Nathan to put it in his bank account but really as I'm now living with Nathan I'm not sure."

"What about the business? Are you still promoting your brand?"

"Well, since the accident I've been a bit nervous. I think it's because I was on a business trip when it happened and was planning on staying in Denver but I just seem to have lost it."

Ellie and Linda, her mum, continued chatting until Nathan came back downstairs from his shower.

"I'm going to have to go now; we're off to see David." Ellie then said goodbye, gave her love to her dad and then hung up.

"Sweetheart there's something I want to ask you," said Ellie

"Sure, what's that?" replied Nathan.

Ellie returned the phone to the lounge and sat down on the chair. "I'd like you to put the insurance cheque in your bank account," said Ellie looking at Nathan all sweet.

"Erm I'm flattered sweetheart but there could be a problem there."

"What do you mean?" asked Ellie inquisitively.

"Well during my, let's say younger days, as an instructor I was classed as self employed. After several years I was spot audited and they discovered I'd come up short on the tax payments. I was taken to court and ordered to pay nearly £23 grand for tax evasion, in fact I was lucky not to get sent down."

Ellie burst out laughing.

"What?" asked Nathan looking coy?

"You, Tax evasion, you're having me on?"

257

"No honest it's the truth. I was lucky to get a job as a pilot after that but it was the number of hours I'd flown that went for me. It took me a while to pay it off but I managed it," said Nathan.

"I just can't imagine you being a naughty boy at all. Come on let's get going," said Ellie laughing.

They both made their way out to the car as Nathan picked up the car keys and shut the door behind them. While Nathan was locking the front door a car drove past that caught his eye.

"Silver Astra!" shouted Nathan and pointing.

"Did you see it? Did you see who was driving?"

"No, the windows were dark, I didn't see anything," said Ellie has she stood by the car.

Nathan backed out of the driveway and drove on to the Surgery. "I swear that was the same Astra that has been following us, I would love to know who it is and what they want." "Maybe we should go to the Police?" asked Ellie.

"No we can't, what if it's something to do with, well you know, with what's been happening."

"I suppose so yes, although it could just be a coincidence, at least I know it's not going to be Jason this time," said Ellie.

Nathan gave her hand a rub and said, "I will do my best to look after you now."

Ellie smiled back at him with a huge smile feeling really happy.

"We've come to see David and Diana," said Ellie to the receptionist.

You couldn't tell anything had happened as they walked through the corridors. Everywhere clean and white with the usual smell of a hospital.

Diana was sat at David's side with a drip attached to her arm as Nathan and Ellie both walked onto the ward. Nathan rushed ahead to David who was semi conscious and talking to Diana.

"I've just been bringing David up to speed with what's been happening. How are you both," said Diana.

"We're fine," said Ellie as she caught up.

"Nathan," said David. "Good to see you. Diana tells me you finally found the love of your life?"

"Yes, I'd like you to meet Ellie. Ellie this is David, David this is Ellie."

"Pleased to meet you," said Ellie as she sat on the bed next to him. "Nathan has told me so much about you; in fact he's not shut up about you."

Nathan started to go red as he looked at David.

"Didn't you know? These two are soul mates, they were virtually inseparable before the accident," said Diana.

"How come I'm in a private Surgery instead of hospital?" asked David.

Ellie just looked at Nathan. She knew he would have to tell David the truth on what had happened but was now the right time?

"Erm well it's a bit complicated there's something I need to tell you both but I'm not sure now is the right time."

David tried to pull himself up right and succeeded in pulling the pulse monitor off his finger. A loud beeping noise alerted the Nurse nearby who came over and reinserted it onto his finger.

"You need to take it easy David," said the nurse.

While she was with David she took his blood pressure.

"That's all good and normal," said the Nurse as she filled in the patient sheet and then left.

"Maybe we could talk more tomorrow?" suggested Nathan.

"Yes I think that might be better. I do hear that you have been a bit of a hero in this place mind. I am sorry to drag you into all this," said David.

"What do you mean," said Nathan but his question came too late. David had fallen unconscious again.

"The Nurse said this was normal considering what he had gone through," said Diana. "Do you know what he meant by sorry to drag you into all this?" asked Nathan.

Diana turned her chair to face Nathan. "I told him about the crash to which he can remember, even going through the windshield but the odd thing is, when I told him about the guys who came in here in the black clothes, knocked Ellie out and held a gun to you he just didn't seem surprised. He didn't even comment on their intentions to find those container things, it was as though he knew about them," said Diana.

"Jesus, I wonder if David has something to do with it. But if I remember rightly the two gunmen didn't know who David was as they had to ask who he was and what was wrong with him," said Nathan.

"Nathan," said a slow voice. "David, David what do you know?" asked Nathan quickly.

"London, Heathrow. The container is in London, there is only one," said David as his eyes fluttered and blinked several time before shutting.

"Shit," said Nathan. "Why didn't he tell me, and what the hell as he been doing?" asked Nathan sounding annoyed. "This isn't like David, he is the most honest and trustful man that I know. If he was doing anything bad, he would have hidden it from me to protect me. He must know what the containers are or as he said container and knows what's in it and why it's worth killing for."

"He didn't say too much too me about it or let anything on, but he was very pleased to hear about you two becoming an item," said Diana.

Nathan got up and walked over to Diana's bed and sat on the side. "Diana there something I need to tell you before David wakes up again."

"What's that Nathan you killed someone?" she said laughing as Ellie came over to join him.

"Well you're not far from wrong," said Nathan.

Ellie came and sat by his side and took hold of his hand for support. "While you were unconscious, both you and David needed organ transplants in order to stand any chance of surviving. The thing is you were based down in the London Trauma Hospital and was on the transplant waiting list. You can just imagine the transplant waiting list; it is huge with a lot of people waiting."

Nathan paused for a second and took a deep breath. "The truth is I didn't want to lose you or David. We found a surgeon friend that would be willing to do the transplant, no questions asked, in return for a slight favour. I have a friend that dabbles in Surgery and came across a list of bad people with the same blood groups. These people were rapists and murderers and kind of ended up dead, with their organs being transported here while their bodies were disposed of. It meant that you and David would survive."

Nathan was feeling nervous now on how she would react but she just burst into tears. "It's a bit much to take in," said Diana, "but I think I understand why you did it for us. What if these friends of yours get caught?" asked Diana.

"I don't think there's much chance of them getting caught. I think you might have already met one of them, Dr Gunter. He performed the Surgery on both you and David," said Nathan.

"You're joking?" sniffled Diana as she wiped her nose. "I just met him this morning; he seems quite a nice guy."

"He really is good," said Nathan.

Nathan, Ellie and Diana continued chatting a while catching up on the past few months with details of the accident and how they met. They chatted about the terrorist's and what the container might contain. Nathan was interested to hear that Diana was making progress and feeling better, but was eager to talk to David. This however would have to wait until David was conscious.

CD Links
~ Chapter Thirty Nine ~

"Shiva Lawman, served 8 months for killing four people," said Neil.

"Only eight months?" asked Claire. "That's not right surely."

"He was originally sent down for life but on appeal it was found that the evidence had been incorrectly stored with procedures not being followed."

"So he got off on a technicality?" asked Claire.

"Yes, he did indeed," said Neil as he thumbed through the paperwork turning the pages. "He was re-arrested some years later on suspicion of killing eight people in Ingoldmells, on the east coast, but was released due to an issue with the evidence."

"I can remember that on the news," said Claire as she continued driving her way back to headquarters.

"I remember both cases and helped co-ordinate the investigations," said Neil.

"Do you think the evidence was tampered with?" asked Claire.

"You mean did he pay off someone on the inside to get him off? Well he came across as an educated smart man but as for is financial status he wasn't that well off, so if he did get someone in the force to tamper with the evidence it would have to be a close friend or he threatened someone. There was an internal investigation but nothing ever came of it. I personally think it was a coincidence but I could be wrong."

"What about the eight people in Ingoldmells? How did he manage to get away with that one?" asked Claire.

"Well the evidence that was collect was circumstantial. He was in the area and several witness statements were collected that described him at the scene, but there was no motive or physical evidence put him there," said Neil.

After arriving back at the Police Headquarters both Neil and Claire quickly learnt of the missing person, Jason.

"Come on I want to go and check this one out," said Neil.

"But it's just a missing person," said Claire.

"So were Margaret and Marcus, and all the others."

Claire picked up the paper work and started reading through it as they made their way back to the car and on to Jason's house.

The duty Sergeant in charge of the scene bought Neil up to speed. "We thought this might just be another missing person, but when his mate called round he found blood on the sofa. The Scene of Crimes Officers found blood on the fence on the back garden. It also appears that the back door was forced open."

Neil bent down to look at the back door and could indeed see the back door had been forced open.

"What are these marks on the frame?" asked Neil.

"It appears the door was jacked open making the frame wider than the door so the door pops open," said the Sergeant.

"Would this have made a noise do you think?" asked Neil already knowing the answer.

"To be honest I'm not sure. If I was to guess, I would say the only noise made, would be the click of the door opening."

"How many witness statements have been collected?"

"About twenty, we made door to door enquires and turned in all statements. From what I've read nothing showed up as out the blue."

I'll be the judge of that thought Neil. "Pass the statements on to my assistant Claire and have SOCO sweep for finger prints on this door," said Neil.

"Yes Sir," said the Sergeant has he left to go and collect the statements from his officers.

Neil wandered through the kitchen looking around for any disturbance while making his way through to the lounge. On the floor next to the TV and Stereo System was an untidy pile of CD's. *It's the same person* thought Neil instantly as he bent down to look at the CD's. Seeing the case from the Smurf's greatest hits he began to wonder if it was teenagers or even kids doing this but quickly dismissed the thought when he realised it would take some muscle to cart a person through the house and over into a field. But why was he taken from here and where is he now.

Neil took the time to search the rest of the house while Claire sat in the car reading through the neighbours statements. Claire didn't yet know that Neil was linking this crime to the recent others.

It didn't take Neil long to figure out that a quilt-cover was missing from the bed and probably used to carry the body out the house and over the fields.

Neil tried to follow the footsteps of where they had gone, walking from the bedroom, down the stairs, into the lounge, through the kitchen and out into the garden. He made his way over to the fence where he got one of the Scene of Crimes Officers to help him over the fence and into the field. The grass was a little damp and had been trodden down. He tried his best not to disturb any evidence and began to follow the trial of disturbed grass. He walked down to the bottom of the field, where he had a good view of the back of the houses, and that's when he spotted the alleyway between the houses.

That's how they did it. They used the quilt-cover to carry him through the house and over the fence and then carried him up the alleyway and into a waiting car or as he was beginning to suspect, a waiting bus he thought to himself

Race Against Time
~ Chapter Forty ~

"Don't worry I won't be leaving David's side," said Diana as she was talking to Nathan.

"How will you know what the container looks like or where to find it?" asked Ellie. Nathan was just about to speak when he saw David move and start to wake up. Nathan helped him up and placed the pillow behind his head. "How you feeling?" asked Nathan.

"I'm thirsty but feel a bit better."

"Can you remember what you said to me before you passed out?" asked Nathan.

"Yes, yes I remember. You need to find the container before they do. It will still be in storage at Heathrow. Find it Nathan before they do." "David what's in the container? Who is after them? David? David?"

David was still very weak drifting in and out of consciousness but was trying to stay awake.

"Nathan, don't trust Ben, he is behind the terrorist's and he's probably following you to find out what you know."

The Silver Astra thought Nathan to himself. "You mean Ben Books our manager?" asked Nathan.

"Yes," struggled David. "I kept it from you to protect you. Ben is well linked into the World Health Terrorist Organisation. He tried to force me to transport the container from Germany to Denver. He threatened to bring down several planes unless I complied. He even got one of the terrorist phoning, sending threats to the company demanding money."

Nathan just sat with his mouth wide open. "So was the crash actually an accident?" asked Nathan.

"I'm beginning to think it was no accident but in fact we were bought down on purpose," said David.

Ellie and Diana had moved over to Diana's bed and were chatting away but partly listening in to David and Nathan's conversation.

"Have you any idea as to what is in the container?" asked Nathan.

"Not really but I can tell you Ben was deadly serious when he said the airline would suffer losses if the container wasn't delivered."

"So I'm guessing the raid in here was something to do with Ben?"

"Yes I guess so," said David "You can bet that the wreckage of LA 1872 was searched for the container and when they found it missing they came after you and Ellie. They probably burnt down Ellie's house as warning and then came here after me."

"But why, I knew nothing about the container"

David sat up a little bit further and rubbed his face with his left hand. He was looking a bit brighter but his pulse rate was a little rapid. The staff Nurse came back over to David. "You need to stop over doing it David and rest," said the nurse as she re-adjusted his pillows.

"Nathan, they will have discovered by now the container is missing. You survived the crash so they think you have it. Listen to me carefully Nathan. You need to find the container and discover what is inside it. What is worth killing for and bringing down an entire aircraft and possibly an airline?"

"I'm scared David," said Nathan as he stood up from his seat and perched himself next to David.

"Take Ellie with you Nathan she may be able help you. The minute you locate the container open it. They will stop at nothing Nathan they have already proved that, so time is of the essence."

Nathan took hold of David's hand, "We will leave for London now David and do our very best."

Nathan stood up and called over to Ellie, "We have to go now Ellie."

"I know sweetheart, I'm ready when you are."

Nathan and Ellie had just arrived at Nathan's house when Ellie turned to face Nathan. "At this storage depot that David mentioned, how will you know where to look or know what you're looking for?" asked Ellie with a puzzled look on her face.

"Well to be honest I'm not sure what the container will look like but they are usually labelled with the flight information, origin, destination and the recipient details. The storage depots are pretty well organised so I'm hoping it will be easy to find as all

LA 1872 cargo should have been shipped out on the flight," said Nathan.

"I just can't believe Ben is involved in all this I mean involved with terrorists and crashing planes. I've known Ben for years and he never came across as that sort of person. He is a pilot himself and worked really hard to get where he is. It makes me wonder if he hasn't been forced to do this or a threat made on his life. He just didn't seem the sort of person to do this sort of thing."

Ellie just sat listening to him and could tell that he was in shock. "It's okay, just take a deep breath and we'll think this through. To stop anybody else getting hurt we first need to locate that container and find out what the hell is inside it."

"Yes I agree," said Nathan still looking shocked.

"What is it?" asked Nathan as Ellie suddenly went quiet. "Oh it's nothing really. I was just going to say a need to nip back to my place to pick a few things up when it dawned on me, my place burnt down. I don't think the incident at my flat as really hit me yet."

Nathan put his arm around her and gave her a cuddle. "Come on let's get sorted."

They both spent the next few minutes packing a few light things into their suitcases for the trip down to London. Nathan was used to packing a case but looking over at Ellie he could tell she wasn't so good. "Just pack light cloths, underwear and a change of shoes, and just one pair mind; I know what you're like," said Nathan laughing.

"Okay I get it, I'll pack light and one pair of shoes," said Ellie pushing her bottom lip out.

Upon packing their cases Nathan took them to the boot of the car and they set off for the several hours trip down to London. "It's 11:36am with a bit of luck we should be at Heathrow Storage Depot by about 3pm," said Nathan.

Transplant
~ Chapter Forty One ~

Gunter had received Jason's heart from Shiva in the early hours of the morning but had decided at the last moment to postpone the transplant. In Gunter's medical opinion David wasn't well enough to undergo the surgery and decided David's body needed to rest for a further 24 hours.

In order for Jason's heart to survive outside of a body it would need to have blood constantly pumping through it.

While in Germany, practising at the Ludwigshafen Hospital, Gunter had been pioneering a method of placing a heart into a semi animated state. This involved infusing the heart with what looked like a green slushy liquid. It was in fact a super chilled solution of vitamins, minerals and plasma. The liquid slush was then mechanically pumped throughout the heart using a dialysis machine.

It was just after 1pm when David was prepared for surgery. He was waiting in the Pre-Op suite semi conscious and feeling very relaxed from the Pre-Med Metoclopramide injection. After assembling the medical team and briefing every one, Gunter was scrubbed and ready to operate.

David was wheeled into the theatre for the third and hopefully last time and was injected with 10mg of Thiopental before being asked to count to ten. He managed to get to four before he was out cold.

While in the theatre a mask was placed over his mouth by the Anaesthetist. So he would stay unconscious, he was given Halothane to breath in through the mask along with oxygen.

The medical team that consisted of five surgeons, two assistants and an Anaesthetist got to work, first covering David with a green sheet that had an opening which was placed over the area of the heart. "Suction please," said Gunter as he made a ten inch incision below David's left breast. The incision was seeping blood and had run down the side of his chest and onto the surgical sheet. At each end of the incision, Gunter made an additional V shaped incision and clamps were clipped onto each piece of flesh and flapped out and over to give access to the ribs. Using an electronic surgical saw, Gunter started to cut through and remove the 2nd, 3rd, 4th and 5th ribs. This now gave clear access to the heart, valves and arteries.

The assistant surgeon to Gunter's left was removing Jason's heart from the dialysis machine and flushing the heart through with saline solution while

Gunter was cutting through the main valves, arteries and connecting the Heart Bypass Machine.

Gunter now needed to stop David's heart from beating before he could cut through the remaining valves. One of the technicians across the table handed Gunter two small defibrillator paddles that had been pre-gelled. He placed a paddle on either side of David's heart and in a firm clear voice said "Clear."

The antithesis removed the mask from David's face and stepped back along with the surgeons and technicians. A jolt of electricity was zapped from one paddle to the other through David's heart which stopped it instantly.

"Stay focused," said Gunter as the mask was placed back over David's face and everyone resumed their position. The last valve was carefully detached and suction was applied around the heart and cavity to remove the excess blood that had built up.

Carefully sliding his hands down each side of the heart and underneath, Gunter slowly lifted out David's heart turned round and placed it into an oval shaped bowl behind him. He was then handed Jason's heart that was in a kidney shaped bowl to which Gunter placed in front of him. He carefully picked up the new heart and lowered it into the empty cavity in David's chest.

It had taken Gunter and his team just a little over an hour to remove David's failing heart and now was preparing to transplant and connect the new heart, Jason's heart.

David's old heart was disposed of and would be incinerated while Gunter was carefully placing sutures around the Superior and Inferior Vena Cava along with the Pulmonary Arteries. The last part was to suture the Pulmonary Vein and laser close the Aorta.

Once completed the clamps were removed from the various arteries and veins as the heart started to swell and fill with blood. Having checked and re checked for leaks, the last job was to restart the heart.

Gunter again placed the paddles either side of the heart, hit the discharge button sending 200 Joules of electricity coursing through the heart. After a short while, the heart began to pump David's blood around his body unaided since before the last few hours.

After re checking all the connection and removing the last of the pipes from the Heart Bypass Machine it was time to close David's chest. The clamps were removed from the muscle and skin leaving them to *flop* back into their original position. Gunter began to close the cavity by suturing the muscles together and to reduce the amount of scaring, he used the laser to close the skin.

David's mask was changed over to 100% pure oxygen while the relevant paper work was filled in noting his BP 104 over 67 and heart beat 72 bpm with his O2 Stats at 99%.

David's chest was scrubbed clean, and then a large wad of cotton padding was stuck over the wound area. David was then injected with 1000mg of aspirin and 10mg of Morphine to thin the blood and prevent clotting with the morphine to manage the pain.

While being wheeled in to the recovery room, David was beginning to come round when he started to pull the mask off of his face. The nurse in charge, who was sat next to him, stood up and placed the mask back on his face. "How are you feeling David?" asked the nurse in a slightly raised voice, but David's reply was somewhat incoherent.

Watch and Learn
~ Chapter Forty Two ~

"I think we should set up a covert surveillance team at the bus garage," said Claire as she was looking through a bunch of statements.

"I'm not sure we really have enough to go on at the moment and the department budget is stretched thin as it is," said Neil.

"But Sir, we have several witness statements stating they saw or heard as bus and Shiva Lawman works at the bus depot as a somewhat tainted record," said Claire as she put the statements down on her lap.

Neil didn't say anything as he turned into the Police Headquarters car park and activated the electronic barrier.

They both stepped out of the car and began walking over to the CID department at the other side of the complex. "Okay, organise a two man surveillance team from tonight," said Neil as he opened the door for Claire.

"According to his employment record and job description, he is responsible for taking home the drivers in the evening and early hours, so we could have the surveillance team in place from 1am Sir," said Claire.

"Yes that's good. I want Jamie and Dominic on the team. If Mr Lawman is our man then they are the best we have," said Neil.

"Yes Sir," said Claire as they finally reached the CID department.

Claire sat down to brief both Dominic and Jamie as to the surveillance job that lay ahead.

"Across the road is the Horse and Apple Public House," said Claire. "You should be able to park up in amongst the other cars and have a clear vantage point of the main depot entrance."

"Are we using one car or two?" asked Jamie.

"I want you to use two cars. Dominic you stay at the car park, Jamie you follow the bus. If a second bus comes out the depot I want you to follow it Dominic," said Claire as she was jotting notes down on a piece of paper.

"Both of you stay in touch and both report back to HQ every fifteen minutes. Make no joke about it; Shiva Lawman is a cold blooded killer. Each time he has been caught he has slipped through our fingers due to a lack of evidence or incorrectly cataloguing the evidence. Take the camera cars so we can capture every move and every piece of evidence," said Claire energetically.

"What time do you want us there from?" asked Jamie.

Claire finished writing some more notes and said "I want you both down there around 1am but don't both arrive together. Stagger you arrival by about ten minutes. If at 4am nothing as occurred then you can call it a day. This is a two day operation authorised by Neil himself so don't miss anything up."

Claire finished writing some more notes and then stacked all her paperwork together. "Go get your selves a coffee while I get these briefing notes typed up and organise photos and descriptions," said Claire.

Claire quickly got the briefing notes typed up and attached a photograph of Shiva along with his Police file. She typed out a short email to the control room briefly describing the surveillance teams objectives in case anybody was to report them as suspicious or if any other team or officers working in the area. She then made her way down to the canteen to find Jamie and Dominic and handed over the paper work.

Missing
~ Chapter Forty Three ~

Nathan and Ellie had been driving for several hours down the M1 and onto the M25. They had spent a little over 50 minutes on the M25 before they pulled off at Junction 14 and onto airport Road.

"We should be there in about twenty five minutes," said Nathan as he slipped some sweets into his mouth.

"Just look at the state of you, you're drooling all down yourself," said Ellie as she started to wipe his mouth and the top of his shirt.

"Thank you sweetheart," said Nathan slurping on his sweets.

"Freight Storage is straight ahead," said Ellie as she sat with a map on her knee. "Have you ever been here before?" she asked.

"I've been here a few times during my training days," said Nathan, "but I imagine it hasn't changed too much."

Rounding the next corner, Nathan pulled into the huge car park and parked up. The Audi which was given to him by Harold Gillespie had an authentic Lufthansa Staff ID in the windscreen that would identify him as a Lufthansa employee.

The storage unit was a single story pre-fabricated type building on top of a brick shell. The upper metal structure was painted dark green with the lower brick level a light beige colour. The road and pathways outside were dry and dusty but a few trees around the sides added a warming effect to the building. Down the rear side was about eight metal green roller shutters pulled down slightly with forklift trucks buzzing around going in and out of the building and several staff wandering around wearing high visibility yellow jackets.

The main entrance was made of new type brick which looked aesthetically pleasing and modern. Walking up to the entrance Nathan and Ellie were greeted by a large brown wooden door with an intercom and card swipe entry system on the right. The intercom was lit up with an orange glow with a button that said *Reception*. Nathan reached out and pressed the button. In doing so a buzzing noise could be heard in the distance.

"How can I help?" asked a voice over the intercom.

"I'm Nathan Taylor, First Officer with Lufthansa to sign out a container from Flight Lima Alpha 1872."

"Hold your ID up please." asked the voice.

Inside the intercom was a small camera where the receptionist could see both Ellie and Nathan.

Nathan was fishing around in his wallet looking for his Company ID Card while Ellie was tinkering around with her hair. Once Nathan had found his ID Card, he held it up to the intercom for a few seconds when the door buzzed and clicked. "Come through," said the voice.

Inside they were greeted by a middle aged slim looking woman. "Hi Nathan I'm Lucy Clarke, can I check your ID again please?"

"Yes, sure," said Nathan as he presented her with his ID Card.

"Thank you," said Lucy as she clipped his ID Card on to her Clip Board and wrote down his Employee ID Number, Branch Number and Authorisation Code and then handed him the card back.

"Fill out this form in triplicate detailing the container Description, Storage code and Storage Date along with your personal details," said Lucy.

"This may present a problem Lucy," said Nathan.

"Erm okay come and take a seat and explain," said Lucy.

"We were flying flight LA 1872 out of Heathrow to Denver; however Captain David Benson removed a container from the plane before we set off as there was no clear destination marked on the container. From what I can tell the container is the size of an average suitcase," said Nathan.

While Nathan had been talking, Lucy was chewing the end of her pen and never took her eyes off of him. Ellie seeing this, was starting to get annoyed and fidgety when Lucy looked at Nathan and said "Leave it with me sweetheart and I'll see what I can do," she then left the room with her clipboard and closed the door behind her.

"She definitely fancies you," said Ellie looking straight at Nathan but Nathan just chuckled at her and got up for a walk round.

The office section they were in had a glass partitioning window as Nathan walked up to it and peered through. Ahead of him he could see the forklift trucks that were still buzzing around with their flash orange beacons pulsing and people darting around up and down the aisles. From the window, the place looked massive, the size of a football field. The floor appeared to be laminated or though it could have been an anti slip paint. There were hundreds of strip lights that hung down from the roof clearly lighting up every inch of the building and making the floor shine.

Around the outskirts of the building were metal racks that looked like scaffolding. They were stacked six shelves high with approximately two metres in between them. Each shelf was stacked to the top with container and boxes of all shapes and sizes. On the floor there were pallets stacked on top of one another housing a similar set up of wooden container and boxes of all sizes and wrapped in cellophane. Towards the end of the building he could just see that the shelving units had been placed in rows and aisles.

He noticed that each box or container no matter where it was stored or how big it was, it was printed with an eight digit code of some sort and a fairly large bar code.

A minute or two had passed when Nathan noticed Lucy talking to a young man and was waving her arms around.

"Looks like someone's getting a roasting," said Nathan. Ellie came over and stood by his side as they both watched Lucy arguing.

After about five minutes, Lucy came back in to speak to Nathan. "I'm sorry for the delay but we are struggling to find any container from flight 1872. I'll be back in a moment; meanwhile help yourselves to tea or coffee." Lucy then left looking a bit nervous.

"There's something not right here Nathan and I don't like the way she looks at you either," said Ellie.

"Don't worry, we shouldn't be here much longer," said Nathan taking hold of Ellie's hand.

"Do you want a coffee?" asked Nathan.

"Yes, I'll do it," said Ellie walking over to the Coffee Percolator. She took two mugs off the mug tree and placed them on the side before pouring the coffee and adding a little milk and sugar. "There you go," said Ellie as she passed a mug of the coffee to Nathan.

"Thank you," said Nathan as he took it off her and went and sat down.

They spent the next 40 minutes talking and trying to guess what could be inside the container and why people were killing to get hold of it.

"Maybe it's loaded with Gold or Diamonds," said Ellie.

"Nahh, I don't think so. More likely to be high grade weapons or some form of chemical if it's terrorists that are after it" said Nathan.

"Could be drugs like cocaine or heroin? Just think what if it's a mummy or an ancient Egyptian Artefact or something," said Ellie laughing.

"Maybe," said Nathan but I guess we should find out any minute. We've been here ages."

Just as Nathan was walking over to the window, Lucy came in through the door looking all flustered.

"What's wrong?" asked Nathan.

"Take a seat please," said Lucy.

"There seems to be a problem with your container."

First Watch
~ Chapter Forty Four ~

They had been on surveillance duty for about an hour when Dominic poured himself a cup of soup from his flask and sat with his hands wrapped around the cup.

"Mobile One to Mobile Two, receiving over?" asked Jamie.

"Go ahead," said Dominic.

"All quiet at the moment except for a few piss heads larking around," said Jamie.

"All received, I can see them coming down the hill now," said Dominic.

"Standby One," said Jamie. "We have movement at the entrance."

The radio went silent for a few moments until Jamie said, "There's a Midi-Bus pulling out from the bus park entrance. There seems to be the driver and a smallish bloke stood next to him wearing a dirty yellow jacket. I'm following and observing."

Jamie followed Shiva all the way through to Ilkeston, Trowell and on towards Nottingham. Before arriving at Canning Circus they pulled up just before some road works and switched the engine off.

That's odd thought Jamie as he pulled up some distance behind them. He pulled a pair of binoculars out from under the passenger seat and held them up to see what they were doing. It took him a few seconds to refocus the binoculars and point them towards the Midi-Bus.

Shiva pulled his cigarettes and lighter out of his pocket and lit one. With the cigarette hanging out the corner of his mouth, he sat in the driver's seat with one foot on the dashboard. Meanwhile Lenny was pulling the temporary bus stop down from the back of the bus and out onto the pavement.

The temporary bus stop was made from the inner metal part of a bus wheel with a scaffolding bar welded to the middle. The wheel would act as a base while the flag was attached to the other end of the pole. Surprisingly enough they were incredibly heavy which was showing as Lenny was struggling to pull it down the bus.

He managed to get as far as the platform near the doors when he stopped for a moment, removed his thick rimmed glasses and wiped the sweat from his face.

"Can you give us a hand Shiva?" asked Lenny in his croaky baby voice.

Shiva just looked at him and raised his eyebrows then went back to chuffing on his cigarette. Lenny wiped his face once more and replaced his glasses after tutting at Shiva.

The temporary bus stop went with a thud as it rolled off the platform and onto the pavement. He spent the next few minutes positioning the temporary stop just before the traffic road works and then grabbed a roll of tape off the bus. He ran up and past the traffic road works until he came to the proper bus stop. Using his dirty nailed grubby fingers he piddled the end of the tape back and wrapped the tape around the flag on the bus stop before writing *Out Of Order* on the tape.

Bloody typical thought Jamie has he peered through his binoculars. "Mobile Two, are you receiving?"

"Go ahead," said Dominic.

"I've followed the bus to Canning Circus. There is road works up here and they are pushing out a temporary bus stop," said Jamie.

Jamie stowed his binoculars back under the passenger seat and switched the engine back on as he continued to follow Shiva and Lenny.

45 minutes had passed before Shiva indicated and turned back into the bus depot. Jamie appeared a few minutes after and turned back into the pub car park and turned off the car's engine. He reclined his chair slightly, poured himself a cup of soup and began to fill out his report.

Spain
~ Chapter Forty Five ~

"How can you lose a container?" snapped Nathan pacing up and down. This was the first time Ellie had seen Nathan starting to lose his temper and become angry.

"Well it's not strictly lost," said Lucy.

An elderly man came through the door and handed Lucy some paperwork. "Thank you," said Lucy as the man then disappeared back through the door.

"A few weeks ago," explained Lucy "We converted our filing system over to CSASN and Barcode. During the transfer over, the last digits were recorded incorrectly on your container forcing it to be automatically detected and transferred to another Freight and Storage, Depot. It seems we now know where your container is Mr Taylor."

"Malaga!" said Ellie "You're having a laugh aren't you?"

"I'm really sorry miss but accidents do happen. I don't know what else I can say," said Lucy as she handed one of the Documents to Nathan.

"This is the address in Malaga where the container has been shipped, it should be there waiting for you."

"Lucy," said Nathan, "Do me a favour. If anyone else turns up looking for this container, could you tell them there is no container to collect?"

"Erm, Yes of course," said Lucy. "It's the least I can do for you."

Nathan and Ellie left the storage unit and headed back towards the car.

"What now?" asked Ellie as she took hold of Nathan's hand.

"How are you fixed for going to Malaga?" asked Nathan.

Ellie just smiled at him.

They spent the next hour driving the 45 miles round the M25/M23 to Gatwick airport then twenty minutes driving around the airport car park looking for a space. "Over there," said Ellie as she pointed across. They parked the car up quickly before anyone else jumped in the parking spot and removed their suitcases they had previously packed.

"Which terminal do we need?" Asked Ellie as she picked up her suitcase and chucked her overnight bag over her shoulder.

"We need the North Terminal," said Nathan has they started walking over to the main building.

A few minutes later they arrived at the British Airways ticket desk where Nathan purchased and paid for two return flights to Malaga.

"I would have thought you'd get free travel," said Ellie.

"I wish," said Nathan as he tucked his credit card away and handed her a ticket.

They made their way over to the *Check In* desk and then on to the Departure Lounge The next flight wasn't due out for two hours so they had a walk through the duty frees and on to a café for a strong coffee.

"I think I'm going to phone Ben," said Nathan.

Ellie shot him a glance as if to say *what!* "Do you think that's such a good idea?" asked Ellie taking a sip from her double Cappuccino.

"I want to hear what he as to say for himself and admit to being involved." Nathan did no more than pick up his mobile and rang Ben.

"Hi Nathan, I was going to call you. How's David?"

"David's just fine Ben in fact he regained consciousness yesterday and I had quite a conversation with him this morning," said Nathan.

"Erm, oh rite, Erm what did he say?"

"I think you know what he said Ben. You've been following us since the meeting in London haven't you?" asked Nathan in a stern voice.

"Nathan, listen, there's more to this than meets the eye. You really don't want to medal around in affairs that you don't understand."

"Oh I understand alright you little prick, you burnt Ellie's house down and attached a device under my car and you've been following us everywhere. What gives Ben?"

Nathan was getting upset and annoyed when Ben told him he had nothing to do with Ellie's house or the incident at the surgery.

"Nathan, this is not my doing. I'm in the same predicament as you," said Ben in a weary voice.

"What do you mean?" asked Nathan sounding interested.

"I was approached some months ago to transport a secret container to Denver and on to America. However the good David Benson found out about the container onboard flight 1872. He rang me to tell me there was an unidentified container onboard. I was caught off guard and demanded the container stay on board to which I thought had happened. If it did not reach its destination then they would blow up further planes and kill my family. I thought that when the plane crashed that you or David had taken the container and hidden it. I need to find that container Nathan, please you have to believe me."

By this time Nathan had moved to a quiet corner of the Café and had placed the phone on hands free speaker phone so Ellie too could listen in.

"Why the hell should I trust you Ben, you tried to kill David and burnt down Ellie's house?"

"That was THEM; you have to believe me Nathan."

Nathan paused a moment to think. "What's your involvement with the World Health Terrorist Organisation?" asked Nathan.

"I'm not involved with them, that is THEM. It's them who are after the container like I told David. They have my family and have threatened to kill them. Please Nathan, if you know where it is you must help me, I don't want my family to die."

"Do you believe him Ellie?" asked Nathan.

"Yes I do, I can hear the desperation in his voice Nathan."

"What should I do though?" asked Nathan feeling all confused.

"Tell him when we find the container we'll tell him where it is if he makes them back off," said Ellie

"Ben, if we find the container then you have my word I'll tell you where it is, as long as you swear to tell them to back off," said Nathan.

"If they think you don't have the container but are looking for it, they will kill you. Do you hear me Nathan? They will kill you!" said Ben in a serious voice.

"Just tell me where it is Nathan and I will get it."

"Erm, we don't know where it is Ben."

"Flight British Airways 523 to Malaga now boarding at Gate 4, flight British Airways 523 to Malaga now boarding at Gate 4." repeated the voice on the tannoy.

Nathan quickly hung up the phone and turned it off not wanting Ben to know they were at the airport. "That's us Ellie, come on," said Nathan as the flight was announced again.

Nathan and Ellie boarded the plane and took their seats. Ellie was holding Nathan's hand really tight as the plane began to taxi down the runway.

"There's nothing to worry about Ellie," said Nathan as he turned to look at her and gave her a warm smile.

"You're kidding aren't you? I still have the bruise on my bum from the last plane crash I was in. Anyway how long is the flight for?"

"Well," said Nathan, "It's around 1050 miles to Spain depending on the airport. This 747 will cruise at about 565 mph, so I would say a little over two hours taking into account holding vectoring and taxiing to the stand, and I know you still have the bruise on your bum, I've seen it enough times." winked Nathan.

"You cheeky bugger," said Ellie as she playfully nudged him in the ribs.

They continued their flight in peace unaware of the dangers that lay ahead of them.

Jump Ship
~ Chapter Forty Six ~

"You don't have a choice," said Maggie as she slammed her fist down hard on the table, "tell me where the container is!"

Mason had been interrogated now for several days with only water to drink and no food. Maggie could see that he was starting to break but it was going to take a little more time, however she had other plans on her mind.

Walking behind him she could see the dried blood stains on the table where his head had hit the table several times, busting his nose and forehead. Maggie placed her hand on the back of his head again and said to him "Tell me what is in the container!" but Mason sat bolt upright and said nothing. Again Maggie smashed his face hard into the table sending splatters of blood everywhere.

Mason was tired, in pain and hungry. He didn't know how much more he could take. The shear pain in his head was obscuring his thoughts and clouding his vision, when he felt a hand behind his head smash his face into the table yet again.

Maggie removed the table and pulled her chair in front of him and sat down just inches from him. She took a cigarette out of her pocket and lit one. She signalled to one of the armed guards to unfasten Mason's handcuffs.

Maggie could see the look of relief on his face as he alternated rubbing his wrists. Offering him a cigarette she knew she now had a bargaining tool. Mason took the cigarette off her and lit it before he inhaled a huge lung full of smoke. Blowing the smoke out he looked up at her and said "I represent *The World Health Terrorist Organisation* and I'm following orders to find the container from flight LA 1872. It doesn't matter how much you torture me, I can't tell you what is inside it because I don't know. I'm simply under instruction to retrieve the container and deliver it to London."

Maggie thought about what he said for a few minutes while smoking her cigarette. She beckoned over to the armed guard for the handcuffs and placed them on the table by her side.

"How much are you being paid to retrieve the container?" Asked Maggie as she looked at the handcuffs and then back to Mason.

Sensing she was giving him a warning to speak up or be cuffed again Mason said, "£ 150 thousand up front and a further £150 thousand upon delivery."

"Who else knows about this?" asked Maggie as she lit another cigarette and handed Mason another one.

"There's me, Nolan, Ben Brooks and the Organisation Co-ordinators."

"Tell me a bit about Ben Brooks," said Maggie.

"Ben is a Manager at Lufthansa. He was recruited by our Organisation to ensure a safe passage for the container but he failed. He too has now been tasked with locating it."

"So, since the demise of Nolan, there is just you and Ben looking for the container?" "No," said Mason. "Back at the Surgery was the First Officer from flight LA 1872, I don't trust him, nor do I trust the Captain who was there too but I think he had died or something before you lot came bursting in."

"It seems you could be right. Intelligence tells me Nathan Taylor the First Officer and Ellie Fox a passenger where flagged leaving Gatwick, bound to Spain a few moments ago, although David Benson is very much alive having received a private heart transplant. What can you tell me about Nathan?"

Mason took another drag from his cigarette and blew the smoke out. "Only that he was the First Officer on flight LA 1872 with David Benson the Captain. It was Ben who led us to Nathan at the Surgery suggesting he might know where the container is."

Maggie thought for a while again while rubbing her chin. "You know the government could always do with good men like you," said Maggie.

"What you mean Jump Ship and work for you?"

"Yes that's exactly what I mean."

"What would be in it for me?" asked Mason.

"Well your life for one," said Maggie very sharp. "I would pay you £1 million if you successfully delivered me the contents of that container. I think you now get the picture how badly The British Government wants their container back," said Maggie rubbing her hands together.

"£1 Million you say? How do I know you will pay up and this isn't some sort of setup?" asked Mason.

"This is the MI5 you prick not some kindergarten *Mickey Mouse* outfit." Maggie then lit another cigarette.

"Okay," said Mason, "you think the container is in Spain don't you?"

"Yes I do and I think Nathan and his little friend are trying to find it!" said Maggie.

"Okay, I'm going to need an anonymous flight into Spain to the same airport and I'm going to need a few toys," said Mason.

"As I said, this is MI5 Mason, we specialise in toys," said Maggie with a very cheesy grin.

An hour or so later, after being briefed on MI5 procedures, Mason was issued with phone numbers and an *Access Code* before he was washed, dressed and on his way to Spain in a private jet courtesy of The British Government.

He spent the best part of the flight checking and cleaning his weapons, a Sig Sauer P229 pistol with several 9mm Luger rounds and a Silver Colt Mustang 380 backup ankle gun. He carefully checked the internal barrels cleaning and checking for pit marks.

The P229 was always his favourite weapon of choice which he learnt to love and cherish during his training days. He checked the sights on the 380 and happy that all was good, slipped it into his ankle holster and fastened the safety buckle. Checking the sights on the P229 he engaged the safety catch and returned it to its holster under his left arm.

Secrets Out
~ Chapter Forty Seven ~

Stepping down from the plane and onto the tarmac Ellie felt the warm breeze splash across her face. "Where is it we're going?" asked Ellie.

"Camino de Campanales, Mijas Costa," said Nathan in a Spanish accent. "It's near Fuengirola. We'll be there in about 30 minutes. According to the map it's only 15 miles away." "I didn't know you could speak Spanish" said Ellie. "I know a little bit from my stays over in Spain but only enough really to get me by."

"Come on," said Ellie as she took his hand and started to walk briskly. "We're going to hire a car."

Twenty minutes or so later Ellie was holding the keys to a Volkswagen Caddy, freshly hired from Dragon Van Hire at the airport. They had decided to hire a van as it would be more convenient to pick up the container

They found the van without any problem and set off from the airport and down the A-7 and into the town of Mijas. They found the building very easily using the vans GPS.

Britannica Southern Stores looked nothing like the Freight Storage at Heathrow airport. It was a much smaller unit made of corrugated white metal with a medium size roller shutter at the front of the building in the centre. Just to the right was a small office window where to the right of that was the office door.

Nathan and Ellie parked up in the small car park out front while Nathan locked the van using the remote key fob. They walked the small distance over to the office door and walked in.

Inside the office was very small and dusty with paperwork and folders in piles on top of filling cabinets. Sat at the desk to the left of the door was a thin looking middle aged man with grey hair.

"Hola puedo ayudar?" asked the gentleman.

"Do you speak English?" asked Nathan.

"Yes I do, my names Adrian Núñez can I help you?"

"Yes," said Nathan as he handed him the paperwork. "I'm here from Lufthansa to collect a container that was transferred from Freight Storage at Heathrow."

Adrian looked through the paperwork and said, "You'll need to fill out a NIE Certificate and I will need to see your Company ID and Passport Sir."

Nathan took the document and a pen from the table while Adrian disappeared through the doors to retrieve the container. "Frigging paperwork," said

Nathan. "Everything has to have frigging paperwork. I fly a multi million pound aeroplanes run by computers but still has to have the frigging paperwork before I can move it," said Nathan as he sat down and began to fill in the paperwork. Ellie just shook her head chuckling at him.

A few minutes later the paperwork was completed and Adrian returned with the container. It was about a metre wide by a foot high and looked like a wooden suitcase. The wood was dark in places and stained. There were several numbers printed on the top with an oversized Barcode at the side of the numbers.

Nathan handed over the completed NIE Certificate along with his Passport and Company ID Card. Adrian took a few minutes to examine the documents and paperwork before saying, "Yes that's fine." He then handed the Passport and ID Card back.

"Have a good day Sir," said Adrian as Nathan picked up the container and left.

"We need to go somewhere to open this," said Nathan placing the container in the back of the van.

"Why can't we open it here?" asked Ellie.

"No," said Nathan, "It's not safe."

Ellie climbed into the passenger seat and took a map out of the glove box while Nathan started the van and they drove out of the yard and back across to the A-7.

Fifteen minutes or so later Ellie said, "Turn left in here and pull up." Indicating left, Nathan pulled off road onto a small piece of wasteland that was obscured by trees.

"This is perfect," said Nathan checking his mirrors that no one had followed them.

They both got out of the van and slowly walked to the back. Looking at Ellie, Nathan slowly opened the doors. In front of them, laying there waiting to be opened at long last was the container.

Nathan sat just inside of the van and took hold of the tyre lever that was fastened to the side panel. He forcefully slid the tyre lever under one corner of the lid. Wiggling the lever up and down, he moved it all the way around the lid until it broke loose.

Checking no one was around, both Nathan and Ellie took a deep breath and then Nathan removed the lid to the container.

Second Watch

~ Chapter Forty Eight ~

Shiva had just received a phone call to inform him that the road works were completed at Canning Circus and the Temporary bus stop was no longer required.

Once he'd hung up the phone he shouted to Paul and Lenny who were outside the cabin having a smoke. Lenny popped his head round the cabin door having heard Shiva shout. "Yeah?" asked Lenny.

"Bring the bus around to the front," said Shiva, "We are going to Canning Circus." "No problem." replied Lenny.

A few minutes later, Lenny had parked the bus in front of the cabin just as Shiva got up and went outside. He took his cigarettes out of his pocket and lit one, then took a long soothing drag and blew the smoke out through his nose and up into the cool night air as he closed his eyes and cocked his head back.

Shiva was just climbing onto the bus when Paul shouted, "Shiva, wait!"

"What?" replied Shiva sounding annoyed.

"I need to nip to my house to feed Twinkle."

"Can't she wait till you go home?"

"No I've got to do it as soon as possible. She's not been fed all day."

Shiva frowned, sighed and took another drag on his cigarette. "Go and put Jake in the cabin and hurry up then."

"Thank you Shiva," said Paul. He quickly went and put Jake in the cabin and then ran back to the bus as the doors hissed and closed behind him.

Jamie and Dominic were just about to wrap up their shift and drive back to the station when Dominic saw lights flickering from the depot entrance.

"Mobile Two to Mobile One, receiving over?" asked Dominic.

"Go ahead," said Jamie.

"There are flickering lights at the entrance; it looks like someone may be coming out." Just then a red Midi-Bus appeared at the entrance.

Dominic got his binoculars out of the glove compartment and looked towards the entrance. "I'm going to follow and observe."

"Received" said Jamie. The Midi-Bus had pull out and was on its way down the road when Dominic started his engine then slowly and discretely began to follow.

They drove through Ilkeston, Trowell and then on towards Wollaton before reaching Nottingham. Approaching Canning Circus they pulled up a few feet from where the road works were. It would be a bit easier putting the bus stop back on the bus this time because there were two people to lift it into the bus.

Lenny stepped off the bus first followed by Paul who took a step back, slipped off the kerb and was flat out on the floor. Lenny bent down, with one hand still on the bus stop and burst out laughing. Shiva raised his eyebrows, rolled his eyes and shook his head at them. "Kids!" Shiver muttered under his breath.

Once they had got the bus stop on board and to the back of the bus, Shiva closed the doors as they hissed loudly.

Upon closing the doors Shiva noticed a pool of blood underneath the door.

"Okay which one of you idiots cleaned the bus out?" asked Shiva.

"Erm we both did Shiva," said Lenny, "Why?"

"There's dried blood under the doors you pair of pricks, from when we collected Jason."

"Oops, Sorry Shiva," said Lenny,

"Yeah sorry Shiva," said Paul, "We'll scrub it clean when we get back to the depot," Shiva started the bus and began to pull away.

"Ooo don't forget to go to my house on the way back Shiva," shouted Paul from the back of the bus.

"Yeah okay, whatever." mumbled Shiva.

Dominic started to follow them and soon realised that they were not on the same route back to the bus depot.

"Mobile Two, receiving over?" Jamie jumped up out of his seat. The crackle of the radio had made him jump.

"Go ahead Mobile Two."

"I have followed the Midi-Bus to Canning Circus; they have picked up a temporary bus sign and are on the move again. However, they are not on route back to the depot though, over."

"What is your current position? Over."

"I'm on the A610, Nuthall Road at Cinderhill, over."

"Keep me informed of your location, over," said Jamie.

Dominic continued to follow the bus all the way down the A610 towards Woodlinkin.

Paul lived at 53 Andrew Drive in Aldercar, just off the A610. When they reached Aldercar, they turned off the A610, down Upper Dunstead Road and took the second right into Andrews Drive.

When they arrived, all the lights were on in Paul's house. This was typical of Paul as he'd forgotten to turn them off before he left for work. "Don't be long," said Shiva.

His front garden was kept nice and neat with flowers down the edge of the path. He searched each and every pocket for his house keys. Then it dawned on him. He screwed his face up and said. "Oh shit, shit, shit, bugger and shit! I've left my keys in the bloody cabin." He walked back to the bus. "Shiva."

"What?"

"I've left my keys in the cabin back at the yard, have you got your tools to open me door for me?"

"Why?"

"I need to feed Twinkle like I said Shiva; she's been in all night with nothing not even a bean,"

Shiva shut his eyes and gave a small sigh and replied "Okay."

"Ooo thanks Shiva,"

Shiva got the bus tool kit from behind the driver's seat and headed down the path of Paul's house.

Dominic had parked up about 500 yards back up the road. He grabbed his binoculars and his radio. "Mobile Two to Control, are you receiving over?"

"Go ahead Mobile Two."

"I am at Aldercar on Andrew Drive. My suspects have got off the bus and all three are outside 53 Andrew Drive. It looks like they are attempting to gain entry to the house."

"Hold your position Mobile Two; I am dispatching an Armed Response Vehicle to the location."

"Received, I'm holding position on Andrew Drive Aldercar, over"

Shiva decided he would pick the lock on the front door. He had done this so many times that it took seconds to access Paul's house. Paul went in and picked up his cat Twinkle and gave her a fuss.

"Mobile Two to Control, they have entered the house."

"Hold your position Mobile Two the ARV's are on route, ETA 1 minute to your location."

Dominic continued to watch as heard sirens approaching from the distance. As they grew louder and louder, Dominic could see a tinge of blue lights lighting up the night air as they got brighter and bright. The sirens continued to get louder as Dominic turned round to see three Black Ranger Rovers shoot past like scolded cats one after another, so fast that his car shook. He was blinded by the blue lights as all three Ranger Rovers parked sideways on to Paul's house.

Shortly after a Silver BMW X5 shot past Dominic's car also shaking it from side to side. The sirens wailed loudly and the blue light rebounded off nearby houses now filling the night air.

Parking to the rear of the Range Rovers, a team of firearm officers alighted from the BMW. Stepping out of the BMW, Carson was holding a Taser gun and pointed directly at Shiva from between the windshield and the door frame.

"GET DOWN ON THE FLOOR," shouted Carson. Shiva just turned round and looked at him.

Shiva was just about to reach for his cigarettes when another Officer pulled out his COLT M1911 and pointed it at Shiva. "ON THE GROUND NOW!" Shouted several officers as they all suddenly drew their weapons.

Carson was very well built, and stood about six foot three inches, square and straight like a proper military man. He wore a navy baseball cap, with the letters ARV stitched in white, navy blue t-shirt with a bullet proof vest on top and black trousers with pockets everywhere.

"GET DOWN ON THE FLOOR!" repeated Carson. Dominic drove down and pulled up behind the bus and got out. A few seconds later three more Police cars turned up with blue lights that shone illuminating the street and sirens howling and echoing through the night.

If Shiva refused or gave any form of resistance, Carson would result in using the Taser to make him cooperate. A Taser or *Thomas A. Swift's Electric Rifle*, works in a unique way that actually disrupts the body's ability to communicate with its muscles, making you collapse. They are only usually dangerous if used on someone with a heart condition.

Dominic and the other officers went and cuffed Lenny and Paul while Carson cuffed Shiva.

Paul shouted "Hey, what are you doing? This is my house, get off me!" The officers ignored him, took a hold of him and shoved him into the back of the Police car. Paul wondered why he had been arrested in his own house. Shiva and Lenny had both been placed in separate cars.

Dominic thanked Carson for his assistance. Just as they were about to leave the scene and head to the Police Station, detective Neil Curtis turned up as Dominic got out his car to meet him.

"Which car is Shiva Lawman in?"

"Erm, He is in the Volvo V70 Sir." Neil went over to the Volvo V70 opened the back door and grabbed Shiva's arm. He dragged him out of the car and rammed him against the back of the car.

"You will not get away with it this time you bastard. You're going down years for this."

Shiva grinned and raised his eyebrows and said, "Yeah we'll see about that."

Neil dragged him across the road to his car, opened the door and threw him in the back.

"I want this bus towing back to the station for forensics!" Shout Neil.

Making their way to the Police Station, Shiva could see Neil grinning through the rear view mirror. It was as though he had won an ongoing battle, but Shiva knew that he was an exceptionally clean and methodical worker. They couldn't possibly have anything on him. It would be proven that he was entering Paul's house. So he had not committed a crime and had nothing to worry about, but then he remembered the blood under the door.

When they arrived at the Police Station, they were all placed in separate interviewing rooms so they could not confer with each other.

Neil went to interview Paul while Claire went to interview Lenny. They both gave exactly the same story.

Paul's story, "We drove to Canning Circus to pick up a temporary bus stop, which was placed due to road works. We then drove on all the way down the A610 to Aldercar where we turned off. We drove along Upper Dunstead Road and went down Andrew drive where I live. I forgot my keys; I left them back at the bus depot in the cabin, on the table. I walked back to the bus and asked Shiva if he had the bus tool kit to open my door. He got it out and unlocked my door for me."

"Is that everything?"

"Yes that's all that happened. Here is my driving license. It has my picture and address on it."

Having both been interviewed, Lenny and Paul were released.

About ten minutes later, Lenny came out of the Police Station.

"I wonder where Shiva is?" asked Lenny.

Both Neil and Claire went to speak to Shiva.

"What were you doing at 53 Andrew Drive in the early hours of this morning?"

Shiva began to speak, "We had a phone call from the road works company to inform us that the road works were complete and that they no longer needed the bus stop. Paul had forgotten to feed his cat, so afterwards we drove to his house, he got off and realised like the twat he is, that he had left his keys on the table back at the cabin. He asked me if I had the tools to open doors."

"Why would you have tools to open doors?" asked Claire.

"If you let me finish. There is a small tool kit kept behind the driver's seat. Anyway, I got off the bus and opened the door for him. He was just about to feed his cat when you lot arrested us."

"Quite a while ago, you were charged with killing about twelve people but due to a lack of, or misplaced evidence you were released. We now have witnesses and signed statements that have seen your bus in the same location that several people have been murdered or gone missing."

"And your point is?" asked Shiva.

"I'm going to prove that you were driving that bus and you murdered those people," said Neil in a harsh voice.

"You have nothing on me."

"Well due to extenuating circumstances I am charging you with murder."

Shiva just shook his head and laughed at Neil.

"What's so funny?" asked Neil.

"You have nothing on me and you're just clutching at straws. If you had any evidence of any wrong doing, you would have arrested me before now. You have obviously been watching me for some time and you haven't any evidence, then when you saw me at Paul's house you just jumped to the wrong conclusion. As I said, you would have arrested me some time ago."

"We'll see," said Neil, although he knew Shiva was right that the evidence he had, was circumstantial. Neil started to wonder if indeed he had the right person in custody but then dismissed the thought. Meanwhile, Shiva was wondering how he would explain the blood in the bus.

The Truth Within
~ Chapter Forty Nine ~

"What is it?" asked Ellie all excited.

"I don't know, I've not seen anything like it before," said Nathan looking shocked.

He sat down on the edge of the boot and tried to gather his thoughts. He was holding a small vial of fluorescing orange liquid. Holding it up to the sky the liquid sparkled and glistened.

"There must be over a hundred of them," said Ellie peering into the container. "Hang on there's a load of documents underneath them."

Ellie pulled out several greyish folders and past one to Nathan before opening one herself.

They both sat on the edge of the boot of the van reading the documents. The documents were cream coloured paper with *TOP SECRET* printed in bright red lettering across the top. It had the official *House of Lords* Logo in the bottom right hand corner. "Frigging Hell," said Nathan, "These Vials are

Hydratetralynx CC60. According to these documents, Hydratetralynx CC60 can cure all known cancers and repair the damaged caused within sixty minutes!"

"You're kidding me?" asked Ellie.

"Nope it's right here," said Nathan showing her the document.

"What's Bromate?" asked Ellie looking puzzled.

"I've no idea," said Nathan, "Let's have a look."

Ellie passed the documents to Nathan as he began to read them. A few minutes passed when Nathan looked up at Ellie like he'd seen a ghost.

"What? What is it?" asked Ellie frantic. "What is it?"

Nathan cleared his throat. "Water, it's in water," said Nathan in a slow shocked croaky voice.

"What is?" asked Ellie getting agitated.

"When water is disinfected it leaves behind a chemical compound called Bromate. The Bromate is then supposed to be removed by other means. This document proves that the Bromate is being left in the water."

"So what's bad about that then?" asked Ellie looking confused.

"Bromate causes cancer, and this proves cancer is Man Made and that The British Government is killing British people."

What Next?
~ Chapter Fifty ~

Mason sat in his Mazel Lancia with its crunchy black leather interior and soft top roof, as he watched Nathan and Ellie having removed the container lid. He would have to make a move soon to get his hands on it, but being a professional he wouldn't make any irrational decisions or just jump in.

Peering through his binoculars, he could see Nathan reading a piece of paper and Ellie holding what looked like to be a large orange test tube. Mason still had no idea what was in the container nor did he care, but he did know how much it was worth to him, a cool £1,000,000.

He decided to continue to watch and observe what they were doing and what they would do next before he planned his next move.

Broadcast
~ Chapter Fifty One ~

"So what do we do now?" asked Ellie.

"We need to tell someone," said Nathan panicking slightly.

"Are you sure this is right and not some sort wind up?"

"As I see it," said Nathan as he put the papers down, "This would be the government's way of controlling the population. It makes sense really that that is what they have been doing. Imagine how many babies are born in the UK each day and how many people come to live in this country each day. The UK population is around 63 million people, if just 1% were to give birth each week along with 1000 new people entering the country each week and say 100 illegally entering the country, in two years the population would have doubled."

Ellie thought about what Nathan was saying for a moment and said "Well when you put it that way it does suggest that the population growth is being controlled. I've never really thought about it to be honest. It must mean that a lot of people die each day. It's sad really but it's not right. You're right, we need to tell someone, we need to tell everyone."

"Vernon!" snapped Nathan, "Vernon could publish these on the internet and tell everyone."

"Yes, yes he could," said Ellie enthusiastically. "I think we should take this container back to the storage depot and have them mail it out to Vernon, what do you think?" asked Ellie. "Yes that's a good idea. We would never get through customs with it, so that is definitely a good idea. I think we should put the documents and vials in your suitcase Ellie, that way it won't look suspicious if someone starts nosing around," said Nathan.

They emptied Ellie's clothes into Nathan's suitcase then carefully transferred the documents and vials into Ellie's suitcase.

"What do we do with the container?" asked Ellie.

"I've got an idea. We could store the container back at Britannica so that it confuses people if they come looking for it," said Nathan as they both shut the van doors together and got back in the van.

"I like it," said Ellie.

They made it back to Britannica Storage within minutes and took the container back inside along with Ellie's pink and flowered suitcase. After giving Adrian Vernon's address and paying him, Nathan and Ellie set back off to the airport.

Tricked
~ Chapter Fifty Two ~

Seeing Nathan and Ellie come back out of Britannica Storage without the container, Mason knew that they would either be storing it for safe keeping or sending it back England.

"The two people, the man and women that came in with the wooden container. Where is it?" asked Mason.

"Erm I'm sorry Sir but that is confidential," said Adrian shuffling some paperwork together and sitting back down.

"I don't think you heard me right," said Mason, "I want that container and I want it now." Mason pulled out his gun and pointed it at Adrian.

"Okay, Okay I'll get you the container." Adrian stood up and walked into the back of the storage room followed by Mason. He retrieved the container from a rack of other containers and boxes and handed it to Mason.

Mason refused it and told him to take it out front. Placing the container on the desk Adrian turned round to see Mason pointing the gun straight at his head.

The room lit up like a strike of lightening as Mason pulled the trigger. A small trickle of blood ran down his forehead and onto his nose as the back of his head exploded behind him leaving a crimson trail of splatted blood and bone up the wall and across part of the ceiling.

Adrian's eyes were still wide open and staring at Mason as he slumped to the floor in a heap. Blood was still gushing from his head and forming into a pool as Mason holstered his gun, picked up the container and left.

Mason now had the container in the back of his car and was considering what he would do with all the money. He was no longer interested in Ellie or Nathan as he now had what he wanted. *I've always fancied a yacht,* he thought to himself as he headed back to the airport to the private jet that was on standby waiting for him.

He parked the car and handed the keys to a steward whom had taken the container and placed it on board the jet. The steward noticed some blood on the side of the container but knew better than to say anything. He had been doing his job for some years working as a steward and had seen and heard some scary and sometimes weird things.

The Gulfstream IV Jet taxied to the runway, and after clearance accelerated full speed down the runway and took off into the evening sky. They had been airborne about 30 minutes when Mason decided he wanted to know what the fuss was about and what was in the container. He unclipped his seat belt and wandered down the back of the plane to where the container was stored. Removing the lid and peering inside Mason was horrified to see the container was empty. Instantly panic started to set in. Where were the contents, what was the contents. After the initial panic, Mason started to fill up with an overwhelming urge of anger and rage.

Guessing Nathan and Ellie would still be waiting at Malaga airport waiting to fly back to England, he knew now he could use the element of surprise. Nobody made a fool of Mason. Tonight Mason would teach Nathan and Ellie a lesson they would never forget.

Unlucky for Some
~ Chapter Fifty Three ~

In light of Shiva being charged with murder, he was now considered a flight risk, and therefore would be held on remand until the day of his trial.

Neil placed Shiva in handcuffs and took him outside to a waiting Prisoner Transport Van. Neil opened the back doors and the Officer, who was driving the van, came and unlocked the steel grey mesh door. It was obvious Neil despised Shiva has he rammed him inside the back of the van.

Shiva slipped and banged his head on the steel mesh partitioning as Neil chuckled to himself and said "What a twat." The metal door was locked and Neil slammed the back doors shut. Shiva managed to sit himself up, but he could feel a trickle of blood running down his forehead.

The route to the Prison was very bouncy and rough as they were heading to the Nottingham Prison on Perry Road. The Prison accommodation was set in different wings, D, E, F and G Wing. Shiva would be in *G Wing* which was for first night inductions and short stays. Shiva would be only staying a short while unless he was convicted of murder by the court.

When they arrived, they emptied his pockets, took any jewellery, belts, shoe laces etc. and then placed them in a tray. He wouldn't be allowed these items back until he was released from Prison. Shiva believed he wouldn't be on remand long, but he couldn't help thinking about the pool of blood under the bus doors, even though it was only circumstantial.

He was placed in a small cell for the night while he waited for the news of his court hearing.

Paul was sat at home on the sofa stroking Twinkle who was lying on his knees, when he heard a knock at the door. He put Twinkle on the sofa next to him and went and answered the door. It was Lenny.

"Paul, I've been thinking about the pool of blood, we cleaned that bus from top to bottom, and when we left there was no blood at all on the floor."

"Calm down Lenny and come in, I've been thinking the same thing. How could we miss a pool of blood near the doors?"

"I'm beginning to wonder if I'm starting to go blind Paul." said Lenny.

"Don't be stupid," said Paul, "You're not that old yet."

They both started to chuckle.

"Was the bus on service yesterday afternoon?" asked Paul.

"I'm not sure, it might have been," replied Lenny.

"I think that we should go and enquire about it at the depot in the morning."

They sat talking for a while and just before Lenny left, they arranged to meet at the depot, in the morning, to see if the bus had been used during the day. If it had been used in the day, somebody could have fell and cut themselves on the steps.

Shiva was sat in his cell reading a newspaper when an Officer unlocked the observation hatch, which was about half way down the door, and placed a grey tray of food through the hatch. "Ooo lovely," said Shiva in a sarcastic voice. There was corned beef hash, as his main meal with apple pie and custard for pudding.

"Looks like something that a cat chucked up," he said as he looked down at the food. Not having a choice what he had, he made do and ate it.

The next morning Lenny and Paul met at the reception at the bus depot.

"Morning Paul," said a polite voice from behind the desk. "What can I do you for?" "Hi Cathy, How are you? I've just come to see if someone used bus 426 the Midi-Bus last night?"

Cathy checked on the computer for yesterday's logs to see who if anyone had taken the bus on service.

Cathy was 52 years old and about 5' 1" tall. She had blonde curly frizzy hair and always had it up in a pony tail on the top of her head. She was very wrinkly and had huge black bags under her eyes from all the late nights on duty.

A few minutes later she replied, "Yes the bus was used yesterday afternoon for two hours then was brought back."

"Did anybody injure themselves on the bus?" asked Paul.

"No not that I am aware of but I'll just go and ask the driver to make sure."

"Thanks." said Paul.

A moment or two later, Cathy returned, "The driver has said that there were no injuries while he had the bus."

"Right, Erm okay" said Paul.

"Out of curiosity why did you ask about any injuries?" asked Cathy.

"Well, there was a small pool of blood near the door, yet the bus was cleaned the day before. We wouldn't have missed it."

"Ah that's strange," said Cathy, "If you need any more information or anything, you know where I am, don't be a stranger."

"I won't and thanks again Cathy."

Paul climbed in his car as Lenny joined him. "So even though we aren't sure if the blood is Jason's or not, do you think that it is worth attempting to gain access to the bus and cleaning it?" asked Lenny.

"If I'm totally honest with you, I don't know what to do for the best. I wish we could talk to Shiva about it. He would know what to do."

"You never know Paul; he might be allowed a phone call. I bet he will call us if he does."

Shiva wasn't fussed about being in Prison as he had been inside before. There were TV's, Pool tables, Tennis courts and loads of other facilities to help rehabilitate prisoners. Shiva had requested an in cell TV for the duration of his time inside and they allowed it. He just sat there in a small room with his newspaper and TV, he wasn't bothered, but he was beginning to miss Jake. He loved taking him for walks and rides round in the car, he was the most loyal loving dog he had ever come across but knew Lenny would be looking after him.

The small cell that Shiva was in had very dim lighting with dull, painted grey walls. The door was black and there was also a window on the outer wall that was tinted and had bars to stop prisoners looking outside or to plan escapes or get any other ideas. The bed that was in there was just like a step really it was raised about four bricks high with a fairly hard mattress on the top but Shiva liked the idea of a hard mattress because he had a bad back and it helped to ease the pain. He was given a pillow and two fresh blankets which were changed daily.

Paul had decided that he was indeed going to break into the Police Compound. He wasn't sure how yet but was trying to come up with a plan. He had already involved Lenny. He will be waiting outside in the car just in case they had to get away a bit lively. He would have to keep an eye on the Police Station to see when Neil and Claire were off duty. Their best bet would be to break in, in the early hours of the morning when the place would be at it's quietest.

He had to work out how he would get in without being questioned if he was seen. The only plan so far that he could come up with was to get a plastic disposable all in one dust suit. He was also thinking of a dust mask and goggles so that he wouldn't disturb any of the circumstantial evidence too much. He would have to get a pair of plastic disposable shoe covers and gloves, so that he wouldn't leave any prints behind.

Paul didn't come across as a smart person but after all the years of working with Shiva, he too had picked up more knowledge on how to tidy up after himself and make sure that there would be no evidence which is why he didn't really believe it was Jason's blood.

One of the officers opened Shiva's hatch and took the dinner tray away. The Officer on duty informed Shiva that he could make a phone call. Shiva sat down and thought about it for a while. He knew that Paul and Lenny would want to hear from him to see what was happening but it would be too risky. All the incoming and outgoing phone calls that were made were recorded and monitored by the Prison Officers. If there was information about the crimes they had committed, the officers would inform the Police.

Shiva was starting to get bored with his newspaper and had requested to leave his cell and go and play a game of pool with some of the other inmates. The senior Officer had come round and unlocked his door. Because he was in for murder they didn't want to let him leave his cell, however, he had been well behaved so they decided to let him out for an hour. They didn't know what Shiva was capable of yet but they still let him roam around to stretch his legs and have his game of pool.

About 30 minutes later an Officer approached Shiva. "Oi," shouted the Officer. "I've got something for you."

"I have a name and it's not hard to remember. What do you have for me?"

"It's a letter that contains the date that you're going down my friend."

"I ain't your friend, never have been never will be," said Shiva as he snatched the letter off the Officer who then backed off, back to his colleagues in the office.

Shiva began to read the letter that was from the court. His hearing date was on Friday 13th of January. Friday 13th was unlucky for most people, but not for Shiva.

The phone rang as Shiva decided that he would telephone Paul.

"Hello?"

"Paul, its Shiva, this phone call is being recorded so be careful what you say."

"Okay" replied Paul.

"I'm ringing to tell you that my court hearing is tomorrow. Could you let Gunter, Nathan and Ellie know?"

"Yes of course I can Shiva. Have you got their numbers?"

"Yes, they are written down on the notepad in the cabin back at the depot."

"No problem Shiva."

"Before I go, how's Jake?" asked Shiva inquisitively.

"He's really happy. Lenny has taken him to his house so he can look after him properly. I didn't think that it would be a good idea that I had him because of Twinkle." "That's great, I'm glad he's okay. I have to go now but I'll see you soon," said Shiva. "You sure will," replied Paul, "Bye."

Deciding they would attempt to gain access to the Police Compound, Paul went on-line looking for a fake Police Identification Badge. He was surprised how cheap and easy they are to get hold of as he ordered one for both himself and Lenny.

The ID cards arrived the next day and Paul noticed that they had printed a long number across the bottom of the card and they had even printed the photos on the cards that he emailed to them making them look very genuine.

It was 2:30am when Paul and Lenny both but on a plastic disposable all in one dust suit, got all of their gear ready and headed to the Police Compound. When they arrived there were no cars in the Police car park, this was a good sign because there wouldn't be hardly anyone about to confront and ask awkward questions. Plus, now that they had their ID cards they would get even less awkward questions.

When they were planning on breaking into the Police Compound, they originally planned for Lenny to stay in the car but Paul changed his mind at the last minute and Lenny went inside with him.

They walked into the Police Station and went to the front desk. "How can I help you?" asked the woman at reception.

"Hi, we're from the Forensic Team, we're here to examine the bus that was seized from Andrew drive in Aldercar," said Paul in an official manner.

The woman at the reception didn't ask for any Identification because it was clipped to their chest pockets and they were dressed as a typical Scenes of Crimes Officer.

"Follow me and I'll direct you to the compound."

Both Paul and Lenny followed her to a flight of stairs.

"Right, if you go all the way to the bottom floor, until you can't go any further, go left through the first door, follow the corridor all the way to the end and the compound is through the last door on the right."

"Thank you," said Paul as the woman headed back up the stairs to the reception desk. Paul and Lenny went to the ground floor and followed her instructions as they found the bus easily.

Once they had entered the room, Lenny used his initiative and locked the door behind them. Paul opened the bus doors and the pool of blood emerged. In their bag of goodies, they had loads of kitchen roll to absorb the excess blood before pulling out a bottle marked 'Biolactosin'. Before opening the bottle, Paul put some heavy duty gardening gloves on over the top of his rubber gloves and they both put on goggles and dust masks because the smell was so potent. This would give them the best protection possible. The chemicals in Biolactosin can destroy the slightest trace of blood and is extremely harmful if comes into contact with skin. If Liquid Luminol was sprayed over where the blood stain was, there would be no traces left.

It took Paul and Lenny just under twenty minutes to clean the blood up and leave. Leaving the room, there was an Officer walking down the corridor.

The Officer nodded his head and smiled, as if to say *alright gentlemen?* Both Paul and Lenny nodded and smiled back. The Officer continued down the corridor, Paul turned round slightly to see which room the Officer was going into. He went to put his hand on the door handle of the room that led to the compound, but changed his mind and entered the room on the left. Paul closed his eyes and breathed a sigh of relief.

Paul and Lenny went up the stairs and through the fire exit onto the third level and out into the car park. They put all their gear in the back of the car, jumped in and drove back to Paul's house to get changed dispose of their dust suits.

The Unexpected
~ Chapter Fifty Four ~

Nathan and Ellie's return flight BA523 was due to land in ten minutes at Gatwick as Mason stood nearby watching their car. He checked his gun was loaded and the safety was on as he attached a silencer and then re-holstered it. The anger inside him was overwhelming as he waited in the shadows for them.

"I don't think I'll ever get used to flying again," said Ellie as they walked hand in hand through customs carrying their bags and Nathan's suitcase.

"I must say you have done really well though, this is the third time you have flown since the accident. I promise you that it will get easier," said Nathan as they began the short walk through the airport and across the car park.

It was beginning to get dark and cold outside as Nathan fiddled around in his pockets trying to find his car keys. "Need a hand?" asked Ellie in a naughty voice just as he pulled the keys out. Nathan smiled at her and moved over and gave her a peck on the cheek.

He pressed the key fob to disable the car alarm and opened the boot. They had both chucked their bags in the boot when from out of nowhere Ellie received a sharp blow to the back of the head knocking her out instantly and falling into the boot.

Mason slammed the boot shut with his left hand has he held his gun in his right hand pointing at Nathan.

"Get in," said Mason. Nathan climbed slowly into the driver's seat as Mason got in the rear seat and sat behind him. Under the cover of the falling darkness nobody had seen what had happened as Mason told Nathan to drive onwards.

"What do you want?" asked Nathan, but Mason didn't reply.

For about half an hour Mason directed Nathan across to the M25 in the ever growing amounts of traffic to several junctions up, they had been driving for about forty minutes when Mason instructed Nathan to pull off the M25 and on a country road. The night had fallen quickly as the lights from Nathan's car lit up the road into the distance. Nathan was becoming really nervous wondering where they were heading as they just kept driving past houses and fields.

Nathan was just about to ask Mason where they were going as he heard Ellie's screams as she'd woken and was banging on the boot lid. Ellie had no idea what was going on, only that the back of her head was throbbing like hell and it was pitch black inside the boot.

"LET ME OUT," screamed Ellie as Nathan was instructed to shut up and keep driving. They continued driving into the countryside to an out the way spot where Mason ordered Nathan out of the car.

"Get out," ordered Mason as Nathan stopped the car and turned off the engine. Nathan stepped out the car taking the car keys with him, but feared the worse.

Standing by the car, the nearby street lights shone an orange glow onto Mason's face as Nathan recognised him.

"You're from the Surgery aren't you?" asked Nathan but Mason didn't answer him. Mason motioned to the boot to let Ellie out as the screaming and banging was getting louder. Nathan inserted the keys and opened the boot. Ellie shot up straight away and hugged Nathan.

"What's going on?" asked Ellie as she saw Mason.

"I don't know. He's just bought us here. It's the same bloke from the Surgery if you remember?" asked Nathan.

"That's twice the bastards hit me," said Ellie climbing out of the boot with Nathan's help.

Ellie started to run over to slap Mason but Nathan stopped her just as Mason pulled out his gun.

"Where are the contents of the container from flight LA1872?" asked Mason.

"What you on about you twat? You frigging hit me!" Mason pointed his gun and shot Ellie. The gun only made a small metallic sound due to the silencer Mason had fitted as the bullet flew out and hit her in the shoulder. Nathan and Ellie were blinded by the flash as Ellie fell to the floor from the white hot pain of the bullet entering her flesh.

Mason had shot her in the same shoulder that she had dislocated in the crash making the pain intense and near unbearable.

"Where are the contents of the container from flight LA1872?" asked Mason again. "Don't tell him," screamed Ellie in pain.

Nathan was kneeling by her side pushing on the wound to stop the bleeding. Mason who was now standing about six metres away lifted his gun, pointed it at Ellie's head and pulled the trigger.

The Verdict
~ Chapter Fifty Five ~

Today Shiva was feeling a bit anxious being the date of his court Trial. The day before, Lenny and Paul had visited and bought him a new suit to wear. He now stood wearing a dark blue suit with a crisp white shirt and blue tie.

"Are you ready?" asked Hanna who was one of the Prison Officers, as she tapped on his door and opened it.

"Ready as I'll ever be," said Shiva as he straightened his tie.

Andrew, another Officer, followed Hanna into Shiva's cell and placed one half of a pair of handcuffs on Shiva and the other half on Hanna.

"Comfortable?" asked Andrew to the both of them as they both nodded. Andrew then escorted them to the waiting Prisoner Transportation Van outside in the Prison car park.

Shiva never spoke during the trip to the Courthouse but stayed silent, so silent that you could hear a pin drop. His mind was all over the place thinking, *what did Paul and Lenny mean when they said everything had been taken care of. Did this mean they had somehow disposed of the blood evidence or removed all traces of blood from the bus? How could they of done this?*

He knew he had trained them well in many aspects of their secret goings on but could they have really pulled this off? Shiva was beginning to believe that's what they had meant which meant the only evidence against him was circumstantial witness statements. Shiva started to grin raising the corners of his mouth to reveal his smoke stained teeth.

They arrived at the Courthouse some twenty minutes later and drove past the front of the building to gain access to the rear car park. There must have been around thirty people out front taking photos of the van and filming as they slowly drove past.

There had been quite a few mixed opinions in the press with most of the reporters now outside the Courthouse. A few more onlookers had gathered out of interest and were now making their way to the public gallery.

Once through the main gates, Shiva was escorted down to the holding cells below the Court Room where the handcuffs were removed. Shiva rubbed his left wrist with his hand where the cuff had been as Hanna said, "You'll have to wait here a moment until the Judge calls you." Shiva just looked at her and smiled. He was convinced now that he had nothing to worry about and *business would resume as normal after this minor interference had been cleared up*, he thought.

The cell gate was slid closed and Shiva went and sat down. The cell was very narrow and dimly lit with a fixed bench down one side and a silver stainless steel toilet at the far end. The walls were painted in a calming light green, but the cell gate was painted cream and was starting to peel and blister.

Shiva was sat on the bench leaning forward with his elbows on his knees and his hands cupped together as he listened to the people arrive and take their seats on the floor above him.

A moment or two later, a smallish women appeared from down the corridor dressed in a black robe and cream coloured legal wig.

"Mr Lawman? I'm Louisa Murdock; I'll be representing you as your defence. Well if you don't have any questions then we are ready for you." Shiva stood up from the bench and followed Louisa up the steps to the dock.

"Take a seat," said Louisa as Shiva was then joined by two escorting officers. She then went and took her seat in front of the Judges bench.

The Court Room looked old fashioned with everything made out of dark wood. The walls were made of dark wooden panels and decorated with pictures of Judges past and present and several images of the Queen. The room had a warm feel to it but appeared very dusty as several beams of light shone through the high stained glass windows and fell upon the desks and benches below.

"All Rise" said the Court Usher.

Everybody stood up as Judge Harry Langford entered the Court Room from a side door.

Upon the Judge being seated the Court Usher said, "All be seated." Everyone then took their seats and listened to the Judge.

"Mr Shiva Lawman, you are charged with three counts of murder. How do you plead?" asked Judge Langford.

"Not guilty your honour," said Shiva already looking bored.

The Judge motioned to the prosecution to proceed as Laurence Kennedy stood up and walked over to Shiva. Laurence was representing the Crown as the prosecution and was of middle age but looked much older as he stood wearing the same black cloak and cream legal wig.

Shiva chuckled to himself thinking he looked like some sort of wizard with a pot noodle on his head but after swearing on the bible, Shiva had begun to be questioned.

"Not guilty you say, mmm not guilty," Laurence repeated sarcastically while tapping his fingers on the table edge. "So Marcus Truman, Margaret Hanson and Jason Fletcher, let me guess. You've never heard of them have you?"

"Nope," said Shiva rolling his eyes.

"You're a night shift worker at Brenton Buses?" asked Laurence looking down at some paperwork.

"Yep."

"So you have access to a fleet of buses during your night shift?"

"Erm, no, not really. I only use one of the small buses."

"Indeed you do! In fact you drive a Solo Midi-Bus that was seen on the nights in question that Marcus, Margaret and Jason was either murdered or went missing. How do you explain this?"

"Coincidence," said Shiva opening his eyes wide and shaking his head side to side as he spoke.

"A not guilty plea and now a coincidence, very good. You were previously arrested on suspicion of murder but were found not guilty due to a lack of evidence?"

"Objection," shouted Louisa.

"Sustained," replied the Judge "The Jury will disregard the question."

"So your Red Solo Midi-Bus was spotted and heard on each night in question and a clear description was given but you state it wasn't you?"

"Correct, it wasn't me. That could have been anyone!" said Shiva

"Oh yes, a coincidence, we'll see about that. No more questions your honour," said Laurence as he sat down. He didn't want to play all his cards right now but just take it easy to start with.

Louisa stood up and walked over to Shiva, "Mr Lawman, can you tell the court what your night shift involves doing?"

"Erm, yes. I am responsible for the fleet of buses at night time and with deploying and fetching temporary bus stops. During the late evening to early hours I take the service bus drivers home and fetch drivers in, first thing in a morning."

"And do any of these drivers live in Lenton or Ilkeston?" asked Louisa

"Yes, there are one or two drivers that live over at Ilkeston and several live in Lenton as well, In fact, the drivers live all over the place, even out towards Matlock," said Shiva

"So you taking drivers home could be the reason your bus was spotted, and a description given of you?"

Shiva liked where she was going with the questions, proving that there could be doubt and that in deed he did have a legitimate reason for being out and about in the early hours and to why he was spotted and a description given of him.

Laurence and Louisa spent the next few hours examining and cross examining Shiva until Lenny and Paul were called to stand.

They both agreed that they were witness to taking drivers home with Shiva and that was his main job.

Karen Moss was next called to the stand to give evidence against Shiva but as Louisa pointed out she had a small child that had kept her awake for several nights plus it was dark. Therefore it could have been anyone that she had seen and her statement could not be relied upon.

Next to be called was Neil. He had been waiting for this moment a long time. He knew that Shiva was guilty but he had just learnt that the blood evidence on the bus had been tampered with and was now fuming. He knew that somehow Shiva had got to someone on the inside but he didn't know who or how. He would now have to use all his knowledge and influence as a Detective to prove Shiva was guilty but knew it would be a struggle; he really did hate Shiva Lawman.

"Mr Curtis, can you tell the court who you are, and what role you played in the capture and the subsequent arrest of Shiva Lawman?" asked Laurence.

"Yes, I'm Detective Chief Inspector Neil Curtis from the Organised Crime Unit based in Derbyshire. For several months I have been following an evidence trail left by a very sadistic killer. In the run up to the end of the year over forty people have gone missing or been murdered in similar circumstances linking the cases together. I have worked very closely with my team to collate statements and preserve evidence for over two years. In my twenty years as a detective I have never come across such a callus and brutal killer. I have submitted several witness statements, photographic and blood evidence from the last few crimes and several hundred witness statements, fingerprint and trace evidence from the last two years putting the same killer at each crime scene."

Pleased with Neil's statement, Laurence smiled. "No further questions your honour."

Louisa quickly stood up and walked over to the stand. She had a gut feeling that Neil wasn't telling the whole truth and nothing but the truth.

"How long have you been in the Police Force Mr Curtis?" asked Louisa

"Just over twenty years."

"So you're fully acquainted with Police Policy and Procedures?"

"I would say so yes," said Neil looking like he didn't understand the reason for the question.

"And you say you have . . ." she looked down at her notes, "Statements, Blood and Trace evidence and fingerprints?"

"Yes, yes we do. These were submitted to the prosecution."

"Mr Curtis, could you tell the court in your own words what led to the arrest of my client?"

"Yes, it was only in the last three cases that we managed to link all the cases together and started to see reports of a red Midi-Bus being sighted near or at the crime scenes. Together with my assistant DS Claire Sheppard we both visited the closest bus depot to see if there was a night shift and if anyone had access to the buses. The bus company co-operated very well giving access to personnel files of the night staff. This is where I discovered Shiva Lawman was working the night shift for the company."

"I don't see what relevance that has Mr Curtis," said Louisa

"Well as I said, I've been in the job for over twenty years both man and boy and I've seen some real hard cases. There is always a few that stick out. One of them was the case of Shiva Lawman."

"Objection, the defence is leading the witness!" snapped Laurence

"Overruled!" bellowed Judge Langford, "The witness may continue."

"Please continue," said Louisa.

"As I was saying, the case of Shiva Lawman stands out as he was accused of murdering eight people in Ingoldmells some years back but was later released due to an issue with the evidence. This set off bells ringing so a two night observation was set in place to watch the bus depot."

"What happened the first night?"

"Nothing of interest, just Shiva taking a temporary bus stop into Nottingham," said Neil

"Mmm nothing of interest, so what about the second night?" asked Louisa

"Well the second night was different. After fetching the bus stop back from Nottingham, he was then observed breaking into a house not too far from the bus depot."

"Was he alone?"

"No, there were two other people with him."

"And who were these two other people?" asked Louisa in a smart tone.

"Lenny Briggs and Paul Baker, two of the cleaners at the depot."

"What happened next?"

"Well the Officer observing them breaking into the house radioed in for backup. Because of the nature of the crimes of the suspect, a full Armed Response Unit was authorised and deployed to the address. Once in custody I then arrested Shiva Lawman on suspicion of the murders of Marcus Truman, Margaret Hanson and Jason Fletcher."

"Very good, so how has the evidence been collected for this particular case?"

"The same as all other cases. In line with strict protocols, procedures and guidelines."

"The evidence that has been submitted. You said there were fingerprints?" asked Louisa

"Yes."

"And do any of these fingerprints match my clients?"

"No they don't."

"And did any of the trace evidence point to my client?"

"No," said Neil, starting to feel uncomfortable.

"The blood evidence?"

"The blood was tested and the DNA profile matched that of Jason Fletcher. This would place Jason on the bus."

"And where are the photos of the blood that was collected?" asked Louisa sifting through a collection of photographs.

Neil didn't want to answer the question knowing where it would lead but decided he had no choice.

"There aren't any photos," said Neil reluctantly.

"What do you mean, there aren't any photos?" asked Louisa knowing that she had him.

Neil didn't say anything but just sat there thinking.

"Please answer the question Mr Curtis," said Judge Langford.

Neil sighed, "We have the sample of blood but, the blood evidence on the bus was accidentally cleaned off before any photos could be taken."

A few People in the Gallery and Jury could be heard whispering and shuffling around as some of them were taking notes.

"ORDER, ORDER IN THE COURT," shouted Judge Langford.

The Court Room went quiet again as Louisa continued. "How can this happen when as you put it *evidence is collected in line with strict protocols, procedures and guidelines*?"

Laurence held his head in his hands as he saw Shiva smile at him with a crooked grin. He couldn't argue the case against him without any strong evidence and was beginning to feel the pressure.

"So there is no photo's of the blood evidence or fingerprints linking my client to the scene, in fact there is nothing is there MR CURTIS? If truth be told you hate Mr Lawman?"

"Objection!" said Laurence

"Sustained!" said Judge Langford, "Please stick to the facts Mrs Murdock."

"Yes your honour. Is there any evidence whatsoever that puts Shiva Lawman at the scene of any of the crimes?" asked Louisa.

"We have witness statements." said Neil.

"Yes, you have witness statements from a young mum, in the middle of the night don't you? Thank you your honour, no further questions."

Neither Louisa nor Laurence had any further questions so the Judge asked them to wrap up their case. This involved both of them giving a statement to the Jury in defence of Shiva and against him.

Laurence stood up first, and slowly walked over to the Jury as if to savour the moment. "Here before you, stands trial, an evil man accused of murdering three innocent people. Three normal people going about their daily lives. Three people with family, children and friends who have been murdered or are missing. There are several witnesses that have testified to seeing Shiva Lawman in his bus. Witness statements that clearly put him at the scene. See reason and find him guilty or maybe, just maybe one of you could be his next victim."

Laurence thanked the Jury and sat down just as Louisa stood up and also made her way over to the Jury and addressed them.

"I concur with my learned friend Mr Kennedy, that there were indeed witness testimonies to the fact that Mr Lawman was in the area the night Marcus, Margaret and Jason went missing but these testimonies cannot be relied upon. There have however, been no bodies, no fingerprints and no solid evidence to prove Mr Lawman was even at any of the address's in question and he was simply going about his nightly duties and tasks. I therefore urge you not to convict an innocent man but to find him not guilty."

It was now time for the Jury to decide Shiva Lawman's fate and future. Everybody stood as the Judge left and the Jury retired. Shiva was then led back downstairs to the Courthouse holding cells.

Given that his behaviour had not been disruptive, the guards decided to leave the handcuffs off.

Only an hour had passed when Shiva learnt that the Jury had already reached a verdict. He was immediately escorted back upstairs and into the dock just as the Jury was being seated.

"All rise" said the Court Usher as Judge Harry Langford entered the Court Room again and took his seat.

"Would the defendant please rise," said Judge Langford.

Shiva stood up as the Judge turned to face the Jury. "Foreman of the Jury, how do you find the defendant?"

Bill, who had been elected foreman, stood and faced the Judge.

"We the Jury find the defendant Shiva Lawman . . . Not guilty"

The Court Room erupted as several reporters dashed outside ready to take photos and people phoning the papers and their editors.

"Shiva Lawman, you have been acquitted and may leave the Court Room," said Judge Langford.

Leaving the Courthouse a free man, Shiva was joined by Lenny and Paul who were looking up at Shiva and smiling.

Lenny took Shiva's hand and gave him Jakes lead. Jake was running round in circles and wagging his tail as he was so please to see Shiva.

Walking down the steps, onto the street and past all the video cameras, Shiva ignored the requests for interviews and photo's as he overheard a reporter giving a report on the Court Room events.

"Just a few moments ago at this very Courthouse, Shiva Lawman was acquitted in the murder trial of Marcus Truman, Margaret Hanson and Jason Fletcher. A majority verdict of 11 to 1 saw Shiva Lawman walk free from the Courthouse. So the burning question that remains is who is the real killer and are we safe in our homes. Derek, back to you in the studio."

Shiva chuckled to himself as he knew the answer to that question. He also knew that he would have to lie low for a while before he struck up any other deals with Gunter, but the money was very tempting.

Shiva continued walking and chatting to Lenny and Paul as they made their way over to Paul's car without a care in the world having just stepped out of a Courthouse previously charged with murder.

"Come on let's go back to my place for a drink," said Shiva

"Ooo yes, thank you Shiva," said Lenny still smiling and looking really pleased.

Arriving at Shiva's house, he unlocked the door and sent Paul into the kitchen to make a drink as he hung his coat up.

This was the first time in many years that Lenny and Paul had visited Shiva's house so this was a really special treat for them.

They all sat in Shiva's front room chatting as Lenny noticed that his CD collection had grown considerably.

"Wow Shiva, how many CD's have you got now?" asked Lenny inquisitively.

"248," said Shiva as he returned the Smurf's CD to its case.

"Did you buy all of these?" asked Paul in an astonished voice.

"No, they were all gifts," said Shiva with an evil grin.

Revenge
~ Chapter Fifty Six ~

"Wait, wait, just wait," shouted Nathan standing up holding his hands out. Mason had shot Ellie in the shoulder first then fired his gun at her head. At the very last second Nathan had pulled her away saving her life. He was now pleading with Mason to see reason.

"They're in Nottingham," pleaded Nathan, "They're in Nottingham." He stood in front of Mason with blood all over his shirt. His trousers were dirty and slightly ripped where he was kneeling next to Ellie.

"They?" asked Mason.

"Yes, the documents and vials, they have been sent to Nottingham in Ellie's suitcase."

"What documents and vials," said Mason sounding a bit dumb.

Nathan was beginning to realise Mason had no idea what was in the original container. "Do you know what they are?" asked Nathan as Mason lowered his gun by his side. Mason didn't answer but just listened.

"The documents are Blue Prints for water disinfection. The chemical, Bromide is created when water is cleaned and disinfected. Another process is then used to remove the Bromide but the Blue Prints clearly show and explain that the Bromide is left in water."

Mason re-holstered his weapon. He had been in service working for various organisations and knew there was top level corruption in the government but this; this straight away told him that something wasn't right.

"What does Bromide do? Why is it so bad?" asked Mason now sounding very interested.

Nathan could see he was winning over Mason so took the opportunity to help Ellie. He helped Ellie to her feet and took off his tie to use as a sling for her.

"Put pressure on the wound, front and back," said Mason.

"Thank you," said Nathan shocked that he was trying to kill them one minute but now helping them. It sprung to his mind that Mason was really interested in the documents and vials but really didn't know what it was about. "The vials," said Nathan "are Hydratetralynx CC60."

"Hydratetralynx?" repeated Mason.

"Yes, Hydratetralynx. The Bromide is the cause of all cancers in humans and animals alike. The Bromide should be taken from the water but it is left in. So every time we drink water we are drinking Bromide and exposing ourselves to the risk of cancer. The Hydratetralynx CC60 is the Cure for Cancer and can reverse the damage caused by the cancer in less than 60 minutes."

Mason didn't know what to say or think but decided to tell Nathan what he was doing. He walked over to Ellie and took out a small first aid kit from the back of his belt. He pulled down the top of her blouse to reveal her shoulder. "Rip off some of your shirt," said Mason. Nathan quickly ripped his shirt and passed it to Mason whom began to clean up the wound. The bullet was a *Through and Through* and had only entered the flesh. Mason spent a moment cleaning the wound and applying a pressure bandage, dressings and plasters. "Don't worry, it's only a flesh wound, you'll be fine in a few days."

"Why are you helping us now?" asked Ellie. Having been shot and nearly killed had calmed Ellie right down to the point that she was shaking slightly.

"I worked for the World Health Terrorist Organisation and was tasked with transferring the container from England to America so the contents could be sold to the Americans. However when your friend David found out about Ben and the container everything started to go wrong. Ben followed you for several weeks and told us that you were visiting David at the surgery and that he would know where the container was. Nolan was killed and I was arrested by MI5 but some bitch at their headquarters offered me £1,000,000 to find and return the container back to The British Government."

"You sound a bit shocked," said Ellie as she opened the car door and sat half on the seat with her feet hanging out. Nathan took off his jacket and placed it around her shoulders.

"Thank you," said Ellie.

"Yes I am shocked if I was to tell you the truth. My wife and daughter both died of cancer last year. And now I'm tasked with returning the very thing to the government that killed them. My daughter was 22 when she died from Colorectal cancer. For the last six months of her life she suffered in extreme pain. My wife died a month later of Breast cancer. I endured a year of watching my wife and daughter suffer in extreme pain. I've never been the same since," said Mason. Mason had sat down on the floor and was drawing in the dirt with his finger. "I want revenge," said Mason standing up and dusting himself off.

"What do you want us to do?" asked Nathan being a bit cautious.

"If what you say was in the container is real then we need to come up with a plan," said Mason.

Mason had brushed himself down and had holstered his weapon as he was now pacing up and down.

"Whereabouts in Nottingham are the documents and vials?" asked Mason holding his chin with his right hand and his left arm tucked under his right armpit while pacing up and down.

"They were posted, hidden in my suitcase guaranteed same day delivery to my old college friend Vernon Cooper," said Ellie.

"Why did you pick him? What was he going to do?" asked Mason now stood in front of her.

Somehow Mason seemed different like smaller than he was before and very less intimidating. Still thinking of what had happened to his wife and daughter, Ellie was starting to feel a bit sorry for him.

"Vernon is an expert in computers. It was our plan for Vernon to hide the vials, broadcast the documents on the internet and send copies to the local and International news Offices. To be honest he should have received them by now and have begun working on a plan of attack. He really is the best at what he does," said Ellie.

Ellie could tell that Mason was in deep thought and wondered what he had in mind. "What are you thinking?" asked Ellie speaking to Mason.

"The British Intelligence MI5 is willing to pay £1,000,000 for those documents and vials. I think I know a way both parties could be made happy," said Mason rather cryptically.

Mason took a note of Vernon's address and arranged to meet Nathan and Ellie there at noon the following day.

Mason quickly parted company, while both Nathan and Ellie stood in shock.

"Come on let's get you to hospital and checked over," said Nathan.

After climbing back in to the car and making their way back to the main roads, Nathan followed signs for the local hospital.

Betrayed

~ Chapter Fifty Seven ~

"How did you manage to do this?" asked the nurse as she swabbed clean Ellie's arm and shoulder.

"Oh, Erm, we live on a farm and were shooting rats out in the barn," said Ellie thinking as quickly as she could.

The nurse gave her a look of disbelief but didn't say anything. Ellie didn't look under distress so the nurse decided not to pursue the matter any further.

"The shot went straight through the surface of the flesh, so no lasting damage has been done. I'm going to put you two dissolvable stitches in the entry and exit wound. They will dissolve in about two weeks. Just keep them clean and free of any infection and try not to move your arm around too much either," said the nurse reassuringly.

Another Nurse bought over a stainless steel tray with a few instruments and a package on it and laid it out on the table at the side of Ellie. The nurse proceeded to open one of the packets and pulled out a thread with a tiny bent silver needle attached.

Using the tweezers and small forceps, the nurse carefully wove two stitches into the front of Ellie's shoulder. She then crossed her hands several times and twisted them to knot off the ends of the thread and then cut them close to the stitches.

After repeating the same procedure on the back of her shoulder the nurse applied several layers of surgical tape to each wound.

"Ibuprofen will help with the swelling and Paracetamol will help ease the pain," said the nurse. She then signed a discharge note and handed it to Ellie along with a small brown envelope.

"What's this for?" asked Ellie turning the envelope over in her hands.

"It's just a standard letter for your Doctor to place in your medical file so they know what happened and how you were treated."

Ellie thanked the nurse and her and Nathan left. With it being so late, they both decided to pull in at a local bed and breakfast until morning then make the trip up to Nottingham to see Vernon and meet Mason.

"Do you think we should phone Vernon and let him know about Mason?" asked Nathan as he sat on the bed and pulled his shoes off.

"No, I'd leave it to him to be honest. If we tell him about Mason it might scare him or disturb what he's doing," said Ellie

The following morning they woke at 8am, showered and set off for the trip to Nottingham. They had been driving for several hours talking about the documents and the vials and what Mason had in mind. When Ellie asked, "Can you pull in at the Services?"

"Yes, sure. I bet it's all that coffee you drank this morning," said Nathan

"I know but I was so tired, something kept me awake all night."

Nathan just smiled at her as he indicated to pull off the motorway and into the services.

While Ellie had gone to the bathroom, Nathan bought a couple of drinks, a morning newspaper and went and sat down outside. It was a beautiful morning with the sun shining and a warm breeze blowing. This was not your typical October morning but then again this would not be a typical day.

Ellie returned outside to join Nathan and picked up the newspaper.

"Maybe there's something in here about what Vernon is doing for us," said Ellie.

"Maybe, I didn't really notice," said Nathan yawning.

After the papers revealed nothing, they finished up their drinks and made it on to Vernon's house.

"Looks like he's got company," said Ellie walking down the front path.

The front door was ajar as Ellie poked her head round and shouted, "Hello."

There was no reply. "Hello, morning!" shouted Ellie as she pushed the door a bit further open.

"Go on in," said Nathan giving her a nudge, "Go on then, your faffing around now."

Ellie pushed the door wide open and stepped inside. She kept calling out to Vernon but there was no answer. Slowly creeping further inside in case Vernon was playing some game, she made her way down the hall followed by Nathan. "Hello, Vernon, it's Ellie and Nathan," she shouted, but there was no response. She carefully opened the living room door to find Vernon lying on the floor face down. Nathan ran up to him to check for a pulse but there wasn't one.

"Shit, gimme a hand," shouted Nathan, "We need to get him on his back."

Turning him over they discovered he had been lying in a pool of blood. He had been shot twice at close range by the looks of the powder burn marks on his forehead. There was one clean shot to the forehead and one to the heart. Nathan tried to calm Ellie as she was trembling with fear.

"This is Mason's doing," sobbed Ellie.

Nathan stood up from Vernon's side and wandered around the house. Ellie sat on the chair looking at Vernon's body trying to figure out what might have happened.

"We should never have trusted Mason," said Ellie.

"Yes your right, it looks like the documents and vials have gone too. Your suitcase is in the kitchen but there are no signs of them," said Nathan as he walked back into the living room.

"Looks like someone has trashed the computers as well," said Nathan walking over to them.

The computers had been pulled out from under the desk and were now sat on top of it instead. The sides had been removed and some of the internal components were missing including the hard drives and memory modules.

"It looks like Mason wanted to cover his tracks and remove what Vernon had been doing. These computers are in a right mess," said Nathan as he was fiddling with the wires that were sticking out from the side of the computer.

"So you agree with me this is Mason's doing?" asked Ellie, "He must have been planning this last night, and this is what he meant by *he had an idea.*"

"What we going to do with Vernon?" asked Nathan, "I mean the Police are going to be all over this wanting to know what we're doing here and how we know Vernon. There could be a lot of awkward questions that I think neither of us need right now."

"So what do you suggest?" asked Ellie rubbing her nose with a tissue, "we just leave him there on the floor in a pool of blood? He's dead because of us; we got him into this mess. Without us interfering in his life he would still be alive. If only I could have thought of someone else."

"But if it wasn't him it would have been someone else just the same. There's nothing we could have done. We did know when we started out, that some people would get hurt," said Nathan as he comforted her.

"I just feel so sorry for him," said Ellie, "we should let Gunter and Shiva know straight away. I think we should leave now and call the Police from a phone box anonymously."

"Yes, I agree, that's a good idea," said Nathan rubbing her shoulders.

A moment or two had past when they heard a noise near the front door. Nathan put his finger to his lips as if to say *shush* as he walked over to the living room door.

Just then Mason came strolling in. "The door was open," said Mason

"This is your doing isn't it?" asked Ellie pointing towards Vernon's body.

"I don't think so, I've just arrived. So what have you pair been up to?" asked Mason smiling.

"So if it wasn't you then who was it?" asked Nathan in disbelief, "and what do we do now?"

After thinking for a moment Mason said, "First things first is, calm yourselves down. Secondly do you have a company phone Nathan?"

"Erm, yes, yes I do," said Nathan reaching into his pocket for it. "Why do you ask?"

Mason said nothing as he took the phone off Nathan, removed the battery and dropped the phone to the floor. He then stamped on the phone sending bits of plastic up into the air. Nathan just looked at Ellie not knowing what to think or say.

Mason opened the left hand side of his jacket to reveal his gun to both Nathan and Ellie as a subtle warning.

"If you ever repeat what I'm about to tell you, you'll wish you never had," said Mason in a low voice as he then picked up the pieces of phone and handed them to Nathan.

"Every single mobile phone that has been manufactured as been built with two added *features* shall we say, that the end user is unaware of. Embedded into the circuitry is a sophisticated listening device with a GPS tracker. The government can activate the tracker via GCHQ and track you to within an inch anywhere on the planet. The listening device is activated by dialling the user's phone number prefixed with a secret ten digit code. The user's phone doesn't ring but activates into a super listening mode that can hear every conversation in a room or building. Ben as been monitoring you and following you ever since he gave you this phone. He also is not working alone now either but I'm unable to find out who he's working with."

Nathan just stood with his mouth wide open. Ellie however not surprised to hear this said, "Close your mouth Nathan, we're not catching flies." Nathan as if on cue snapped his mouth closed.

"So every conversation me and Ellie's had, Ben as been able to listen too?" asked Nathan in pure astonishment.

"Yep," said Mason.

"But why put a tracker on the car if he could track the phone?" asked Ellie

"That's a good question," said Mason, "GCHQ or The Government Communications Headquarters is the British *Eyes* and *Ears* of the electronic age, they can monitor every phone conversation to every single email sent right through to every broadcast made, however they do have to operate within the law. It would be very difficult to activate the tracker without MI5 intervention. So he had to track the car separately."

᾿ "Well that will make me think twice about where I leave my phone in future," said Ellie, "but I just can't believe that someone with this code can

361

listen in through anyone's telephone. I mean how is this possible and why would the government allow such a thing?"

"And a few days ago Ellie, you would have said the government is doing their level best to help people and also doing their bit for charities like Erm, let's see, cancer Research," said Mason trying to make a point.

"Yes I suppose your right," said Ellie in a lowered tone, but really she was thinking *sarcastic twat.*

Mason followed his nose into the kitchen and returned a few minutes later with several bottles of kitchen cleaner, oven cleaner, alcohol and bucket.

"What you doing with them?" asked Ellie looking inquisitively while wiping a tear from her eye.

"We need to get rid of all the evidence," said Mason abruptly.

He disappeared out to his car and came back a moment later with a small bottle of brake fluid and a bottle of weed killer he found near the front door. He carefully tipped the fluid along with the kitchen and oven cleaner, alcohol and some of the weed killer in to the bucket. After a second or two of mixing the liquids, vapours started to pour out of the bucket. The reaction of mixing the chemicals would result in an acid like formulation. Mason walked over to Vernon's body and carefully poured some of the contents over him and some over the computers with the rest poured over Ellie's suitcase. The liquid started to fizz and gradually burn its way through the computers, suitcase and started to burn and fizz away at Vernon's face.

Mason dropped the bucket to the floor and walked into the kitchen followed by Nathan and Ellie.

"What are you doing now?" asked Nathan.

"Cleaning up, my friend. In about ten minutes you don't want to be here," explained Mason.

"Why what you going to do?" asked Nathan

"We need to get rid of any evidence of what Vernon was doing and remove any trace of you two being here."

"But I thought we was going to ring the Police and report it anonymously?" asked Ellie.

"Yes but we need to remove all links and implication to any of us. The Police will be all over this place and could link you to his murder. So we need to clean this place to remove any evidence."

Looking around, Mason found in the kitchen there was a small cupboard with a *Combination Water Heater Boiler* inside. He turned off the heating and hot water controls as he then took a multi tool from his belt, extracted a screwdriver bit and proceeded to remove the front cover and the safety glass exposing the flame igniter. He placed the front cover on the floor and then set the heating to come on in fifteen minutes time.

Nathan had started to get an idea of what Mason was up to as he walked over to the cooker. In turn Mason lit all four rings and turned them up full. He then bent down opened the oven and lit that too.

"Not bad," said Ellie, "A man who knows how to work an oven."

Mason just chuckled as he stood up but Nathan looked at her as if to say *behave yourself.*

"Come on, we don't have long," said Mason

"What's he done?" asked Ellie speaking to Nathan.

"You'll see, come on we need to get out of here now."

Mason finished off by closing all the windows as they left by the front door.

"Follow me," said Mason as he jumped into his car.

Following Mason, Nathan and Ellie drove away from Vernon's house as quickly as they could without drawing attention to themselves and down the street before driving about a mile away and parking up in a lay by.

Mason stepped out his car first followed by Nathan and Ellie climbing out of their car. Within a matter of minutes they all heard the explosion and saw flames rip up into the air as they all stood watching.

The flames, although from a distance seemed to dance around in the sky before they became engulfed in plumes of jet black smoke. Moments later the sound of the fire engines and other emergency services could be heard racing towards Vernon's house.

Rest in peace and thank you Vernon, Ellie said to herself as held Nathan's hand and lowered her head.

Guess Who's Calling?
~ Chapter Fifty Eight ~

Ben was on the outskirts of London travelling south down the M1 making his way to the *World Health Terrorist's Organisation's* secret headquarters when his phone rang.

"Hi, Ben speaking."

"Ben, I've been waiting for you to ring. What's the situation your end?"

"I have the documents and vials safely with me and I'm about two hours away from the office," said Ben.

Ben was originally approached to transfer the container, containing the documents and vials after they were stolen from The British Government, because of his long term ties in the terrorist underworld. He was well known in the underworld for his radical beliefs and anti government activities but this was just some simple task to him.

Ben and his accomplice had plotted for several weeks to bring down flight 1872 sending terrorist letters and demands till in the end finally bringing down the flight so the container could be retrieved from the wreckage to avoid customs and questions. There were many other ways the container could have been transported but Ben held a damaging grudge against the airline he worked for so this would have proved a reassuring pay back from him. It was only because he believed David Benson knew too much that he failed to allow the container onboard flight 1872 but that didn't matter for the moment, Ben now had the documents and vials and would soon be collecting his £300,000 reward the same as Mason would have if he had found them and delivered them first.

"That's good news, and the loose ends?"

"I just need to send an anonymous call to the Police. Nathan and Ellie will then be framed for the murder of Vernon," said Ben

"You didn't?"

"What, planted evidence in his house? I sure did," sniggered Ben

"Well done my friend."

"Believe me they deserve it, they are more stupid than you can imagine. I've had them running up and down the country doing my dirty work without them even knowing it and even had them retrieve the container from Spain. Now they will not only be charged with murder but also conspiring to bring down an entire airline," said Ben. "The funniest bit is though I told them my family had been taken hostage until I'd returned the container and they believed me."

"That reminds me; I sent the next letter repeating the demands. That will give them a bit of a stir and throw them off our scent."

"But how did you lead the Police to the *Terrorist Cell* in London? I mean the calls were traced?" asked Ben

"That's what the Police said, but the truth was they had a tip off. They didn't find anything on him to do with the plane crash or threats but they did find evidence relating to other incidences, but because of *National Security* the Police couldn't release the details of what he had done, so they framed him for the terrorist threats at the airport instead."

"But why him?" asked Ben

"He'd ripped off a large sum of money for a job he didn't complete so he had to be dealt with. The Police have pinned everything on him because they have nothing with regards to the crash and the threat letters. It's pathetic really. They haven't got a clue."

"Well we have everything in order now, I'm about an hour and a half away so should be with you soon," said Ben feeling pleased with himself.

"What about David Benson? Do you still think he knows?"

"To be honest I'm not sure but maybe we could send Mason back in to take care of him?" suggested Ben

"No, that wouldn't work, not after what happened last time."

Ben continued to travel down to London thinking about David and what he thought he might actually know. Ben had been at work in his office some time back and had accidentally left some paperwork on his table while he'd nipped out to get a drink. When he'd returned David was waiting for him in his office to discuss one of the routine flights and weather. Ben didn't say anything at the time but was sure David had looked through and read the paperwork. This would have given David a good insight into Ben's business and affairs.

"Leave it with me," said Ben, "I'll think of something but are we disposing of David or just a warning to shut him up?"

"I'll leave that up to you Ben; maybe you could have a word with Mason after all and see what he suggests?"

"Thinking about it, we need to keep things very much under wraps so I agree Mason is our man for the job, I'll have a word with him later," said Ben

Ben then hung up the phone and continued his drive down towards London still thinking about David. David was the final loose end to tie up but, he wasn't sure which way he wanted to go. On the one hand David was a friend and a colleague but on the other hand he might have enough knowledge to cause issues for the Organisation. While he thought about it he dialled 999 on a prepaid phone he'd bought from a petrol station on the way down, reported Vernon's dead body and then quickly hung up the phone and switched it off.

A few moments had passed when Ben decided to call Mason and ask for his advice.

"Mason, it's Ben."

"Hi Ben, where are you?" asked Mason

"I'm just going past Junction 13 on the M1 on my way to the office. I've retrieved the contents of the container Mason," said Ben

"Really? Well done, but hey listen Ben, I need to see you, the contents you have might be fakes," said Mason, making it up as he went along.

"Oh, okay, what do you mean fakes? What should I do" asked Ben sounding a bit stunned.

The way the Organisation structure was set out meant Mason had direct authority over Ben as Mason was employed there fulltime. Ben was tasked to retrieve and return the container after failing to ensure a safe passage for it to America. So now was a good time to make sure he had in his car what he should have.

"I'll meet up with you before you get to the office, pull in at Toddington Services and wait for me, I'll be with you within the hour," said Mason.

"Okay, thank you. I also need your advice and maybe expertise as well," said Ben

"No problem, we'll have a chat when I get to you," said Mason before they hung up.

Some time later Ben was indicating to pull off the M1 and merged left onto the services slip road. Slowing down, he came to a slight curve in the road bearing off to the left but continued straight on passing a line of parked cars on his left. Pausing for a minute at the pedestrian crossing to allow someone to cross, he turned left in front of the main building and left again and drove on until he found a parking space. He locked the car and began the short walk across the car park to the front entrance he had just passed.

Opening the doors a warm breeze blew down on him from above as he walked into the foyer. After rounding the corner he popped to the gents before following the smell of coffee over to Costa. Fancying something strong he ordered a *double shot of Ristretto* and went and sat over in the far corner facing the foyer entrance to wait for Mason.

Police Escort
~ Chapter Fifty Nine ~

"You're not going to believe this," said Mason, "but that was Ben on the phone, He has the documents and vials."

"So he was the one that killed Vernon?" asked Ellie angrily.

"It's starting to look that way," said Mason.

"So what is he going to do with them?" asked Nathan.

"He's on his way back to the office at the Organisations Headquarters, but I've managed to arrange to meet him down the motorway at Toddington Services near Junction 12. We only have about 60 minutes to get there and get the documents and vials back, we need to move fast," said Mason.

"Toddington? That's below Northampton and nearly a hundred miles away! How in god's name are we going to get to Toddington in 60 minutes," asked Nathan.

"Leave that to me," said Mason.

Mason took out his wallet and removed the card that MI5 had issued him with and rang the phone number on it.

"Access Code," said the voice on the other end of the phone.

"Alpha - Delta - Seven - Seven - Zero - Nine - Tango - Uniform," said Mason.

"Access confirmed, go ahead," said the Operator.

"The contents of the container have been confirmed as being located at Toddington Services at Junction 12 on the M1, I need an immediate Police escort," said Mason speaking as quickly as he could."

"We are tracking your current position as Nottingham, what's your exact location?"

"We're west bound on the A611 Hucknall Bypass."

The line went quiet for a few seconds as Mason could hear the Operator on the other end of the phone line typing away.

"Continue south to the location, the Police Units have been dispatched and you will be intercepted on route," said the Operator.

"All received. We need the units to break off before the services as a silent approach must be made," said Mason.

The Operator confirmed Masons request as they both hung up.

"Come on you two we have to shift, get in my car," said Mason jumping in to the driver's seat.

Nathan and Ellie were quick off the mark to follow as Nathan sat in the front and Ellie climbed in behind Mason as he quickly sped off.

He made his way back down the A611 and pass Top Valley before entering Bulwell and down towards Nuthall. Ignoring the red traffic lights he accelerated around the island and onto the short dual carriageway in no time as he entered the M1 slip road at Junction 26.

Mason was driving a dark grey Audi A6 coupé with sports leather interior, alloy wheels and a twin turbo charged engine. He had been loaned the car by MI5 as part of the *Toys Package,* as they were now, currently tracking the position of the car and transmitting the position live to the Police Interceptors.

Almost immediately after pulling onto the motorway, Mason noticed several blue flashing lights appearing in his review mirror. Two Police Motorcycles blistered past him with blue lights flashing and two tones whaling, as one of the riders motioned to him to follow. Mason dropped the car into third gear and pushed hard on the accelerator pedal as the car dipped down slightly at the back and energetically burst into life as the twin turbo's kicked in.

The speedometer was showing Mason accelerating to 140mph as more blue lights appeared from behind him. A Silver Mitsubishi Lancer Evolution passed him on the left hand side and pulled in front of him to guide the way.

Travelling now at over 150 mph Mason had two motorcycles way in front clearing the way with their ultra bright blue xenon lights and wailing sirens with two Police Interceptors now to the front of him and one just settling in behind him.

Ellie who was sat nervously in the back hanging on for dear life, checked her seat belt was tight as Nathan said, "Don't worry you'll be just fine, he knows what he is doing."

Ellie smiled a nervous smile as if to say *I know he does.*

Mason was fully focused on the road as Nathan turn to him and asked, "What's the plan when we get there?"

Mason adjusted his review mirror down slightly as he began to reveal his plan.

Recovery
~ Chapter Sixty ~

David was half sat up in bed and feeling much better as Gunter came walking over. Gunter spent a minute checking David's chart and then took his blood pressure as David was chatting away to Diana.

Over the past few weeks David and Diana had spent every hour talking and becoming even closer. Diana had to admit that she was feeling much better and enjoyed the long chats with David. Gunter too could see they were bonding and getting closer as he walked round the side of the bed to David.

"That's normal, 122 over 78; you're looking really good this morning. I don't know if it's the new heart or Diana." said Gunter smiling.

"I think it's a bit of both," said David also smiling.

"Give it a few more days and I think you'll both be well enough to go home but, David you will need looking after and need to take it easy," said Gunter.

David turned to look at Diana. It was obvious that David had feelings for Diana as he looked at her waiting, hoping for her to say what he was feeling. David had a feeling that Gunter had said that to push things along and help him out so to speak as Gunter gave him a wink.

"Don't worry Doctor, I will be looking after David from now on," said Diana as she took hold of David's hand, "If that's okay with you David," she said.

Yes, thank you, thought David as he turned to face her. "Does that mean you'll be coming to live with me then?" asked David.

"Well, if you will have me . . . yes," said Diana blushing slightly.

"I would love that," said David squeezing her hand.

The Plan
~ Chapter Sixty One ~

"The MI5 has offered me £1,000,000 for the contents of the container and that's what they are going to get," said Mason.

"I don't understand, why would you give it back to them knowing what they are doing with it, and how they are responsible for killing British people, and aren't you supposed to be giving them to the Organisation too?" asked Nathan sounding annoyed.

"Simple, MI5 get the documents and vials and we get £1, 000, 000," said Mason.

"We," said Nathan.

"Yes we. You help me get the documents and vials back and I will split the money three ways with you and Ellie. We will take two copies of the documents. MI5 will have the originals, the Organisation will have one copy and we sell the other copy to ALL the newspapers and TV stations and again split the money three ways. I will of course keep the £300,000 from the Organisation for my trouble," suggested Mason.

"Oh my god," said Ellie, "We could net thousands of pounds each and let the British public know what's happening at the same time, so the documents will be useless to the government. That's a genius idea don't you think Nathan?"

Nathan thought for a while, while watching the blue lights from the two interceptors in front light up the inside of the car. Nathan's heart was racing, thinking of the money they could make but was also trying to work out the implications."

"It's a bloody good idea, but the government is going to be extremely pissed with you when they find out you've double crossed them too, and so will the Organisation," said Nathan.

"You would think so but, if anything would happen to me it would look too obvious like a huge cover up. My guess is they will either keep quiet or try to deny what they have been doing. Either way it will stir them up yes but I'm pretty sure they won't be approaching me again, and as for the Organisation, they just want the plans and the instruction on how to re-create the Hydratetralynx CC60 formulae to sell to the Americans. 31% of the world as cancer with America being the highest bidder on the formulae. The amount of money to be made in releasing a cure could run into the billions. The Organisation is out to make money but in this case for all the right reasons."

Nathan and Ellie both agreed with Mason's idea hoping that it would work out but, Nathan wasn't sure how they would retrieve the documents and vials from Ben.

"What are we going to do when we get there, I mean how are we going to get them back," asked Nathan.

"For safety, Ben will have them stored out of sight in the boot of his car. All you have to do is, go in and take them back," said Mason laughing and trying to keep his eyes on the road.

"Very funny," said Nathan, "but how are we to get the boot open?"

"In the glove box, there's a large screwdriver," said Mason.

Nathan lent forward and opened the glove box. Sure enough, inside was a large red handled, flat bed screwdriver measuring about eight inches long.

"As you know, Ben drives a Silver Vauxhall Astra. On the dashboard to the right of the steering wheel is the boot release switch. Now listen carefully. Take the screwdriver to the driver's side window and stand as though you are about to unlock the door with a key. Jam the screwdriver hard between the driver's side glass and the rubber seal. Don't worry nothing will happen yet. Now check around that no one is around or near you. Next is the fun bit, slowly pull the top of the screwdriver back towards the back of the car and twist it hard at the same time," explained Mason.

"What will happen?" asked Ellie leaning forward from the back seat.

"You will hear a quiet *tshhh* sound and the glass will shatter. Quickly push the glass into the car with the palm of your hand. Reach inside with the screwdriver and press the boot release switch," said Mason.

"Are you sure it's that easy?" asked Nathan.

"Yes I'm sure, trust me. Once the boot pops open remove the documents and vials and place them in the boot of this car taking care to shut the boot of Ben's car with the palm of your hand," said Mason.

"What do we do then?" asked Nathan with a puzzled look on his face.

"Just get back in the car and wait for me," said Mason in a voice that said *that should have been obvious.*

"Oh right, okay, but what if something goes wrong?" asked Nathan.

"Just come back to the car and wait for me," said Mason.

Just as Mason had finished speaking the air went quiet and the blue pulsing lights stopped.

"Are we here already?" asked Ellie as the interceptors broke away to the sides and behind them.

"Yes so get ready, you're both clear on what you're doing?" asked Mason.

Both Nathan and Ellie said "Yes" as Nathan slipped the screwdriver into this pocket.

Mason glided the car over the next mile into the first lane and slowed down as he exited onto the services slip road.

He too continued straight on past the parked cars and turned left in front of the main building.

"There's Ben's car," said Mason pointing to it as they drove past.

Mason continued down into the opposite corner of the car park near the petrol station and parked up.

"Okay this is it," said Mason as they all stepped out the car.

Ellie stretched, yawned and rubbed her eyes as Mason left them and headed for the main building. Ellie took hold of Nathan's hand as they walked across the car park towards Ben's car.

Waiting until no one was around Nathan discreetly took the screwdriver out of his pocket and stood square to the driver's door. Checking again no one was watching he forced the screwdriver blade between the rubber seal and the glass, pulled back and twisted. Exactly as Mason described there was a low tshhh sound as the window shattered into tiny little shiny pieces reflecting the sun.

Nathan quickly pushed the glass inwards being careful to use the palm of his hand. With a big enough hole in the glass he poked the screwdriver in and pressed the boot release button as the boot clicked and slowly sprung open.

Clean Up
~ Chapter Sixty Two ~

Having just bought a coffee, Mason and Ben sat back down at the table. Mason was interested to hear what Ben had to say, what he had been up to and also what his plans were, although he despised him very much. In Mason's opinion, Ben was a jumped up little twat that thought he was a lot better than he actually was.

"He should be here any minute," said Ben.

"How long as he been working with you then, I mean he's not employed by the Organisation is he?" asked Mason.

"No he's not employed by them but he works for Lufthansa same as me. He's been working with me for the past year. He helped set up the letters and phone calls as well as helping me track down Nathan and Ellie." Just as Ben was taking a sip of his second Ristretto his guest walked through the main entrance into the foyer.

"Over here," called Ben as he waived his arm above his head.

"This is Mason and Mason I would like you to meet . . . Ron Shaw," said Ben shaking Ron's hand.

Mason stood up and shook Ron's hand before sitting down again. Ben went over to buy three coffees as Ron and Mason sat down to talk.

"Was it your idea to crash the plane?" asked Mason.

"Not really," said Ron, "that was Ben's idea to bring the plane down."

"So how did you both manage to crash a plane without causing suspicion or getting caught?" asked Mason.

"Well actually it wasn't supposed to be as bad as it was. All we had to do was, undo a fuel line in one of the engines. That would have been enough to have stopped the engine and force a landing but Ben took it one step further and pulled the locking pins on the starboard landing gear. The fuel line severely leaked inside the engine and instead of catching fire the whole engine exploded ripping the outer panels off. Instead of a forced landing, the landing gear failed causing the horrific crash," said Ron.

Mason saw Ben coming back and could feel his fingers twitching as he clinched his fist tight. He wanted to put a bullet in Ben's head right now because he hated him so much but he would wait, wait a little longer until the time was right. Ben could have picked a much easier way to transfer the containers but instead used his grudge against the airline and messed things up. Now Mason would clean up the mess, clean up Ben and because he knew so much, clean up Ron.

Just as Ben had sat down Mason turned to speak to him. "So why did you choose to bring down flight 1872 instead of just transferring the container a different way?"

"I've worked for Lufthansa for many years and in all those years I have only been promoted three times and only had five, yes five pay rises. It's bloody disgusting and then last year they announced that they were cutting over time right back to next to nothing," said Ben through gritted teeth.

Mason understood where he was coming from and felt his frustration but business was business. Ben had caused problems for the World Health Terrorist Organisation and now would be stopped.

"Excuse me, I just need to nip to the gents," said Ben.

"I think I'll go too," said Mason seizing the opportunity to get Ben alone.

Both of them walked across the corridor and round to the gents. The gent's door opened to reveal a second door as they both walked through to use the toilets.

Having finished, they both stood washing their hands when the last person in there disappeared out through the doors.

Mason didn't waste any time as he pulled his gun out from under his left arm, pointed it straight at Ben and pulled the trigger. With the silencer fitted there was only a small thwoosh sound as the bullet exited the gun and hit Ben in the chest.

Mason had decided in this case not to choose a head shot so as to minimize the risk of blood and blowing the back of Ben's head off all over the toilet wall.

Instantly Ben dropped to the floor dead as Mason then grabbed his legs and pulled him into a nearby cubicle as quickly as he could, but before he managed to get all the way in to the cubicle the main door opened.

Ben and Mason had been gone a while, so Ron had come over to see what they were up to thinking they might have been chatting away or something.

Standing at the door, Ron looked down at Ben at the blood oozing out of his chest then looked up at Mason. Mason looked back, as Ron turned round quickly and disappeared out of the door.

Mason pulled Ben into the cubicle, tucked his legs round the toilet, stepped over him and closed the door shut. He dashed through the double door system, out into the foyer and outside into the carpark. Spotting Nathan and Ellie looking over at him, he shouted, "Where did he go?"

"He jumped in his car and sped off like lightening," said Nathan who had recognised Ron straight away.

"That was Ron wasn't it?" asked Ellie.

"Yes, yes it was," said Mason as he came running over.

"That explains how he got to the hospital in Iceland so bloody quick. He was already there working with Ben waiting to pick up the containers," said Ellie fuming.

"Mason, there's a problem with the documents and vials," said Nathan in a panic.

"Ben is dead, we need to get out of here now, are they in the boot ready?" asked Mason.

"What do you mean Ben is dead," asked Ellie sounding shocked.

"What happened?" asked Nathan also shocked.

All three of them got back in Mason's car as he started to explain. "Ben was responsible for crashing flight 1872. He tampered with the fuel lines and the landing mechanism which caused the plane to crash. He could have transferred the container to America any other way but due to his own selfish reasons he killed all those people. I know I am no better than him but I was working under orders, he just did it out of spite. So when he went to the bathroom I went too and shot the bastard."

"So he's dead in the toilets?" asked Ellie.

"Yes, yes he his. What were you saying about the documents and vials," asked Mason as he started the car.

"They're not in Ben's boot or anywhere in his car. He didn't have them and didn't get them from Vernon. He picked up the Police National Computer printouts and Hacking records from the QMC database along with the requested lists. He must have thought that was what was in the container," explain Nathan.

Shit, thought Mason as he rubbed his hands up his face and over his head. He sat with his hands behind his neck and his head forward as he tried to think.

Mason had been thinking a few minutes when Ellie broke the silence, "So where do you think they are?"

"I truly have no idea," said Mason, "Vernon doesn't have them, neither does Ron. So that only left Ben and by the sounds of it, that idiot had no idea what he was actually looking for. There was only a very small select group of people that knew about the container so really there is no one else."

Mason put the car into gear and started the drive back up to Nottingham.

"Maybe someone went into Vernon's house and just stole them or something," suggested Ellie.

"Not sure that would work to be honest, Vernon would have to have known whoever it was before he let them in," said Mason.

"Yes I suppose so or maybe Ben told someone else . . . no, that wouldn't be it either. Ben was convinced he had the contents of the container and so must have Ron as he was coming over to meet Ben," said Ellie.

Both Nathan and Ellie chatted away trying to work out what had happened as Mason drove back up the M1. He tried to rack his brain but couldn't piece it together. Mason was just so convinced Ben had the documents and vials.

Sometime later they pulled up behind Nathan's car. Mason agreed to keep in touch with Nathan and Ellie as they got out and walked over and got into Nathan's car.

The pair of them drove back to Nathan's house pretty much in silence as they were both in deep thought. So much had happened over the past few days, in fact so much had happened over the past few months from the plane crash, David and Diana's transplant, the surgery being stormed and Ellie being held hostage to travelling down to London then flying over to Spain. Moments later when they arrived home they both fell asleep in each other's arms hoping that tomorrow would make better sense of what had happened today.

The following morning they both woke around 10am and were showered and dressed about half an hour later. Sitting on the sofa they started talking about the past day's events.

"Do you think Ben really does have them or genuinely didn't know what he was looking for?" asked Ellie.

"I think he didn't have a clue what he was doing to be honest. It was easy to transfer the container because it was marked and labelled so they knew what it was," said Nathan.

"That's true, I suppose it was us to blame though for opening the container," said Ellie with a giggle.

"But it was Ben that was trying to kill us and was following us everywhere or maybe it was Ron that was following us as well," said Nathan.

"I wonder what happened to Ron," said Ellie.

"If I were him I would have packed my bags and left the country," said Nathan as he took a drink from his mug. "If I was honest though, I am still a bit worried what he is capable of doing, I mean he's out there and could be doing anything or even be planning to bring down another plane."

Ellie stood up from the chair and sat down beside Nathan on the sofa and put her arms around him. After kissing him on the lips nose and forehead she looked him straight in the eyes and said, "I love you Nathan Taylor."

"I love you too Ellie Fox, I fell in love with you from the moment I met you," said Nathan as he held her tight.

After kissing and cuddling Ellie suggested, "I think we should go and see David and Diana and let them know the situation and that it's all over. He will be able to advise us better on what to do about Ron"

"That's a good idea, come on we'll go now," said Nathan excitedly.

They both finished their drinks and Ellie washed the cups while Nathan went to the bathroom. Nathan was looking forward to seeing David as he reversed out the driveway while looking and Ellie's dress. "You look absolutely gorgeous," said Nathan but Ellie just gave him a coy smile.

Arriving at the surgery they locked the car and walked across the carpark to the reception. Ellie had got goose bumps as she walked through the corridors as she remembered what had happened only a few weeks before.

Diana was sat by the side of David holding his hand as Nathan and Ellie walked in. "Hello, what's going off here then," asked Nathan as he spotted them holding hands.

"Nathan, I've been so worried about you, grab a chair and sit yourselves down," said David.

They all chatted along for a while about David and Diana and how they had grown closer together over the past few weeks they had been in hospital until David said, "So come on, we know you didn't come here to talk about me and Diana, what happened, what was in the container?"

"Well to start off with," said Nathan as he got comfortable, "we left here and went straight back to my place and packed our bags and a suitcase. We then set straight off down to London to the freight, storage, depot at Heathrow."

"And," said David impatiently.

"As we were waiting we could see out into the storage area and tell something was wrong, sure enough it turns out that they had just had a new labelling system installed along with a brand new container numbering system, the only trouble was that our container had been miss labelled and sent off to Malaga."

"You've got to be joking, so what did you both do," asked David.

"Seeing as we already had clothes and what not with us we drove around to Gatwick airport and waited for the next flight out to Spain. While we were in the departure lounge I decided to phone Ben," said Nathan.

"This gets better," said David.

Diana and Ellie were both glued to Nathan listening to every word with Diana trying to guess and figure everything out and Ellie reliving the experience in her mind.

"It gets better alright. He said that his family had been taken hostage until he returned the container but it turns out he was lying. Anyway I had a funny feeling about him and didn't trust him so I hung up. We managed to get on the next flight to Malaga and hired a van and shot straight off to the Britannica Storage Depot over there," explained Nathan.

"What about the container?" asked David.

"After we had arrived we collected the container. It was smaller than I thought so we placed it's in the back of the van and drove off until we found a quiet spot. It took us a few minutes to calm down but we lifted the container out the back and opened it," said Nathan.

"What was inside? Was it drugs or gold?" asked David.

"No where near or even close, when we opened the container there was a heap of documents and just over a hundred tiny vials of fluorescing orange liquid called Hydratetralynx CC60,"

"Documents and vials? That's what this was all about? Some paperwork and a few tubes of tango?"

Ellie burst out laughing, "No it's not tango, tell him Nathan."

"The documents detail the procedures of water purification. When water is cleaned, a chemical is left behind called Bromate," explained Nathan.

"Okay, I get that but what about it?" said David feeling confused.

"When the water is cleaned it leaves behind the chemical Bromate, further cleaning is required to remove the Bromate but the blueprints show and detail that it isn't cleaned out but left in the water. The treatment used is . . . well false, it doesn't do anything," said Nathan.

"I don't understand Nathan, what's so bad about this Bromate chemical?" asked David.

"Bromate is a carcinogen, carcinogens cause cancer. The government is killing the British people by leaving the Bromate in water. Every form of life needs water so everyone is being exposed to cancer in our water system," said Nathan.

Nobody spoke for several moments while they all took in and thought about what Nathan had just said. David had so many questions now but didn't know where to start.

"I'm not sure I know what to say really but what is the Hydratetralynx for?" asked David.

"The documents state that the Hydratetralynx CC60 will cure all known cancers and reverse the damage caused within 60 minutes," said Nathan.

"Jesus, 60 minutes? This can't be right. There must be some mistake or wind up or something," said David shocked and dazed.

"Nope it's no wind up they really do exist," said Nathan.

"So what have you done them? Where are they?" asked David.

"Considering what they were, we decided it wouldn't be a good idea to drag them through customs. Ellie had the idea to put them in her suitcase and send them via a courier to Vernon, Ellie's computer geek friend who has been collecting the list for Shiva. To throw anyone off the track we gave the container, although empty, back. We then caught the nice flight out to the UK and landed safely but while walking back to the car, the same gunman who was here before had found us," said Nathan.

"What happened?" chirped up Diana.

"It was horrible, Ellie was knocked unconscious and put in the boot, I was then forced to drive into the arse end of nowhere for about 40 minutes. Ellie was let out and we were questioned," explained Nathan.

"About the container for a guess?" asked David.

"Yes, he wanted to know where the container was, he then shot Ellie in the shoulder," said Nathan.

Ellie lifted her sleeve up to show Diana the wound that the bullet had made while Nathan continued describing what happened.

"We didn't want to tell him where the container was but he raised his gun to Ellie and fired again, I managed to pull her away at the last moment or he would have killed her. I pleaded with him to stop and told him they were in Nottingham. The weirdest thing then happened. He lowered his gun and asked what we meant by they. It turns out he had no idea what was in the container. It also turned out that his name is Mason and he had recently lost both his wife and daughter to cancer. We explained what the documents and vials were. He was really upset that there was a cure for the cancer and his wife and daughter could have lived," said Nathan.

David pulled himself up a bit in bed as Diana passed him his drink, "So what happened next?"

"He decided he wanted revenge. In a twist of fate he sort of agreed to team up with us and meet us the following day at Vernon's house. When we did get to Vernon he was dead," said Nathan as his voice drifted off slightly.

"Dead? But who would have done that? Mason?" asked David.

"That's what we thought, Ellie was fuming and upset but within a few minutes Mason walked in, he had nothing to do with it. While he was there he got a phone call from Ben saying he had the contents of the container. Mason arranged to meet him near London after setting fire to Vernon's house to remove any evidence," said Nathan.

"This just gets better, so what happened when you got to London?" asked David.

"We met up at Toddington services. The plan was me and Ellie would get the documents and vials out Ben's car while Mason went in to talk to him. We would eventually sell them back to the Organisation Mason worked for and to all the newspapers and television news people," said Nathan.

"That is a good idea, you could net a few thousand plus make everyone aware of what is happening at the same time," said David nodding his head.

"That's what we thought but it didn't sort of go to plan," said Nathan screwing his face up a little.

"What happened?"

"They weren't in his car; it also turned out Ron Shaw was heavily involved with Ben and had been helping him. Anyway, the next minute Ron came running out of the services and shot off in his car leaving half the tread on his tyres behind followed by Mason. We explained to Mason that the documents and vials weren't in Ben's car but it was too late. Mason had lost his temper with Ben and shot him in the toilets," said Nathan.

"So Ben's dead? Why did Mason shoot him?" asked David amazed.

"Ben held a massive grudge against Lufthansa, he was also charged with transferring the container over to America which he could have just got on and done but instead he tried to put the container on flight

1872. He had previously tampered with the plane planning it to crash so Ron could then retrieve the container from the plane. This seemed to upset Mason something bad so he shot him," said Nathan.

"I knew he was bad Nathan but didn't think he was that twisted. What about Ron? What's happened to him?" asked David.

"That's a good question and one that worries me. He is out there and capable of anything. I just have a gut feeling he won't leave it at that,"

"You mean come after you and Ellie?"

"Yes, either that or cause more damage to Lufthansa," said Nathan.

David paused for a moment thinking about it when he said, "Is Mason going to still keep in contact?"

"Yes he is, he as no idea where the documents and vials are now so he said he would keep in contact as too his progress," explained Nathan.

"I think the best bet would be to let Mason take care of Ron if I was to be honest with you," said David.

Nathan looked at Ellie and in an instant they both agreed. Nathan continued talking to David while Ellie was chatting away with Diana catching up on some gossip.

*   *   *

In the up and coming weeks, Nathan had learnt from Mason that he had finally caught up with Ron who was planning another attack on Lufthansa and had disposed of him. This had come as no surprise to Nathan knowing what Ron was capable of. Mason had also told him that he was leaving the Organisation and all that behind him to work as a Security Consultant.

Nathan and Ellie felt more relaxed now knowing Ron was out of the picture. Nathan had even started back at work flying and Ellie had started back up her fashion label.

It would take David a few more weeks of rest but Nathan was counting down the days when he would be back working with him. Diana and Ellie had become close friends over the weeks when Ellie had learnt that David had proposed to Diana. Ellie was so excited at the thought of a wedding and wondered when her time would come. She knew Nathan was the one and that one day he would ask her to marry him but until that day she was happy to be with him and so in love.

Ellie and Nathan were at talking one morning about Nathan's last shift and how it didn't feel the same without David when there was a knock on the door. Nathan answered the door to discover Ellie had a parcel from DHL.

"We've had this letter for the past month or so with specific instructions to deliver it on this day and to inform you to read the letter first," said the young man holding out the letter.

Nathan took the letter from him and turned it over to see who it was from but there was nothing on the back. After signing for the parcel the young man gave Nathan the parcel and left.

"What is it?" asked Ellie as Nathan came back into the living room.

"I'm not sure, it could be something to do with you fashion label. Did you order some new material?"

"Yes I did but I only ordered them yesterday," said Ellie.

Nathan gave Ellie the letter, "The young chap said that they had had the parcel for a while with instructions for you to read the letter first."

They both sat on the sofa as Ellie got comfortable and opened the letter and started to read it to Nathan.

When I received the documents and vials, I read through all the documents and couldn't believe what I was reading. At the time it would have been a bad idea to publish them with so many people look for them. My main concern was that you didn't get hurt; from the moment we met I fell in love with you but just couldn't bring myself to tell you. I missed you so much and when you rang me I felt like I was going to burst with excitement. The sad bit is though if you are reading this letter then I will have been killed trying to save you as you meant so much to me. I chose this date to have the letter delivered to give things time to settle down, plus it is seven years to the date that we first met. I wish you all the luck in the world with Nathan I really do, he's a good man. Take care of yourselves and enjoy the parcel. You will always be in my thoughts. Vernon Cooper.

Ellie had tears pouring from her eyes and down her face as she put the letter down. She put her arms around Nathan and held him for several minutes before she leant over and opened the parcel. They both stopped still and stared. Inside were just over one hundred vials of fluorescing orange liquid and the missing documents.

Lightning Source UK Ltd.
Milton Keynes UK
UKOW040615220313

208008UK00001B/5/P